MO

"A gift of ——————————— ability to create characters
rich with personality, and originality, is a rare talent and one
that Ms. Lykins has in abundance." —Kathee Card

Echoes of Tomorrow

"Readers will delight in Jenny Lykins's original story and the
twists and turns she makes. With a dash of intrigue, humor and
sensuality, she creates a gem of a time-travel romance."
—*Romantic Times*

"If you like time travel, you'll like this book. If you like a
good romance, you'll love this book."—Rita Hyatt

"Ms. Lykins has a fresh approach to characterization that
shines . . . *Echoes of Tomorrow* is a tour-de-force and moves
Jenny Lykins [to] center stage."—*Literary Page*

Lost Yesterday

"A wonderful time-travel romance filled with unexpected
twists and turns."—Patricia Potter, author of *Diablo*

"Lykins is truly a storyteller extraordinaire . . . A marvelous
blend of romance, intrigue, and surprising twists and turns that
kept me spellbound from the first page. Filled with tenderness,
humor, and love . . . This book is a definite keeper. I loved it!"
—Virginia Brown, author of *Jade Moon*

"Wonderful, powerful, and enthralling . . . Jenny Lykins crafts
an unforgettable story of the joy and heartache of true love."
—Lisa Higdon, author of *Our Town: Whistle Stop*

"Jenny Lykins is a talent to watch. With impeccable romantic
timing and wonderful humor she creates a timeless love. *Lost
Yesterday* is just what the doctor ordered. Curl up and tell the
world to go away!"—Debra Dixon, author of *Playing with Fire*

Jove titles by Jenny Lykins

LOST YESTERDAY
ECHOES OF TOMORROW
WAITING FOR YESTERDAY
DISTANT DREAMS

DISTANT DREAMS

Jenny Lykins

JOVE BOOKS, NEW YORK

TIME PASSAGES is a registered trademark of Berkley Publishing Corporation.

DISTANT DREAMS

A Jove Book / published by arrangement with
the author

PRINTING HISTORY
Jove edition / October 1998

The Penguin Putnam Inc. World Wide Web site address is
http://www.penguinputnam.com

ISBN: 0-515-12368-4

A JOVE BOOK®
Jove Books are published by The Berkley Publishing Group,
a member of Penguin Putnam Inc.,
375 Hudson Street, New York, New York 10014.
JOVE and the "J" design are trademarks
belonging to Jove Publications, Inc.

PRINTED IN THE UNITED STATES OF AMERICA

10 9 8 7 6 5 4 3 2 1

For the Father, who has given me everything I've needed, exactly when I needed it, whether I wanted it or not. And for my family, who has done the same.

Chapter 1

"HOW'D YOU LIKE to get married this afternoon?"
The wiry little sailor in dirty, ragged clothes waggled his
eyebrows at Shaelyn as she enjoyed the brisk summer
breeze in her face. The easterly wind lifted her hair and
swirled it over her shoulders as she gave the question a
moment's thought, then shrugged and turned away from
the ship's well-worn rail.

"Sure. Why not."

Pete, the old seadog who'd been assigned to show her
around the antique vessel, clapped his hands together and
rubbed them as if trying to start a fire without matches.
She just rolled her eyes with a smile and shoved away
from the polished wooden rail. The towering masts, nearly
two centuries old, swayed above her in a crystal-blue sky
marred only by a fluffy white streak left in the wake of a
jumbo jet.

"So, who am I going to marry?" Shae asked.

Pete shoved his frayed knit cap to the back of his head,

rubbed the gold hoop earring in his left ear, and surveyed the men on deck. Dozens of ropes on the three-masted ship snapped in the breeze while wood creaked against wood with every little wave in the water.

"Hmm. Lessee. Well, how 'bout . . . nope, he's already married. His wife might frown on that. Then mebbe . . . nah, he's got to take his car to get worked on this afternoon. I dunno. You get dressed and I'll find somebody."

Shaelyn shook her head and smiled as she stepped over a thick coil of rope.

"I hope there aren't going to be pictures, Pete. I'm already living down a multitude of bonehead things. I don't need physical proof adding one more to the list."

"No guarantee, missy." When Pete shook his head with wide-eyed innocence, Shaelyn felt certain she would live to regret this latest spur-of-the-moment decision. But, she had to admit, she'd never let a little regret slow her down. In fact, she'd had an awful lot of fun in exchange for those few moments of remorse.

Especially here in Cape Helm, where the small town had changed little in a hundred and fifty years. The summer vacations she'd spent here had always made the place feel more like home than anywhere else in the world. But even here, she didn't feel quite right. She was used to that, though—that feeling of not belonging. That's probably why she liked being a writer so much. She never stayed in one place long enough to expect to belong. Then again, she never stayed in one place long enough to meet someone special, either. *That* part, she missed.

Pete took her arm and pointed toward a door leading down into the ship. "There's a trunk with some clothes in the cabin next to the cap'n's. You go get dolled up and I'll find you a boy to marry. The tourists'll start showin' up in about a half-hour. By the way," he stopped and spit over the rail, "I talked with Delores Hawthorne, the town historian. She said she'd talk to you for your article. Give her a call when you have time. She's in the book."

"Aye-aye, sir." Shaelyn gave him a sharp salute. "You're a sweetheart."

He snorted and shook his head. "Go get yourself dressed for a wedding," he tossed over his shoulder as he walked away.

She picked her way over the deck and around the hatches of the ship, which had carried both passengers and cargo in the first half of the nineteenth century, wondering why she always found herself in these odd situations. Nobody else she knew did crazy things. Well, at least she'd have some interesting stories to tell the grandchildren, if she ever got around to having any kids.

She descended steps so steep they were almost a ladder, then blinked and waited for her eyes to adjust to the gloom of the ship's musty, dank interior. Oil lamps dotted the narrow corridor's walls, casting a dim, orange glow. The floodlight that should have lighted her way had a black scorched spot on one side. She'd have to tell Pete that the bulb had burned out.

From her earlier tour she knew that the captain's cabin lay at the end of the companionway. Squinting, she made her way to the cabin next to it.

Just as she reached the cabin door, the ship lurched in its moorings, banging against the dock and bouncing her off the bulkhead. Her notebook and tape recorder slid from her arms and skidded across the wooden floor, ricocheting off walls and coming to rest somewhere in the darker shadows between the feeble light of the oil lamps and the captain's quarters. As she edged toward her wayward paraphernalia, her fingers brushed against a light switch. She flicked it on, and a burst of white light bathed the hallway—then that bulb burned out too. And now, to top it off, white spots danced in front of her eyes and she'd lost sight of her recorder.

"Well, crap."

The recorder and notebook had to be near her feet. She dropped to her denim-clad knees and inched along the floor, feeling around like someone searching for a lost contact lens. She hated to think what the knees of her favorite jeans would look like after she got through crawling around the ancient wooden floors of a two-hundred-year-old ship—not to mention scuffing the toes of her cowboy boots.

Her fingers curled around the mini-recorder just as her knee landed on the notebook.

"Yes!" she cheered. Then, "Darn!" Her favorite pen was no longer clipped to the inside of the spiral.

Patting her hands along the floor, she flicked away pebbles, splinters of wood, and a few other things she wasn't sure she wanted to put a name to. Just as she was about to go in search of a light, her fingers touched something protruding from a crack in the floor. She dug at it with her fingernails until it popped from its prison between the floorboards. Definitely not her pen. She picked up a ring. Part of somebody's costume, no doubt.

"Criminy, Sumner, you go out to do a simple story on the last year of the millennium in a sleepy little town, and you end up in the middle of their living history, play-acting a wedding, crawling on your hands and knees in the bowels of a smelly old ship, obsessively chasing after some worthless pen, talking to yourself . . ."

But she loved being a freelance writer and traveling to all the wonderful places her job took her.

She sat back on her heels and looked at the ring, half-inclined to toss it back to the floor and continue her search. But with one glimpse of it in the stingy lamplight, she saw the flash of a rich, emerald-green stone flanked by what looked like diamonds, set in an intricate, filigreed gold band. It looked and felt real.

Maybe the ring wasn't costume jewelry after all.

The hatch above opened, spilling in enough light so that Shaelyn saw her pen. She pounced on it.

"You dressed yet, missy?" Pete bellowed down the companionway. "I found you a groom."

"Give me five minutes, would ya?" she teased. "It's not every day a girl gets married!"

A wheezy chuckle filtered to her just seconds before the hatch slammed shut.

"Oh, Pete, I found a—"

Too late. Shaelyn shrugged and slipped the ring onto her finger so she'd remember to give it to the man playing the captain. He'd know what to do with it.

Just as the ring slid over her knuckle to settle into a perfect fit on her finger, the ship pitched, then pitched again, slamming her into the rough wooden walls, banging her head and knocking the breath from her, reeling her with a bout of vertigo in the cramped, dark corridor belowdecks. She lost the notebook and recorder again when she bounced off two walls, then crashed through the door to the sunlit cabin and shot across the room, landing on a hard bunk covered with a lumpy mattress worthy of one of the ship's original passengers.

"You guys ever hear of a no-wake zone?" she yelled at the anonymous boater who'd no doubt roared through the restricted waters. "They want no wake for a reason!"

She shook her head, amazed at how dizzy a heaving ship could make her. For a brief moment the room spun around and she drunkenly grabbed the edge of the bunk.

The ship's rocking calmed. When her aching head finally stopped spinning, she looked around the cabin. Had she seen this one on the tour Pete had taken her on this morning? She didn't remember it. At least the cabin didn't smell quite so old and musty as the corridor. In fact, it looked almost lived in.

With a shrug, Shae worked her way to the leather-and-brass trunks against the wall. Their richness surprised her, considering the living history's budget. Someone must have donated them. She flipped open the first trunk to reveal what appeared to be mourning clothes. Perhaps appropriate attire for a lot of weddings, but the tourists would want to see something a little more cheerful. She dug through the clothing, finding only layers of black, wondering with a shudder what reenactment those costumes were for. Leaving that chest behind, she heaved open the lid of the second trunk.

Now that was more like it.

A rainbow of silks, satins, and lace shimmered up at her from the velvet-lined trunk. Shaelyn could hardly believe the opulence of the costumes. A far cry from the raggedy outfits of the ship's crew. Of course, they'd be expected to look like a bunch of ragtag sailors after a long voyage, but she'd never expected the passenger costumes to be so realistic. These gowns had to cost a fortune, or else the town had one heck of a costume seamstress.

She pulled the first intricately folded gown from the trunk and shook it out. Yards of silk rippled to the floor in a waterfall of seafoam green. A short matching jacket lay beneath where the gown had been stored.

Shaelyn unsnapped her purse belt, kicked off her boots and socks, then peeled her snug jeans to the floor and stepped out of them. She doubted that the black grime ground into the pale-blue denim knees would ever come clean. With a belated glance at the door, she threw the bolt, then pulled the plain white tee shirt over her head.

She hated to rummage through the rest of the lush, meticulously folded costumes in the trunk, but she had a feeling that the other participants in the living history might frown on her showing up for an 1830s shipboard wedding in cowboy boots.

Disturbing as little as possible, she excavated the contents, finding matching slippers and bonnet, and a few lacy petticoats that looked as if they might be needed under the gown. What looked suspiciously like a corset lay tucked neatly among the underthings. If Pete thought she was wearing one of *those*, he was in for a disappointment.

The sound of increased activity on deck reminded her that the wiry seaman would be bellowing for her again, so she shimmied into the gown, tied on the petticoats, and breathed a sigh of relief that the costume had an inch or so to spare in size. She strapped the small, flat purse pouch around her waist, under the gown, then settled it low over her hip, like a holster for a gun. The purse had her credit cards in it, among other things, and she wasn't about to leave it lying around unattended. She nearly dislocated her shoulders trying to fasten the bazillion microscopic buttons up her back. Just before a healthy curse managed to find its way past her lips, her gaze fell on the short jacket draped across the lid of the trunk.

"Aha!" She'd managed to get at enough top and bottom buttons that the jacket would cover up what she'd missed.

With her clothing at least outwardly acceptable, she slid her bare feet into a pair of ballet-type slippers that looked and felt remarkably like they'd been made by hand. She hadn't bothered to pull stockings out of the trunk, but surely no one would notice during the few minutes she'd be on deck.

Finally, in a rush to finish before Pete came to fetch her, she bent forward, gathered her long, curly hair into one hand, gave the whole thick mass a twist, then stuffed the ponytail into the enormous bonnet and tied the ribbons into a big bow at her cheek.

Her reflection in the tiny mirror by the porthole surprised her. She'd never been into ultrafeminine clothes, so the elegant simplicity of the pre–Civil War gown suited her taste, but the pale green bonnet with ruching framing her face was more delicate than anything she'd ever worn in her life. With the green a few shades lighter than her eyes, the gown was a perfect compliment to her coloring.

A shiver of déjà vu skittered up her spine as she looked at herself in the mirror, as if she'd seen herself in that costume before. She hated the eerie feeling that always caught her unawares, but she experienced it too often to let it bother her. With a practiced shrug, she shoved the feeling out of her thoughts and turned to the door.

"You clean up pretty good, Sumner," she told herself as she stepped out of the cabin. "And quit talking to yourself."

No one had been around to fix the light in the passage-way. She couldn't even find the switch now in the dim gloom, not that it would do her any good. She made her way to the stairs with only the feeble light from the oil lamps.

"Well, just great," she muttered as she felt her way to the steps. Wasn't anyone worried about tourists getting down there, falling and breaking their necks, then suing the pants off the historical society?

She stubbed her toe on something and nearly went sprawling against the steep set of steps. "Klutz," she grumbled, then looked around to see if anyone had wit-nessed her graceful arrival at the stairs. Fortunately, she was alone.

She hiked her dress to her knees with one hand and used the other to pull herself to the upper deck. The door lead-ing outside stuck the first time she tried it, but, of course, it flew open with ease when she shouldered her way through, sending her stumbling onto the deck and into the blinding brilliance of the sun.

Once she managed to stop her forward motion, she squinted into the sunlight until her eyes adjusted, then looked around for Pete and something that might be the stage for the wedding.

"Wow!" she breathed. *Everyone* had on a costume. She hadn't realized there'd be so many re-enactors participat-ing in this event. But where were the tourists? Was this to be like a costume party where everyone participated?

Shrugging, she turned in a circle, scanned 360 degrees around her, then went in search of Pete.

JULY 29, 1830
CAPE HELM, MAINE

"You're going to do what?" Griffin Elliott for once lost his usual bored-with-life expression, and Alec Hawthorne smiled at being the cause. Alec took another sip of his brandy and repeated himself.

"I'm going to wed Phillipa Morgan."

Griffin leapt to his feet, then flicked spilled droplets of brandy from his fingertips.

"But your brother has been betrothed to her since he was ten years of age! I know he has no desire to marry her, but neither do you, and he *is* her betrothed. Surely your father does not condone . . ." Griffin's voice trailed off, then his eyes widened in realization. "You mean to wed her before he finds out! Saints, Alec, is Charles a part of this mad scheme for you to marry his intended?"

Alec settled back in his chair and cocked his head at his closest friend. If he weren't dreading this marriage so much, he might enjoy Griffin's uncharacteristic agitation. He just wished Grif lived in Maine instead of Baton Rouge, so he could irritate him on a regular basis.

"You know Charles is too honorable to go along with this. But he is mad for that little Templeton girl, and at least one of us should have a chance for a happy marriage. Besides," Alec shrugged, "if Father's intended bride for me had not cocked up her toes with pneumonia last season, I would be firmly wed now anyway, and probably well on my way to becoming a father." *If I had been able to accomplish the deed to create a child*, he thought, shuddering at the memory of the horse-faced girl with the sour disposition. His overbearing father seemed to have a penchant for weeding out babies who would become homely women to betroth his young sons to. Lord knew what his little sister would end up with.

Griffin must have read his mind.

"But you said yourself you saw a glimpse of Phillipa on your grand tour, and even as a child the chit showed promise of being the most ill-favored woman you'd ever had the misfortune to encounter."

Alec sighed and tried to act as if her looks held no consequence.

"All I need do is get a child upon her, to quiet Father's constant harping for an heir. Then she can live her life and I will live mine. It's quite simple, really."

"You're mad, Alec. Even if you manage to find yourself wed, her family and yours will scream for an annulment."

Griffin paced the length of the library, stopping occasionally to glare at his longtime friend.

Alec rose and poured himself another brandy. He would no doubt need a continuous supply of the substance before this day was done.

"She has no family left, except an elderly aunt who is traveling with her. When her father died in London, they closed up the house and sent word they were coming to fulfill his last wish. Had he not been sick these last years, she would have been here long before now."

"But you—"

"I am going to wed her, Griffin. Stop worrying over me like a mother hen."

Griffin's mouth worked silently for several seconds before he snapped his lips into a disapproving line and glared at Alec.

"Do you not have enough to worry about with this smuggling business? Must you go in search of yet another source of—"

"I am going to wed her."

Griffin blew out a dramatic sigh. "This is the 1830s, Alec. Not all marriages are arranged. You could defy your father. Charles could defy him. Refuse to wed this woman."

"Charles will do whatever it takes to keep peace with Father, because he knows how miserable the man can make our lives. We have always bowed to his wishes, but those days are over. By marrying Phillipa, I remove myself from the marriage market, and I free Charles to find happiness. My next goal will be to take Molly off the marital auction block, though the child has shown a knack for scaring away anyone interested, without my help." Alec set his empty glass on the table and looked at Griffin. "I am going to do this."

Griffin rolled his eyes. "Very well. If I cannot halt this insane act, I might as well aid you. How do you plan to accomplish this deception?"

Alec walked to the window and stared through the leaded panes at the expanse of the Atlantic Ocean. Just a few miles to the south, her ship was about to dock. His life was about to change.

"Very simply," he stated, trying to keep his voice carefree. "I plan to introduce myself as Charles, wed her on the spot, then consummate the marriage before anyone has a chance to find out."

Griffin moaned and dropped into the nearest leather wingback, shaking his head and mumbling things Alec was sure he didn't want to hear.

"And how will you know her? Pick out the ugliest woman aboard ship?"

Alec flinched, cringing at how accurate that method might be if he hadn't already known how to recognize her.

"Charles sent her the emerald-and-diamond ring Mother inherited from that odd great-aunt of hers, for the betrothal ring. I suppose I shall look for an ugly woman and marry the one wearing that ring."

Griffin quirked a dark brow and leveled a serious gaze upon him.

"I hope you retain your wonderful sense of humor, Hawthorne. I fear you shall need it in the very near future."

Alec, Griffin, and the traveling minister Alec had retained arrived at the ship just as the gangplank settled against the dock.

"It's not too late to change your mind, old boy," Griffin muttered into Alec's ear. "We'll simply tell her who you really are, deposit her at the inn, and keep her there until we break the bad news to Charles."

Truth be told, Alec had considered that option more than
once on the ride to the docks. Even now he fought the
urge to fetch Charles and let him deal with the unwanted
wife. But he kept reminding himself of the last time he'd
seen his brother with Mary Templeton. Besotted. The both
of them. Unaware of any other living creature, save each
other. And disconsolate that their future together would be
nothing more than a collection of fond memories.

Alec doubted he would ever find a woman who could
captivate him so. He would do this for his brother and end
his father's rantings for a grandson. Killing two birds with
one stone, so to speak.

Yes, he thought with a sigh, *and give me enough rope
and I'll hang myself.*

Before the passengers started to swarm off the ship, and
before he could have any more second thoughts, Alec
strode up the gangplank with Griffin and the Reverend Mr.
Forester in tow, to find an ugly woman wearing his great-
aunt's ring. He'd have had the ship's captain marry them,
but he wanted no one he knew to know of his plan. Captain
Albritton would be busy with paperwork belowdecks while
Alec fetched his bride-to-be. They would be off the ship
and wed before the captain came topside.

Every woman the trio encountered was either accom-
panied by a man or too old to be the woman in question.
With each moment that passed, Alec numbed his mind to
what he was about to do. Finally he stopped to scan the
deck, turning in time to see a breathtaking creature in pale
green silk stumble through a door onto the deck. When
she raised her hand to shield her eyes from the sun, Alec's
entire body jerked at the sight of the emerald ring on her
finger.

The homely, chubby child he'd chanced to see years
earlier, before her nanny had shooed her up the stairs, had
grown into an exquisite beauty. Her flawless skin glowed
pink at her cheeks and wisps of shiny dark auburn curls

framed her face beneath the frilly bonnet. The ocean breeze molded her gown gently against her tall, willowy body, revealing generous curves in the most appealing places.

Alec's spirits lifted considerably.

He strode forward, anxious to get this charade over, but not dreading the deed nearly as much now.

She looked up at him as he approached, a question in her eyes but a smile on her lips.

"Phillipa Morgan?" Alec said as she gazed up at him. She cocked her head and her brows drew together in question. "Allow me to introduce myself. Charles Hawthorne, at your service." He bent over her hand and brushed his lips across her knuckles. Her gaze darted to the Bible in the minister's hand.

"Oh! You must be the man I'm going to marry," she said with an odd accent and more self-confidence than he'd ever encountered in a woman.

He struggled to keep his surprise from showing on his face. Certainly hers was not the coy, retiring personality he'd expected.

"Yes," he mumbled. "May I present my friend, Griffin Elliott, and the Reverend Mr. Forester."

"It's nice to meet you." She looked up at Alec, then glanced around. "So where's the ceremony going to be? Here?"

Again, he schooled his features. He'd been prepared to give a spurious reason as to why the marriage needed to take place immediately, but apparently she expected to be wed upon arriving. Perhaps she had no desire to arrive at his home as an unwed woman.

"Yes. Of course. Here will be fine. But where is your chaperone?"

Her brows drew together again, then she blinked and smiled, as if they shared a private joke. "Oh, she's feeling a little under the weather. Ocean travel doesn't agree with her. But she said we should go ahead with the ceremony."

He could have sworn that she winked at him then, but
surely he was mistaken. He turned to the minister and nodded, ignoring Griffin's accusatory glare.

The Reverend Mr. Forester cleared his throat, and with
the words, ''Dearly beloved,'' a crowd gathered. The minister spoke of the meaning of marriage, the sanctity of
marriage, the trust necessary in marriage.

Alec felt an overwhelming urge to run a finger around
his collar. Was he doing the right thing? Should he stop
this farce now, before it was too late? He glanced down
at the woman beside him. She lifted her face and beamed
up at him, her smile achingly similar to that of Mary Templeton when she gazed at Charles.

''Dost thou take this man to be thy lawfully wedded
husband, to love, honor, and obey, for richer, for poorer,
in sickness and in health, till death do thee part?''

''I do,'' she responded in a slightly breathy voice.

''Dost thou take this woman to be thy lawfully wedded
wife, to love, honor, and cherish, for richer, for poorer, in
sickness and in health, till death do thee part?''

Could he do this thing? Could he deceive this woman
in order to free his brother? He looked down into her wide
green eyes, fringed with ebony, at her smile that made
those eyes sparkle. So trusting.

''I do,'' he heard himself say, appalled that he'd spoken
the words without yet deciding to do so. What had possessed him? Griffin had been right. He was mad, and becoming more so by the moment.

''. . . now pronounce thee man and wife. What God hath
joined together, let no man put asunder.''

What had he done?

Alec drew in a deep breath, then stopped breathing when
she tilted her face up in obvious anticipation of a kiss.

People were watching. Griffin was smirking. And the
minister smilingly nodded in a misguided attempt to condone the kiss.

After a moment's hesitation, Alec bent his head to brush his lips across hers, but her arms snaked around his neck, pulling him close as she came up on tiptoe and pressed her lips to his.

Nothing could have prepared him for the convulsive surge of pure lust that shot straight to the center of his being. When her lips parted, he forgot the crowd, and Griffin, and the minister; he forgot he'd just deceived this innocent woman into marrying him. With a will of their own, his arms curled around her slender back, pulling her closer as he sought her tongue with his, as his head spun and his body responded to her sweetness.

How long the soul-stirring kiss lasted, he had no idea. When he finally raised his head, a cheer rose from the crowd. Phillipa stepped away awkwardly, the pink in her cheeks deepening to the red of a sailors' sunset, yet she still smiled at him, a hint of surprise lighting the depths of her moss-colored eyes.

"Shall we fetch your aunt and be on our way?" Alec asked, trying not to stammer like a schoolboy.

Phillipa blinked, looking surprised at his suggestion. Then that mysterious smile stole across her lips again.

"My aunt said to go on without her. She's going to . . . umm . . . visit some friends. She'll catch up with us later."

Odd behavior for an elderly aunt, but then the girl was uncommonly odd as well. Just look at her manner of speech.

"Very well. I'll have a servant collect your trunks and arrange to fetch your aunt when she is ready."

The minister handed Alec the marriage certificate, which he signed and handed to Phillipa. She glanced at it, laughed, and awkwardly dipped the quill pen into the tiny inkwell. Alec slipped a "donation" to Mr. Forester while Phillipa signed the certificate.

The foursome wound their way to the gangplank. Alec

noticed that Phillipa watched her feet while she walked and still managed to trip over the hem of her skirts twice. His hand shot out to steady her both times.

She looked up at him and shrugged with a smile. "Good thing I don't have to wear these things *all* the time." She forged ahead while Alec puzzled over her enigmatic statement; then he forgot what he was thinking when she lifted her delicate green skirts above her ankles to step onto the gangplank. Not only did she reveal several inches of slender ankle, but she wore no stockings beneath her skirts.

Was fashion so different in England as to allow a lady to discard her stockings?

Her skirts dropped back to brush the gangplank and she continued to watch her feet as she gingerly crossed to the dock.

Ned, his coachman, pulled the horses up to them on the secluded dock and Alec helped Phillipa into the closed carriage. He climbed in beside his bride and made room for Griffin and the minister.

Griffin, however, bestowed a wicked smile and merely stuck his head in the door.

"Wouldn't dream of intruding on the newlyweds, old friend. I'll hire a carriage for the Reverend and me. A pleasure to attend your nuptials, Mrs. Hawthorne." He took her fingers and brushed a kiss across her knuckles, then looked at Alec. "I'll come around in a few days, when the waters have settled."

"What did he mean by that?" Phillipa asked after Griffin left, leaving Alec throwing glares at the traitor's back.

"Oh, nothing," he said, itching to choke the life from his friend. "He often speaks in riddles. No one pays attention to him."

He banged on the ceiling of the carriage and they lurched forward at a healthy pace. They would be home in an hour, and by tomorrow morning this whole thing would be behind him.

"Great carriage. Has it been restored?"

He turned to look at the very odd woman to whom he now found himself married.

"Restored? No."

"Wow! It's in great shape." She drummed her fingers on her lap. "So, when do we go back to the ship?"

Chapter 2

SHAELYN WATCHED THE devilishly handsome man arch jet-black eyebrows nearly to his hairline. What in the world had she said to cause such a reaction? Maybe they were supposed to ride out of sight of the ship.

"How long have you been participating in the living-history thing?" she asked chattily. He didn't look like the type to dress up in period costume and pretend he was someone else.

"Living history?"

"Yeah." Shae had never seen the combination of gold-brown eyes and shiny black hair put together with such devastating effect. She wondered if he was single.

"I have no idea to what you are referring." Those gorgeous eyes had narrowed, and now he looked at her as if he expected her to pick his pocket.

"You know. Living history? What you just did?" When he continued to just stare at her, she decided to change the subject. "So, shouldn't we be getting back to the ship?"

His gaze now turned to a look of total bewilderment.

"There is no need to return to the ship. I've arranged

for your aunt and your trunks to be brought to Windward Cottage.''

A cold chill, like droplets of melting ice, trickled down her spine.

''Heh.'' She forced the laugh from her throat. ''You really get into this, don't you? But, seriously, I've got a date tonight,'' she lied, ''and my clothes are on the ship. So if we could just turn this thing around . . .''

The man—Charles, she believed—shook his head as if he didn't understand.

''What are you speaking of, Phillipa? Are you overly fatigued from the voyage?''

The ice water froze solid in her spine. Had she gotten herself mixed up with a nutcase? *Stay calm*, she told herself. *Maybe he's teasing*.

''Now Charles, you know my name isn't really Phillipa. But I didn't introduce myself, did I? I'm Shaelyn Sumner. Shae for short. I freelance for Atlantic Press News Service.'' She offered her hand to shake, but he merely stared at it for a second, then patted it down onto her lap.

''You're distraught. I'll send someone to fetch your aunt as soon as we reach Windward.''

Shaelyn closed her eyes and took a deep breath. He wasn't teasing her. This guy's porch light wasn't on.

''Look, Charles, I know you guys stay in character while you're performing, but we don't have an audience now. Why don't we just turn around and you can take me back to the ship. You know I'm not 'Phillipa.' ''

He lifted her hand and examined the ring she'd found. Oh great. The ring. Now she had someone else's ring on and it was probably going to be stolen.

Stolen. Heck, she'd give the darned thing to him if it would get her out of this mess.

''You want the ring? Here. You can have it. Just stop the carriage and let me out.'' She pulled on the ring, twisted, turned, but it wouldn't budge over her knuckle. Frantic now, she yanked her hand against her chest and pulled. She spit on her finger and worked the saliva around, but still the ring wouldn't move.

"Phillipa, stop it! I don't want—"

"It's Shaelyn!" she yelled, panicked at his use of the other name. She jumped to her feet and banged on the ceiling. "Stop! Stop the carriage!"

Not until she felt them slow did she stop hammering the ceiling with her fists. She grabbed the handle of the door and shoved, leaping to the ground while the carriage still rolled.

The skirts of her cumbersome gown tripped her as she tried to land. She dropped to her knees, falling into the dirt, rolling across gravel and jutting rocks. Scrambling to her feet, she ran, not caring where, as long as it was away from that carriage. A light shone in the early evening from a window of a two-story house just a few yards away. She yanked up her skirts and stormed across the manicured yard, bounded up the steps, then banged on the door as she tried the knob. Miraculously, the door opened and she burst into the interior, screaming for help, turning wildly around in the dim foyer.

A door opened to her left and a stocky, well-to-do man appeared with a candle in his hand just as Charles burst through the front door.

"Help me! Please! This man's crazy!" She ran to the gentleman, who backed away from her with horror in his eyes. "Call 911! He's crazy! He's trying to kidnap me!" She chased the man into the room he'd just left, where a portly woman sat huddled in alarm in the corner of an antique sofa. She wore a long gown, similar to the costume Shaelyn wore. At the sight of her, Shaelyn spun and took in the stocky man's period garb. Oil lamps lit the room in dim puddles of light.

The couple just stared at her, as if *she* were crazy. Charles approached her, his arms wide, doing a magnificent job of looking like the sane one.

"It's an act, don't you see? He won't take me back to

the ship! I've got a date! People will be looking for me!'' She babbled until she realized calm would get her further with these people. She stopped, took a deep breath, then let it out slowly. Charles moved toward her, but she stepped away and glared at him.

"May I borrow your phone to call 911? This man is attempting to abduct me."

Neither the man nor the woman spoke, but continued to stare as if she had two heads.

"Where's your damn phone?" she screamed. The couple both jumped a foot in the air. The man snatched up a poker and waved it at her.

"I have no knowledge of what a 'phone' is, and I wouldn't lend it to a foul-mouthed madwoman if I did. Get out of my house now, and leave God-fearing people alone."

Shaelyn scanned the room for a telephone, then ran through the rest of the downstairs, checking everywhere. As she went from room to room she realized there were no modern conveniences in the house. No TVs, no radios, no electric lights, for pity's sake. The kitchen was a sparse room with no sink, no cabinets, not even a stove. A thing that looked like a small barrel lay on its side just inside a huge fireplace. Good heavens, the whole place looked like a museum. Had she run into another living history?

Nearing hysteria, she whirled around to run out the front door. She ran straight into the immovable chest of her abductor.

"No!" she screamed, and drove her knee into his crotch. She ran without looking back as he doubled over, the air leaving his lungs in a gasping retch.

She ran past him, through the house and out the front door. The carriage still stood on the street—a dirt street.

Shaelyn staggered to a stop, holding her side and panting for breath.

Where was she? She couldn't be more than a few minutes from the dock. She'd spent summer vacations in

Cape Helm for years, since she'd been a teenager. She knew every nook and cranny of this tiny Maine port.

And this dirt street didn't belong here.

She limped on, holding the stitch in her side, beginning to feel the effects of her tumble from the carriage. She desperately scanned her surroundings for a familiar landmark, spying an intersection half a block away.

Turning her walk into a limping run, she arrived at the cross street; another dirt road. Her heart stopped beating and her breath rushed from her lungs.

On the corner stood a familiar landmark. McBane's Apothecary. She'd spent many hours in that shop as a teen, drinking sodas at the quaint, old-fashioned fountain, pouring over the latest makeup colors with her vacation friends. She'd been in there just the day before, talking to Mr. Edwards about the article she was doing on the last year of the millennium in small-town America and how she'd be participating in the living history on the *Sea Queen,* Cape Helm's newest—or, rather, its oldest—attraction. He'd asked her if she planned to cover the opening of the time capsule, buried by the town fathers in 1830, and she assured him she would be there on New Year's Eve for the final article in her series. They'd even talked about how the stone marking the location of the capsule seemed to be in such a strange place—in a corner of the square so thick with trees that Shaelyn had never even seen it until she went looking for it.

And now she stared at McBane's Apothecary, a fairly new building instead of the nearly two-century-old structure of yesterday, standing alone on the corner instead of surrounded by other buildings, as it should be. The sign that read "Proudly serving Cape Helm since 1825" was nowhere in evidence.

She squinted at the building as icy-hot chills crawled across the back of her neck. Panic seized her, making her earlier struggle with Charles feel like afternoon tea. As she stared at the drugstore, a woman dressed in early-

nineteenth-century clothing stepped out the door, opened
a parasol, then nodded to a man in equally antique attire
as she strolled away. The man tipped his hat, then turned
to admire the view from behind. A horse-drawn carriage
rattled down the street.

Shaelyn's heart tap-danced in her chest. What in the
world was happening to her? How hard had she hit her
head in the companionway? Surely she was hallucinating.

She looked down the street, saw the familiar view of
the ocean, and her breath turned to shallow, panicked
gasps. Though her mind raced for possibilities, she could
find no explanation for what she saw. She turned slowly,
sweeping the landscape with her gaze, her mind vaguely
registering the sight of Charles, bent and limping, making
his way toward her. What registered clearly was the recognition of many of the homes she'd seen for years, newer
now, some a shadow of what their remodeled structures
would be. Dusk fell where streetlights should have brightened the landscape. Another carriage rolled down the
street, and a rider on horseback trotted along at a fast clip.

Strong hands grasped her arms from behind in an ironclad grip. She didn't struggle. She was too numb to struggle. She simply moved one foot in front of the other as
the hands pulled her back toward the carriage.

The grip gentled when she failed to resist, and Charles's
face swam before her eyes as he guided her into the carriage.

Shouldn't she try to run? Shouldn't she scream for help?
But she knew it would be useless to fight him right now.
How could she fight a hallucination? She tried to remember if he had given her something to drink. To eat. How
had he drugged her?

She had no concept of time, no idea how long they'd
been in the closed carriage before it lumbered to a stop
and the door flew open. A fresh gust of cool night air
swirled inside, teasing her numbed mind, stirring a hint of
life back into her.

"We're home," Charles said, the first of his words to penetrate her consciousness. She didn't bother to answer. Stepping from the carriage, she sucked in her breath at the magnificent house before her, perched above the ocean like a sentinel. Built of huge blocks of granite, the home was a sea lover's dream, with sweeping arches, large diamond-paned leaded windows looking out in every direction, and stone balconies with sets of French doors opening onto them.

Ten-foot-tall, double-wide arched batten doors swung inward and a diminutive male figure appeared carrying an oil lamp. Behind him, candles and more lamps illuminated the entry hall that seemed to be lined with portraits.

The now-familiar, now-welcome numbness crept back into Shaelyn's mind. She stood in the crushed-shell drive, staring vacantly at the house until Charles took her elbow and guided her up the wide, shallow front steps.

"Martin, this is my wife. Prepare the east room next to mine," she heard Charles say, as if from a distance.

Seconds passed before the small man erased the shock from his features, said, "Yes, sir," then disappeared into the house.

The carriage rumbled away into the darkness as Charles led her into an entry hall and up a flight of stairs at least eight feet wide.

Nowhere in the house was there a sign of the twentieth century. No evidence of electricity whatsoever. No light switches, no alarm systems, no TVs or radios. This house was no more a part of the twentieth century than the one . she'd run to for help.

The harder she looked for some hidden, overlooked piece of modern technology, the more she receded into herself, until she felt like a small child, peeking out at the world from within a dark, comfortable hiding place. Was she hallucinating the home as well, or had she fallen into a drugged sleep to dream its existence?

A maid garbed in a long black dress and white apron

scurried around the room into which Charles guided her. The young red-haired girl fluffed pillows on a bed big enough for a family of four. She drew back heavy brocade draperies the color of clotted cream, then drew back the matching lace sheers beneath to throw open the leaded, diamond-patterned casement windows facing the ocean.

Shaelyn stood in the center of the room, watching, not moving, until the girl left and Charles asked if she was hungry. She looked up at him and blinked. He seemed terribly uncomfortable for some reason. Why should *he* be uncomfortable? He asked her if she wanted food brought up and she continued to stare. Her mouth didn't seem to want to work, and she wasn't quite sure what the right answer was to his question.

Finally she turned away, a voice deep within telling her to pull herself together. Catching her reflection in a tall pier glass in the corner, she stopped and stared at the familiar face framed by an unfamiliar bonnet. Dirt smudged her cheeks, and her arms had cuts on them from her tumble from the carriage. She reached up and pulled the ends of the bow on the now-battered hat, then dragged the frilly bonnet off and tossed it on a chaise. Her hair tumbled in a wavy mass from where she'd stuffed it under the hat. She plowed her fingers to her scalp and shook out her hair, fluffing curls back into it, working out some of the tangles, trying to clear her mind.

Charles made some odd sound deep in his throat, but she ignored him. Maybe if she ignored him long enough, he and the rest of this hallucination would go away.

Turning her numb thoughts away from him, she slipped out of the short, bolero-type jacket, then dropped to the edge of the chaise and kicked off the soft green slippers.

Another strangled sound came from Charles's direction. He said something about sending someone to help her undress, which she ignored, then he strode across the expanse of the gleaming parquet floor, opened a heavily carved pocket door into the wall, and slid it shut behind him.

Shaelyn wanted nothing more than to shut her mind down and let it rest. Perhaps then she could make sense of these bizarre happenings.

With the skill of a contortionist, she managed to unbutton the top and bottom buttons on her gown. She shed the layers of clothing, unsnapped her pouch purse, slipped it under the mattress, then crawled into bed and fell asleep before her head hit the pillow.

What had he gotten himself into? Had he married a madwoman?

Alec paced the floor while he peeled off his jacket and then his tie. He finally loosened his collar, as he had wanted so badly to do all day. With a yank that nearly pulled the cord from the wall, he rang for a servant.

Within seconds a quiet knock sounded on the open door to the hallway and Margaret stood just inside, waiting to do his bidding. Fiery red curls escaped the prim cap on her head and Alec wondered idly if she'd been indiscreet again with the gardener.

"Please take a tray of food to . . . the lady's room, then see if she needs help undressing." *Even though she only bothered to half-dress to begin with.*

He'd thought Phillipa would offer an explanation when she removed her bonnet and her hair tumbled out, obviously having been merely crammed underneath. But she'd only shaken the curls loose with a contented sigh as if it were a common thing for her to wear her hair in such a fashion. But when she'd unashamedly removed her jacket to reveal a gaping expanse of unfastened buttons, Alec could only conclude that she was either mad or a loose woman, to neither of which he desired to be wed.

He scrubbed his eyes with the heels of his hands and dropped into a chair, immediately feeling the damage her knee had done earlier in the evening.

Never had he done such an insane thing in his life. Indeed, this may have been the *only* insane thing he'd ever done, which only gave justification to all his years of common sense.

He had been prepared to weather the considerable wrath of his father in order to free Charles to find his own happiness. He'd been prepared to be a dutiful, as well as discreet, husband to Phillipa. He'd been prepared to be a good, loving father . . . the type of father he and Charles had never had. And now it seemed he'd better prepare himself to spend a lifetime of making excuses for a beautiful wife who lived in her own world, who said her name was really something else, who only bothered to partially dress, who ran into strangers' homes, babbling incoherently . . .

Alec moaned, long and loud, then stood and shrugged out of his suspenders. He tried not to think as he unbuttoned his shirt and tossed it over the back of a chair.

This day had certainly not gone as planned. He'd expected to wed a homely woman today and then get on with his life. He should be in her room right now, consummating the marriage so that Charles could have a life with Mary. But the woman seemed distraught enough already. He wouldn't do anything tonight to add to her unstable frame of mind.

He'd unfastened the top two buttons of his trousers when a strange, high-pitched sound came from behind the closed pocket doors. Alec stopped and listened, then realized it was the sound of his new wife crying.

He stood at the door for only a moment before sliding it open and crossing to the bed. She'd left every single lamp burning, and Alec could see she was crying in her sleep. He should leave her alone; go back to his room and retire for the night. But her muffled cries were so pitiful, so childlike.

He sank to the edge of the bed beside her. The covers bunched around her chin and she huddled beneath them, her hair curling like silk auburn ribbons across the pristine white of the pillow. Saint's blood, she looked like an angel. A slight frown creased her brow and her dark lashes came to inky spikes from the tears that dampened her cheeks.

Was she crying in her sleep because of him?

Shame swept over him as he stared down at the uncommonly beautiful face. He'd not given a moment's thought to Phillipa's feelings, how she would feel at being swept up and married to a stranger the moment her ship tied up at the dock. And how would she feel when she learned that she'd been deceived, married to a man she had no knowledge of, quite possibly didn't even know existed, instead of the man to whom her family had betrothed her in childhood?

And while he was being painfully honest with himself, Alec had to wonder if he would have given any of this a second thought, were he gazing down at the homely face he'd expected to marry. Indeed, would he be looking upon her at all?

Spurred by the shame he was not accustomed to feeling, he decided then and there to make his unconscionable behavior up to his wife. He would not insist on consummating the marriage until she was ready to take that step. He would do what he could to ease her into the position of being married to a stranger. And he would worry about a possible annulment only if the occasion arose.

She sobbed again and he found himself gently brushing a tendril of hair from her cheek. The moment his hand touched her skin, she shot upright and flew into his arms, wrapping her arms about his neck and burying her face in his bare shoulder.

After a moment of shock, he realized she was still asleep. He started to lay her back down, but the feel of her hair against his cheek, the warmth of her body, her scent, all felt so good, so right, that he brought his hands up to pull her closer.

Bolts of fire shot up his fingertips when they encountered bare skin at her back. The woman had no night-clothes on!

Someone knocked on the bedchamber door and a moment later the door swung inward.

Alec swiveled on the side of the bed when the tray of food in Margaret's hand rattled as if she would drop it. Phillipa jerked awake, jumping away with a yelp, staring first at Alec and then at Margaret. The sheet covering her fell, revealing her lack of clothing in all her glory. Margaret stammered an apology and fled while Phillipa scrambled to cover herself.

"What the hell are you doing in here?" she screamed, loud enough to do damage to his hearing. She tried to shove him off the bed, but he held his ground.

"You were crying in your sleep—"

"I don't cry in my sleep."

"Yes, you do. I came in to see if you needed comforting."

"I don't cry in my sleep, and I sure don't need comforting from a whacko kidnapper! Get out!"

He stood then, some of his earlier shame melting away at her words.

"Phillipa, I realize now I should have waited—"

"My name is Shaelyn! S-H-A-E-L-Y-N! If you were out to kidnap Phillipa, you've got the wrong woman! Just take me back to the ship and—"

"But the ring—"

"You want the ring? Take the stupid ring! Take my credit cards! Take whatever you want! Here . . ."

She struggled to pull her betrothal ring from her finger. He stopped her with his hand but she jerked away and continued to struggle.

"Phillipa, I don't want the ring." He tried to take her hand again, but she turned her back on him. "I see my presence is upsetting you. I'll leave now, but in the morning we are going to have a long talk."

She made a rude noise as he rose, but he simply closed his eyes and shook his head.

When he shut the door behind him, a wave of relief nearly weakened his knees. The woman was indeed mad, but what he could not credit was this strange, over-whelming attraction he felt for her. Almost from the moment his gaze had fallen on her. And then to have her press herself against him, warm and fragrant and naked . . .

With a disgusted sigh, he shoved his arms into his dressing gown and went in search of Martin, whom he found inspecting the kitchen.

"Send someone to fetch my wife's aunt, Martin. Ned should be on his way back with the trunks, and he can give directions to where she's staying. I have yet to introduce her to the staff. I shall attend to that tomorrow."

Martin nodded, his face as impassive as ever. "As you wish, sir."

Fatigue crept into Alec's mind and body, and suddenly all he wanted was to lose himself in sleep and put this day behind him.

"I'm not to be disturbed for the remainder of the night."

"Yes, sir."

Alec climbed the stairs back to the second floor, wondering the whole way if he would find sleep this night, and if he did, would it be without nightmares?

Chapter 3

NED STOOD JUST inside the bedchamber door, holding a canvas bag, crushing his cap in his fists, looking ready to run as Alec gawked at him in disbelief.

"What do you mean Phillipa Morgan is dead? She is asleep behind that door. I married her yesterday."

It was Ned's turn to gawk. When the man swallowed, his Adam's apple bobbed like a buoy on rough seas.

"All I know, sir, is what the cap'n told me. Phillipa Morgan's great-aunt Euphilia took sick and died last week, and not an hour after they buried her at sea, Miss Morgan took to her bed as well. She died two days later. They buried her at sea the same day. The cap'n said he ain't no doctor, so he don't know what they died of. He weren't happy to be having a sickness on his ship. Said he lost six passengers to it."

Alec dropped into the leather chair by the window, trying to absorb the meaning of Ned's words. He flinched when Ned cleared his throat and rolled his eyes in Alec's direction.

"There's more?" Alec groaned. At his coachman's squirming reluctance to answer, Alec stood, poured himself a healthy measure of whiskey and tossed it down his throat. He couldn't recall having ever before drunk whiskey at six o'clock in the morning. Of course, he'd never before had the need. "Out with it, Ned," he wheezed past the fire in his stomach, certain he didn't want to hear more.

"The cap'n said she weren't traveling with nobody else. He let me talk to the crew. Some of the men said they saw a woman on board, after the boat docked, a real looker, but she weren't on the voyage." He wrung his cap between his hands and grimaced as he peered up at Alec. "They said she looked to be getting herself wed to some swell, but they couldn't figure out why they was doin' it on board, since neither one sailed on the ship."

Alec turned to the window and rammed a hand through his hair, but Ned cleared his throat again. Alec let his head drop to his chest before he turned and growled, "Go on."

"The cap'n said Miss Phillipa's trunks'd been gone through, and these," Ned held up the canvas bag, "was found in the cabin. He sent Miss Phillipa's trunks along, since your brother was her betrothed and all."

Alec stomped across the room, took the bag, peered into it, then dumped the contents onto the floor.

A small, odd pair of boots, with intricate stitching, pointed toes, and odd-looking heels clattered to the parquet floor. A pair of faded, pale-blue trousers of heavy canvas-like fabric landed on top of them. He picked them up and studied them. Too small for any man, too long for a boy; the knees had black dirt ground into them and there was a leather patch on the back with the name Ralph Lauren tooled into it. While he wondered about the meaning of the patch, he leaned over and scooped up a wad of white fabric. It was some type of shirt with short sleeves, surely an undergarment. He dropped the trousers and inspected the shirt, shocked to find the name Ralph Lauren again, embroidered in white across the chest. What manner of person walked around with his name emblazoned on his clothing? Not a man, for all these garments were far too small. And a lingering scent clung to them that had nothing masculine about it.

Alec dropped the shirt atop the heap, certain that the person who had been walking around in Ralph Lauren's clothing was the woman who now wore the emerald-and-diamond ring . . . as well as the name Hawthorne.

Who the hell had he married? *Was* he married? And why did she have on his great-aunt's ring?

The answer didn't require a great deal of imagination. The woman had obviously stolen the ring from Phillipa's effects. She'd come aboard after the ship had docked, found an empty cabin, then rummaged through the trunks. What else had she stolen from the dead woman besides the ring and the clothing?

Alec's anger, which had been smoldering since Ned's first words, ignited into a full-blown rage. He stomped to the door connecting the two chambers and slammed the panel back into the wall.

The curvy lump on the bed jerked, rolled over, and dragged a pillow over her head. He marched across the room and threw the pillow onto the floor.

"Get up," he ground through clenched teeth.

She reached behind her and started to drag the other pillow toward her. He snatched it away, then grabbed a handful of covers and yanked.

She yelped and shot upright, grappling for the blankets and jerking them back to cover herself.

"What the heck are you doing? Are you crazy?" she yelled, burrowing deeper into the covers until only puffy, terror-filled eyes peered out at him. Hair sprouted in tangled lumps from her head.

"Who are you? You are not Phillipa Morgan."

The woman's eyebrows shot skyward and she blinked at him several times as she lowered the covers a fraction of an inch.

"If I remember right, I've been telling you that all along. Shaelyn Sumner? Remember?"

Alec had opened his mouth to cut down any argument she might have, but now his mouth merely worked, emitting no sound. Damn the woman.

The ring!

"What about the ring? Why are you wearing Phillipa's betrothal ring?"

The woman brought her arms from beneath the covers, tucked the sheet tightly across her bosom, then yanked on the ring again.

"I found the stupid thing in the passageway of the ship, and I put it on so I'd remember to give it to the captain." She grimaced as the ring refused to slip over her knuckle. "I wish I'd left the darn thing where I found it."

Alec narrowed his eyes at her while she struggled.

"Why did you pretend you were Phillipa when we met? Why did you say your aunt was ill? Why did you lie? Do you realize that because of your lie, we may now be well and truly wed?" His voice had risen to nearly a bellow with his questions.

"I *told* you why I said I was Phillipa. I thought it was an act! I didn't—" She stopped in midsentence, her eyes growing so wide that an expanse of white surrounded their odd green color. "Married? What do you mean, married? It was all pretend! You have to have a marriage license to get married!" Suddenly her eyes narrowed to moss-colored slits. "You were going to marry someone you'd never met? How can you blame me for all this when you didn't even know what she looked like? Why would you marry someone you'd never met?"

"She was betrothed to my brother in childhood—"

"Your brother? You were going to marry your brother's fiancée?"

Alec could have bitten off his tongue. The woman was infuriatingly quick.

"Charles is in love with someone else, so I chose to—"

"Charles?" she bleated. "Charles?" Twin furrows

etched themselves between her brows. "If your brother is Charles, then who the heck are you?"

This was not going at all as he'd planned. She seemed to manage to turn the conversation around every time he opened his mouth.

"Who I am is not important. What *is* important—"

"Not important? You bet your life it's important, bubba! If I'm forced to go looking for an annulment, I want to know the name of the guy who tricked me into marrying him."

Alec's fingers itched to encircle her throat. With as much dignity as he could muster, he leveled a glare at her. "I am Alec Hawthorne. And you needn't seek an annulment. I plan to see to it personally."

"Fine," she said, lifting her chin in defiance, "but you'll forgive me if I make sure it's done right." She threw the thin comforter around her and inched to the edge of the bed. "So if you'll just get the heck out of here, I'll dress and be on my way."

Alec blinked at her high-handed tone. How dare she question his ability? How dare she order him around?

"You'll not leave this house until the ring's returned."

She shocked Alec to the core by uttering a foul curse under her breath, then uttered another when the covers started to slip as she struggled with the ring.

He should have averted his gaze, but he found himself fascinated with the sight of translucent ivory flesh beneath a very low line of sun-bronzed skin. He knew from when the sheet had dropped momentarily the night before that the white strip of skin crossed her breasts, but the skin on her stomach was as bronze as the rest of her. What manner of woman exposed herself to the sun in such a way as to darken her skin, let alone in such forbidden places? Had he married a woman of loose virtue? Her knowledge of curses certainly indicated as much.

"Would you please leave me alone so I can get dressed

and try to get this ring off without you hovering over me the whole time?'' she nearly barked.

He jerked his head back and stared at her, trying not to gape. If she had indeed stolen the ring, she certainly wasn't trying to wheedle her way into his good graces.

''I'll leave you to dress,'' he told her evenly, ''but someone will be watching the windows and door, in case you decide to leave before removing the ring. As long as the jewelry is returned, I will not call the authorities.'' He wouldn't call them at any rate. The last thing he wanted was for this disaster to become public knowledge.

She rolled her eyes heavenward and shook her head. As he walked from the room he heard her mutter something about ''anal retentive.''

Surely she couldn't mean . . .

After her pseudo-kidnapper left the room, Shaelyn kicked off the layers of sheet and comforter and scooted to the far side of the bed, muttering to herself and trying her best not to cuss. Every time she cursed, she gave a hundred dollars to charity. She had an awful feeling that by the time this fiasco was over, she was going to need a charity of her own.

At least her kidnapper didn't seem intent on hurting her. He'd had plenty of time and opportunity to force himself on her, if that had been part of the plan. Instead, he'd been very gentle with her.

A dark red blotch in the center of the snowy-white sheet caught her eye, and suddenly she owed another hundred dollars. She searched her arms until she found the deep scratch that had opened during the night and smeared the bedclothes. Blood had dried in several places on her arms, and now she noticed at least a dozen bruises all over her body.

She almost smiled. Having the chance to drive her knee home yesterday had been worth the bruises.

She turned her thoughts back to getting dressed, washing in the frigid water from a pitcher on an antique stand, scrubbing the scratches on her arms, purposely ignoring the lack of modern conveniences and all that implied.

She found her underthings on top of the rumpled heap of the costume and cringed at not being able to put on clean lingerie. But it was that or none at all, and she'd already goofed once by sleeping without them. She'd never in her life been able to sleep with clothing against her skin, and she'd been so mentally exhausted the night before, she just hadn't thought.

Just as she settled the hopelessly wrinkled gown over her head, kicking herself for leaving her clothes on the ship, a quiet knock sounded at her door and the little red-headed maid who'd fled the room the night before entered with a tray.

The aroma of bacon and eggs and freshly baked bread reminded Shae that she hadn't eaten in ages.

"Can I help you dress, ma'am?" the girl asked, with twin spots of pink brightening her cheeks.

"Yes! Thanks." Shaelyn presented her back and lifted the thick tangle of curls away from the buttons. "I nearly dislocated my arm the last time I tried to reach those things."

"If you'd like, I could iron your gown for you, ma'am," the redhead hesitantly offered.

"Oh, no, thanks . . . what's your name?"

"Margaret, ma'am."

"No, thanks, Margaret. I'm going to be changing into my own clothes soon." Shaelyn stood quietly while Margaret worked at the dozen or so buttons. A thought that Shae had been studiously avoiding kept shoving its way to the fore as she stood still and studied her surroundings.

The view from the window wasn't quite right. She couldn't put her finger on it, but it lacked something. Neon-colored buoys bobbing in the water? Motorboats dotting the blue expanse? The lack of noise almost screamed at her. No sounds of boat or car engines. No airplanes in the distance. No telephones ringing or TVs blaring or even the muffled sound of a radio from deep inside the house. Even the air smelled different.

A spider of apprehension crawled up the back of her neck as her hands came together through her hair and she unconsciously tugged at the ring on her finger.

She cleared her throat once and looked at the ceiling.

"Umm, Margaret, what year would you say it is?"

The movement of fingers against her back stopped.

"Beg pardon, ma'am?"

"What year would you say it is?" she repeated, trying to act as if the question wasn't as asinine as it sounded.

"Why, it's the year of our Lord, eighteen hundred and thirty."

Shaelyn froze as her heart tripped and her breath caught in her lungs. Margaret finished buttoning the gown then stepped away, but still Shaelyn stood there.

"Are you all right, ma'am? Would you like for me to fetch Mr. Alec?"

Shaelyn dropped her arms and sank into the nearest chair.

"No, no. Don't get Alec." The last person she wanted was Alec, she told herself, refusing to think about how good his arms had felt the night before when she'd awakened from her nightmare.

The little maid poured a cup of steaming coffee from a silver urn and handed it to Shaelyn, then turned her attention to making the bed.

She flipped the covers back, glanced at the blood, then pulled the sheets from the bed.

"Oh, I'm sorry," Shaelyn offered. "Last night I . . . I guess . . ." She stopped talking when she realized she was babbling. To be truthful, she didn't think her spinning mind could put together a coherent apology anyway.

Margaret left the room, then reappeared in a matter of minutes with a fresh set of sheets.

Shaelyn hadn't moved. Hadn't even blinked. She just

sat in the chair, twisting the stubborn ring on her finger
and trying to pull her shattered thoughts together.

1830.

She wasn't dreaming. She knew that. She always knew
when she was having one of her weird dreams. This wasn't
one of them.

She hardly ever even drank, so she couldn't be drunk.
She didn't remember getting sick or having an accident,
so she couldn't be in a coma. She was positive she hadn't
eaten or drunk anything before or after meeting Alec, so
he couldn't have drugged her.

A dull throb started at the base of her skull. She closed
her eyes and willed herself to relax.

She could almost believe she'd somehow traveled
through time.

Since her earliest memories, she'd had strange things
happening to her. Once she'd had déjà vu so strongly,
she'd known her way around a city she'd never been to.
She had memories that included people she'd never met,
yet she knew them in her memory.

She'd never quite felt that she belonged, no matter
where she was or who she was with. At first she'd thought
it was some sort of psychological thing from being
adopted, but as she matured she realized that her roots had
nothing to do with her sense of displacement. She'd always
felt as if she'd dressed for a part in a play but put on the
wrong character's costume.

Could she possibly have entered some sort of time
warp? It almost made as much sense as anything else she
could come up with.

Alec refolded the marriage certificate, downed his second
glass of whiskey for the morning, and resisted the urge to
bang his head against the nearest wall.

The marriage document acclaimed to one and all that
on the twenty-ninth day of July, in the year of our Lord,
1830, one Reverend Ezekiel Forester joined Alec Haw-

thorne and Shaelyn Sumner in holy matrimony.

She'd signed her real name. If it was her real name. And he'd signed his.

And, blast it all, that traitorous Griffin had witnessed the document with his sweeping signature, no doubt never once looking at the names.

Alec sighed. Why should Griffin have looked at the names? Alec himself had not bothered to even glance at the paper once it'd been signed.

To make matters worse, Margaret had come to him just moments ago, telling him how the blasted woman had asked her what year it was. No doubt trying to prove insanity, now that she'd been found out. Alec had given the maid some vague story about the woman having been ill on board the ship, and no doubt her thoughts were still muddled from the illness. He'd instructed Margaret to keep the information to herself, since their ''guest'' would be embarrassed if news of her irrational question got around.

He dropped into the chair behind his desk and massaged his forehead with his fingertips. What an absolute mess. Did he still have grounds for annulment? He'd deceived her as much as she'd deceived him.

''You have a caller, sir.''

Charles strode into the room behind Martin, looking as haggard as Alec felt, and much older than his twenty-one years.

''Thank you, Martin.'' His brother turned and shut the door when the butler retreated. ''Alec, we must do something. I refuse to marry this Phillipa Morgan. I'd resigned myself to the fate, but that was before I fell in love with Mary. I won't give her up, Alec, because Father made a business deal eleven years ago. He shall have to build his beloved shipping empire without using me as a sacrifice. I won't marry her, if Morgan Shippers were the largest in the world.''

Well, at least Alec could brighten one person's day out of this mess. How macabre, he realized, to brighten one's day with the news of a death. He shook his head.

"Charlie, you're free to wed Mary. Phillipa Morgan is dead. And I suggest you wed your beloved before Father can shackle you to another fortune. God knows he's been trying to find the highest bidder for me since Daphne died last year, even though I've warned him I'll refuse to bow to his wishes again in the marriage mart. Saint's blood, an arranged marriage for a man of thirty years."

Charles paled as he leaned on the desk with his fists.

"What are you saying? Phillipa dead? When? How? And how do you know of this?"

"Her ship docked yesterday." Alec held up a hand to silence Charles's questions. "I . . . um . . . I appropriated her letter. Fortunately it arrived while I was visiting Mother and Father."

"Have you gone absolutely mad? Father will have your head!"

"And he's welcome to it," Alec muttered. He looked up at his brother leaning over the desk and waved him into a chair. "I'll worry about Father when the time comes. But for now, I'd suggest you find yourself a minister and get yourself wed. Phillipa Morgan and her aunt died during the voyage and were buried at sea."

Alec didn't bother to mention that he'd just been apprised of the facts himself less than an hour ago. Until he decided what to do about Shaelyn Sumner—or rather, Shaelyn Hawthorne—he would keep her existence to himself.

Color seeped back into Charles's face. "How dreadful," he said, more to himself than to Alec. "You know I wouldn't have wished her dead."

"Of course not. Her death isn't your fault. She and her aunt fell ill. Four other passengers died as well."

Charles leaned back into the leather of the chair and rubbed his temples. "I say, I feel guilty at this monstrous wave of relief I—"

"Alec!" The angry, booming voice echoed from the front door.

Alec fell back against his chair and rolled his eyes heavenward.

"Heavenly Father, I know You have a sense of humor, but must You be so zealous in displaying it?"

William Hawthorne stormed through the heavily carved door to the library, veins bulging and nostrils flaring. Alec's mother, Jane, rushed in behind her husband, wringing her gloved hands and whispering, "Not in front of the servants, William!"

He ignored her, as if she were no more than a fly buzzing behind him.

He stopped in front of the desk. Alec and Charles rose, as they'd been taught all their lives to do.

In a roar that would have done the fiercest of lions proud, he demanded, "Explain to me why you have married your brother's betrothed."

Charles's eyes bulged and his neck cracked when he jerked his gaze to Alec.

Their father stood there, trembling with fury, while their mother's entreaties to remember himself went ignored.

Alec continued to stand, soundly cursing the servants' grapevine, swearing to turn out whoever had leaked the knowledge. He knew with a certainty the trail would lead back to Ned's wife. He poured himself his third glass of whiskey that morning, idly remembering the days—only a few short hours ago—when he'd been a temperate drinker.

"I did not marry Phillipa Morgan, Father. She's dead."

That piece of information knocked the wind from the old man's sails.

"Oh my," his mother squeaked.

"I do, however," he went on, "seem to find myself married this morning, since I found the woman wearing Great-Aunt Eleanor's ring on the ship and married her on board. It wasn't until this morning that Ned returned to inform me that Miss Morgan had died. It seems I've married a stranger.''

''*What?*'' his father boomed.

Charles dropped back into the chair, then vacated it immediately for his mother. She snatched up a sheaf of papers from Alec's desk and fanned herself, emitting odd little noises that never quite formed into words.

Alec could almost hear the Almighty chuckling to Himself from above.

''What do you mean you've married a stranger?'' His father continued to bellow—the only means he'd ever known of communicating.

''Perhaps I should rephrase that, Father. She is no more a stranger than Miss Morgan was to Charles, or Daphne Witherson was to me.''

William Hawthorne's face turned from mottled red to a hue resembling Alec's favorite claret.

''I demand to know why she was wearing the betrothal ring!''

Alec calmly poured yet another whiskey while he pictured the celestial Power slapping His knee with mirth.

''It seems,'' his gaze wandered around the room, landing on shades of green that matched his wife's eyes, ''that she found it on the ship and slipped it on to remember to give it to the captain.''

The angels, he was sure, were pounding each other on the back now, holding their sides and gathering to peer over at the comedy being played out in the library of Windward Cottage.

For a moment Alec thought his father would climb over the desk to get to Alec's throat. In a rare moment of self-control, William managed to stop himself. Instead, he turned, grabbed the nearest vacant chair, slammed it onto the floor, then threw himself into it with a glare.

''You will start at the beginning and explain to me why you married a woman because she found your great-aunt's ring, and then I will meet this woman myself.''

Alec spent the next thirty minutes trying to weave the truth into some semblance of a sensible explanation. Only then did he realize that his actions—when put into words—weren't nearly as logical as they'd seemed at the time. His only defense was that he hadn't had the luxury of time to come up with a better plan. And, truth be told, he was not experienced in spur-of-the-moment activities.

"I refuse to believe, Alec Christopher, that you do not see that the woman stole that ring and then posed as Charles's betrothed when she saw the opportunity to snare a rich husband. Thought it all an act, my eye."

"There's no proof to that, Father." Why was he taking up for her, when he himself had made the same accusations no more than an hour before? Even now he had her room watched because he didn't trust her.

Because, you great fool, for some strange reason, you want to believe her.

"Where is this woman? I daresay when we delve into her background, we shall find her history as larcenous as it is thespian." While he spoke, his father neatly bent Alec's favorite letter opener into a quaint, silver rainbow. "Have one of your people bring the girl here."

Alec bristled at being ordered about in his own home. Returning his father's glare, he circled the desk and went to the door.

"I'll fetch her myself." Before stepping into the hallway, he turned back to the little group. "And, Father, please do not waste all your charm on her at once. Or at least until we get to the truth of the matter."

"Alec." His father's voice stopped him once more. "Is there any reason why you cannot pursue an annulment?"

Alec's jaw popped when he ground his teeth.

"No, Father. In fact, she wishes one."

The only sound when he left the room and strode to the stairs was that of his mother fanning herself with the morning's invoices.

With one foot on the bottom step, he happened to glance

out the window of the formal parlor. With a curse, and the
sound of celestial laughter pealing from the heavens, he
changed directions and ran for the back door.

Shaelyn prowled the confines of the bedroom, picking up
knickknacks and setting them back down without even
looking at them. The more she prowled, the angrier she
got.

How dare he lock her up and put guards on her, as if
she were a criminal? That's what she got for wanting to
return that stupid ring. No good deed goes unpunished.
That was the motto her college roommate had lived by. If
she got out of this alive, she might very well adopt the
saying for herself.

She paced the perimeter of the room, opened the door
to glare at the man sitting in the chair in the hall. She
slammed the door, then stomped to the window and
growled at the sight of another man propped under a tree,
eating an apple. When he nodded at her she slung the
drapes closed.

Oh!

She marched around the room, kicking at the skirts of
that stupid, stupid gown. What she wouldn't give for her
jeans and tee shirt.

She passed the pocket door that separated the room from
Charles's. No. Alec's. Her captor's name was Alec. On
her second pass, she stopped and pressed her ear against
the carved wood. She could hear no sounds on the other
side. With all the stealth of a cat burglar, she slid the door
open a crack and peeked in.

Empty.

Heart drumming in her chest, she slipped through the
opening, tiptoed to the window on the far side of the room,
and peered out. She saw no sign of anyone watching
Alec's windows.

Ha! Male superiority underestimates again.

Without a second thought she pulled the sheets from his

bed, ripped the Egyptian cotton into several strips, and within five minutes had them tied together, one end tied to the stone balcony and the other dangling a few feet from the ground. Not until she started to climb over the balcony did she realize the problem her clothing might pose. She yanked off the petticoats, grabbed the back hem, pulled it between her legs, and tucked it into the front of her waistband, giving the gown the look of a Middle Eastern eunuch's garb. She tested the knot in the sheets, scrambled over the stone railing, and lowered herself hand-over-hand down the side of the house.

Just a few more feet.

"Going somewhere?"

An ironclad grip fastened around both her ankles.

In one startled gasp she upped her charitable donations by another hundred dollars.

"With language like that, dear wife, one might find cause to wonder about your breeding."

"Oh, you can take your breeding and—" She stopped herself. She'd be da . . . darned if she'd let him stir her enough to curse again. "Let go of my feet!" She kicked out, but his grip remained solid.

"Let go of the rope, or should I say what's left of my favorite sheets."

"No!" She peered down at him. Her feet hovered nearly a foot and a half above his head, yet he held her with ease. Her stomach flipped when she looked down. It had to be from the height. It certainly wasn't because of that smug, heart-stopping smile of his.

"I daresay, Shaelyn, I'll wager that I can hold your feet longer than you can hold onto those sheets."

Her hands were already beginning to slip. And it wasn't as if she had any hope of escaping now. With an evil grin, she looked down, calculated her trajectory, and let go.

"No, wait! I didn't—OOPH!"

He fell flat on his back with Shaelyn sprawled on top of him. She managed to land a knee dead-center in his stomach. Even though he wheezed for breath, he managed to get his arms wrapped around her and hold her so tight she could do no more damage.

"Let go of me! Let go!" She struggled against him, but it was like struggling against steel bands. She stopped her squirming and glared at him. He glared back. And then a hint of a grin curved his lips. She felt her own lips twitching and fought to stop it. He didn't bother to stop his. In moments his laughter boomed in her ears, and she found herself laughing with him. At what, she didn't know, but suddenly everything seemed ridiculous. They lay there in the dirt of the flower bed, surrounded with the scent of crushed pansies, howling with laughter and gasping for breath. When her neck started to hurt, she rested her head on his shoulder and giggled into his shirt.

And suddenly neither of them found anything funny anymore.

"Shaelyn." His voice was almost a whisper, and she raised her head to look at him. Golden-brown eyes studied her, sent hot little shivers racing through her blood.

He raised his head and she watched his mouth come closer. The warmth of his breath mingled with her own. This was insane. She didn't know him. She'd tried to escape him. She'd melt if he kissed her. She'd die if he didn't.

"May we presume this is your wife?"

Chapter 4

ALEC STOPPED, HIS mouth a fraction of an inch from Shaelyn's. He turned his head, and so did she, to look up at a man glowering down at them, a woman fanning herself, and a younger version of Alec. Charles, perhaps?

"Why, yes, Father. May I present my wife, Shaelyn . . ." He turned back to her with an irreverent glint in his eyes. "What was your surname again, darling?"

"Sumner," she supplied sweetly.

"Oh yes. Sumner. Shaelyn Sumner Hawthorne." He loosened his steel grip for the first time before helping her to her feet. "May I introduce my mother, Jane, my father, William, and my brother—"

"Charles?"

The young man in question looked surprised that she would know of him.

"Why, yes," Charles said.

Alec dusted off the back of his clothing, then brushed Shaelyn's skirts as if it were the most natural thing in the world. The gesture, however, felt more like a caress with all her nerves still tingling from that near-kiss. Thank heavens her skirts had come untucked from their harem-pants fashion. She fluffed them around her as if she always picked herself up out of petunias to meet people.

"It seems my bride tired of waiting for me to procure the annulment," Alec said in way of explanation.

"Yes," Shaelyn smiled. "And I have an aversion to being held prisoner, especially for something I didn't do." She smiled as if she were accustomed to making such statements on a regular basis.

Alec looked a little uncomfortable at that. Could he be having second thoughts about believing her? And why was he being so nice, when earlier he'd all but threatened her?

The woman named Jane stood wringing her hands while William grabbed Shaelyn's hand and studied the ring.

"Take it off," he barked, then shoved her hand back at her.

She managed not to jerk from having the order boomed in her face. Somehow she maintained her sweet smile and held her hand back out to him.

"I'd be happy to take the ring off, Mr. Hawthorne. And you have my permission to try. Maybe if you continue to glare at it, my finger will wither and the ring will fall off. Heaven knows, I've tried everything else."

It would have been impossible for William Hawthorne to intensify that glare, so he shifted his attention to Alec.

"What does she mean she's being held prisoner?"

Alec opened his mouth to answer, but Shaelyn bristled and stepped in front of him.

"I can answer for myself, thankyouverymuch. Your son has put guards on me, for fear I'll leave with the ring. But I can assure you, as soon as the ring comes off, it will be returned. I don't want the ring, and I don't want to be married to your son." Why did that last statement feel like a lie? She ignored the odd, foreign feeling of belonging that had started to uncurl when Alec had almost kissed her. She turned to her questionable husband and gave him an innocent, irreverent smile. "I'm sorry I tried to escape, but I usually do the opposite of whatever people order."

Disapproval emanated from his father, as thick as the fog that rolled in from the ocean, but Alec expected nothing less. Indeed, so far his father had behaved with boring predictability. And Alec had long ago stopped quivering in his shoes at the sight of William Hawthorne's glare. Charles and his mother simply stood there: Charles with his mouth agape, his mother making worried little noises.

Even though he no longer feared his father, he was grateful that Shaelyn hadn't launched into her extraordinary story about being some sort of journalist. He had enough to contend with, without a hue and cry to send the woman to an asylum.

"If you'll not confine me to a room, I promise I won't run away. After all, where would I go? I don't know anyone here."

From the corner of his eyes, Alec could see his father's disapproving stance. If for no other reason than that, Alec chose to grant Shaelyn her request. She seemed surprised that he capitulated, and he had to admit that he surprised himself.

Defying his overbearing father brought him a sense of satisfaction. Perhaps he would do it more often.

"Alec, I want to see you in the library. Alone." William issued his order, then turned and marched off, his stride telegraphing that he expected nothing less than absolute compliance.

Alec turned back to Shaelyn. She frowned at his father's retreating back before turning a questioning gaze to Alec.

"You may leave your room. I apologize for locking you in earlier. Blame it on my temper. But if you leave the grounds, I ask that you take someone with you."

"Fair enough," she nodded.

He studied her face for a moment, wondering at her odd language, and then wondering if her body, too, had come alive when they'd almost kissed. While she'd lain atop him, he'd felt like a youth again. An irreverent, devil-may-care youth. It had felt like heaven.

With a sigh he broke the gaze and turned to make his way to the library. When he arrived, he found his father sitting behind the desk—Alec's desk. His knuckles popped as his hands curled into fists.

William leaned back in the chair with his arms on the armrests, like Henry VIII waiting to dole out judgment on a hapless subject.

"I want your immediate annulment from this... woman."

Alec's fingernails bit into the palms of his hand at his father's king-of-the-castle attitude. William had used the word *woman* as if it were interchangeable with *slut*.

"I'd already planned to start proceedings as soon as I see my attorney. You needn't worry—"

"Needn't worry?" William blasted. "My eldest son sets out to deceive me! Marries the woman he thinks is his brother's betrothed! The woman her father and I arranged for him to marry! All in the name of *love*." Again, he'd pronounced the word as if it were the vilest of curses. "You get the annulment, Alec Christopher, because I've betrothed you to someone else!"

For the first time in his memory, a surge of anger tore through Alec with such violence it left him light-headed.

"You have done what?" Though he spoke his words quietly, they carried all the force of a bellow.

"I believe I enunciated that statement quite clearly."

"Father, has it not come to your attention recently that I am a man of thirty years? Do you not find it at all ludicrous to even contemplate arranging my marriage?"

William's neck bulged over his pristine collar as his face turned the color of a ripe tomato.

"I am still the head of this family! A man marries to further his business and his social standing. I won't have our good name and our business threatened because some little thief has outdeceived you!''

Alec closed his eyes and wondered why he ever bothered to have a conversation with this man. But with the closing of his eyes came the image of Shaelyn, dangling from the torn, knotted sheets, the ring still on her finger. Enough time had passed to convince him that the almost-kiss and all that followed had been nothing more than defiance against his father.

He massaged his eyes before looking back at the man behind the desk. He might as well find out the identity of this latest marriage acquisition. Then he would disabuse his father of any notion that he might comply with yet another arranged marriage.

''Would you care to enlighten me as to the name of this hapless woman, no doubt too homely to acquire a husband in the normal manner?''

Leather creaked as William settled back into the chair and picked up the letter opener he'd earlier mangled.

''Faith Almany.''

''Faith . . .'' Alec's heart lodged in his throat. *Faith.* The one name he would have never imagined. The woman he'd fallen in love with twelve years earlier. The woman his father had forbidden him to marry . . . because he was already betrothed to a woman ten years his junior with a face and disposition less appealing than a jackass's. ''But she's married. She moved to Boston with her husband years—''

''Dead. Nearly a year past,'' his father interrupted. ''She'll be back here by October. You'll wed before Christmas.''

A string of emotions warred in Alec. He would defy his father to his dying breath over this latest chess move if the woman had been anyone but Faith.

Faith. His first love. Just the thought of her brought a warmth to his heart, a tenderness to his soul. Much as Charles must feel when thinking about his Mary.

Alec squared his shoulders and turned his gaze back to his father's smug face.

"When Faith arrives here, she and I will discuss the matter. *We* will decide if and when we shall marry."

Amazingly, his father chose not to bark out a contradicting order. Instead his face contorted into the closest thing to a smile Alec had ever seen; then he rose from the chair and left the room without a word.

Shaelyn walked the rocky beach for hours, most of that time spent tugging on the ring that refused to leave her finger.

She had no doubt now that she had somehow traveled to 1830. Since the moment she stepped out of the ship's cabin, she hadn't seen one single modern convenience. No telephones, no light bulbs, no cars, no motorboats. The sky held no sign of airplanes. Indeed, the very air smelled cleaner, perfumed with the scent of ocean and flowers and whiffs of freshly scythed grass instead of car exhaust and cigarette smoke.

And she had no doubt that the emerald-and-diamond ring stuck on her finger was the key to how she'd gotten to the past. Why else would Alec have recognized it? The ring was even responsible for keeping her a virtual prisoner at the home of a man who was far too charming for Shaelyn's comfort. The last thing she needed was to fall for a guy from 1830. Talk about a different time zone.

She shook off that roller-coaster feeling just the thought of his grin caused and concentrated on getting the ring off. Once it was off, she had a feeling that she would return to 1999.

What were they thinking in her time? Had anyone even noticed she was gone? Had Pete gone looking for her and found nothing more than her tee shirt and jeans and cowboy boots?

A tingly shock raced up the back of her neck. Pete wouldn't find her clothes and boots because she'd had them on when she "traveled." The memory of the ship pitching with such violence and the vertigo she'd felt after slipping on the ring came rushing back to her. The cabin had smelled fresher, looked lived in. The clothes had been Charles's fiancée's.

If she hadn't been convinced before that the ring had caused all this, she was now. She redoubled her efforts, wincing at how sore her finger had become from all the tugging.

She sat atop a large boulder jutting from the sand and stared out at the islands dotting the horizon. She didn't know how long she'd sat there, hours maybe, before she got that creepy feeling that someone was watching her.

The tide had come in while she'd stared out to sea, and the shore was a good twenty feet behind her now. Alec stood at the edge of the water, his mood obviously different from when she'd left him. The glaring hadn't returned, but he looked decidedly uncomfortable.

She stood up on the rock she'd perched on and scanned the water. No way around it, she was going to have to wade back to shore. After slipping off the old-fashioned shoes that were a tad too big, she hiked up her gown, threw it over her arm, sat back down, and inched her way off the rock.

"Stay there," he called, but the water lapping around the boulder drowned out anything else he said. Shaelyn, of course, ignored him, then lowered her head as she picked her way across the slippery rock bottom.

"I told you to stay there!"

When he grabbed her arm, she started so violently she lost her balance. Alec grappled with her, both of them thigh-deep in the water, and then she went down, dragging him with her. She came up laughing, he came up sputtering.

"Blast it all! I told you to stay put! I would have carried you to shore."

"Oh, really! I was doing fine until you started helping."

She laughed and raked a handful of clinging, spiderweb hair from her cheeks, then automatically reached up and smoothed an inky, dripping spike from his forehead.

The moment her fingers touched his face, she knew it was a mistake. His angry gaze softened, and they stared at each other while cool waves tugged at her skirts. His eyes gentled more than she would have ever dreamed they could, and her fingers ached to trace the outline of a jaw that would do a sculptor proud. *Don't kiss me*, she thought. *I don't need to make this complicated.*

Would his kiss taste as good as he looked?

His head slowly bent toward hers, and against her better judgment she lifted her face to meet him.

A moment of confusion lit in his eyes, then he jerked upright and plowed his fingers through his dripping hair as he spoke to a point above her left shoulder.

"You should get out of that wet gown. You'll catch your death." Without waiting for a comment, he grasped her elbow and guided her toward shore.

Shaelyn stumbled on her hem, then yanked her arm back, wadded the fabric in her hands, and trudged across the submerged rocks alone, numb with rejection.

She didn't need this. She didn't need to be stuck in the past, with this man who ran hot and cold toward her. She didn't need to have this big, empty feeling in the center of her chest.

She needed to get home.

"Shaelyn, wait!"

Alec took her arm again just as they reached the shore. Shae dropped her sodden skirts and pasted a neutral, in-quisitive look on her face before turning around.

He bowed his head and massaged his brow before speaking. "I'm sorry about . . ." He shook his head. "I came out here to tell you that my solicitor will be back from Boston in three days. I'll apply for the annulment then."

She nodded, then turned back toward the house, ignoring the little drop her heart had taken.

"I'm sorry I've put you through this." His words stopped her and she turned back once more. "I had no right to do what I did."

Shae sensed this was a man who did not often apologize. It touched her that he chose to do so now.

"I've never thought to ask," he continued. "You must have family or friends you were meeting. They must be worried."

She studied the rock-strewn beach while she shook out her dripping skirts. How could she tell him the truth?

"No. No one," she said, then looked up to meet his gaze. "I have no one here."

He seemed uncomfortable with the honesty of her statement. After tugging on the wet collar of his shirt and searching the sky for a moment, he swung his gaze back to her and gave her a hesitant grin.

"I could be your friend. After all, I am your husband." He shrugged like a little boy in trouble. A devastatingly handsome little boy who made all the little girls' hearts flutter.

A smile of her own tugged at her lips while she ignored the butterflies that grin caused.

"You have a point, I suppose. I could use a friend right now. After all, I'm getting an annulment. And I'm not going anywhere until I get this ring off my finger."

"An unreasonable blackguard surely, who has put you in this position." Alec took her arm and they started back down the beach.

Shaelyn shook her head and shrugged with a smile. "And a confused one. The poor man isn't even sure what his name is."

He cringed at that, then laughed. With the sound, her heart rose back into her chest, and for the first time since the carriage ride there, she had a lightness to her step.

"Can I ask you something?"

He helped her over a large cluster of rocks. "I am an open book."

She waited until she had solid footing before posing the question.

"Why did you do it? Why did you marry someone you didn't know?"

Alec clamped his hands behind his back and stared at the rocky shore as they walked.

"I'm afraid you'll not think better of me when the story's told."

"Hey, you don't have much to lose," she teased. He swiveled his head and stared down at her until she gave him enough of a smile to ease his conscious. He drew in a deep breath and let it out.

"I was trying to kill two birds with one stone, so to speak. Give my father another branch on the family tree of heirs, and free Charles to marry the woman he loves."

Shaelyn listened, astounded at Alec's story. If she had not already concluded that she had somehow traveled to 1830, she had no doubts about it now. Arranged marriages, fathers joining businesses via their children, creating business dynasties.

If not for the death of Alec's fiancée, he would already be a married man and Charles still would have been free to marry whomever he wished. At least Shaelyn could thankfully see no connection with her appearance there and the cause of Phillipa's death. Would anyone who slipped that ring on travel through time? Apparently not, if Phillipa had worn it. If Shaelyn managed to get the ring off her finger, would she go back to her own time? And if so, would the same amount of time have passed? Would she remember where she'd been? How many other people had experienced time travel?

Her mind spun with more questions than she would ever have answers to. But one thing she felt instinctively was that the ring had brought *her* to Alec; that another woman might have slipped the ring on in 1999 and never felt the vertigo, never opened her eyes in another time, never felt more than pride at the beautiful, antique diamond-and-emerald jewelry adorning her hand.

Alec's hand steadied her arm as he helped her over another patch of large rocks. She glanced up at him to smile her thanks, then froze.

Wave after wave of déjà vu washed over her like the ocean washing over the rocks on the shore. She'd been here before, seen this picture of Alec, lived this moment in time. She'd heard the water lapping against the beach, seen the clouds skimming across the sky. Alec's face would turn to her, smile, then turn serious. He would ask her if she was quite well.

"Shaelyn, are you quite well?"

She blinked and studied his face more. She'd dreamed this. His was one of the faces in the dream that always left her crying. Alec's face, and Charles's. And Alec's parents. These were the faces in her memories. Memories of people she'd never met.

"Shaelyn, are you well?"

In the distance there would be a cry of a bird, and the sun would come from behind a cloud to glint off Alec's softly blowing hair like sunshine on black, rippling silk. His golden eyes would catch the light and come alive with sparkles.

Blood roared in her ears when the bird called out. A dizzying tingle crept from the pit of her stomach to the top of her head when the cloud blocking the sun scudded across the sky, lighting his eyes with an inner glow, bouncing black diamonds off ebony strands of hair.

The déjà vu passed then, the sense of precognition gone. But she knew now that she'd been destined to live through this. From the moment of her birth to unknown parents, fate had guided her to this moment in time. And all she could think about was the tortured anguish that drove her from her sleep when the dream came and left her aching with an emptiness that tore at her soul. Would she relive all of her bouts of déjà vu now, here in the past?

She looked away from Alec and continued their walk.

"Tell me about the ring, Alec." She tried to keep her voice calm, conversational, with no trace of the apprehension tumbling in her chest. "Was it new, or is there some history to it?"

Alec took her arm as he guided her toward the path away from the beach. That simple touch soothed her soul and eased the roaring in her ears.

"The ring most certainly isn't new. However, no one knows the true story behind it. It is said to be an heirloom handed down from Celtic ancestors. The last owner was a great-aunt who, kindly worded, was more than a little eccentric. She used to spin tales about the ring having powers, changing lives. No one paid heed to her words. She was never the same after her husband disappeared. I would not be surprised to find that she acquired the ring from a jeweler, then fabricated the Celtic ancestors and all the other stories from her poor deranged mind."

Shaelyn tried to stop her hand from trembling as she splayed her fingers to look at the ring. The setting wasn't particularly feminine. A man quite possibly would have worn the ring on his little finger, especially in the days when men wore white makeup, rouge, and beauty patches. Had the great-aunt's husband come from another time, taken the ring off, and returned to his time?

She tugged again at the circlet on her finger.

"Don't." Alec stopped her by taking her hands in his. "Your finger is red and swollen. You'll do more harm than good. There is no rush now. I know you had no intentions of stealing it. This whole debacle is my doing."

She let him continue to labor under that misconception for the time being. Now wasn't the time to explain exactly *when* she'd put the ring on.

Chapter 5

"Y OU HAVE PUT me in a pickle, Alec Christopher."
His mother sat across from him with her teacup daintily
hovering at her lips. He noticed more silver strands thread-
ing her jet-black hair, but her skin still looked as youthful
as a girl's. "If she attends the masquerade ball, do we
introduce her as your wife? And, if so, how do we explain
the annulment later? Do we introduce her as a family
friend? Do we simply not invite her? Your father, of
course, insists she not come. This is a pickle, Alec Christopher."

Alec tossed back the last of his tea and wished it were
something stronger. Masquerade balls. With everything
else, with the latest shipment to meet, he now had to worry
about a masquerade ball. But he could little complain.
He'd brought the mess upon himself.

"Excuse me." Shaelyn stepped into the room, pink
staining her cheeks, looking fresh and touchable in a gown
of palest blue in some summery, wispy fabric. She must
be making the contents of Phillipa's trunks available to
herself, since he knew she'd sent for no other clothing. He
would have to order her more garments, or make sure she

sent for her own. He would send for a seamstress immediately. "I . . . I overheard the conversation as I was coming down the stairs."

His mother made a little apologetic squeak and suddenly
found it necessary to pour another cup of tea.

"Anyway, I thought I could solve your problem for you.
You don't have to invite me. In fact, I'd rather you didn't.
I don't know anyone. I . . . well, it would just be simpler
for everyone if I wasn't there."

"I didn't mean to imply that you are not welcome,
dear," Jane insisted. "It is just so . . . confusing. And Mr.
Hawthorne is being so fussy about the whole matter."

When Shaelyn smiled, a fist squeezed Alec's heart.

"Shaelyn, we will bow to your wishes, since I am the
one who put you in this awkward position," he offered.
"If you wish to attend, you shall attend. If you would
prefer not, we will not expect you to—"

"Well, the newlyweds. What a charming picture."

Griffin marched through the parlor doors, slapping his
riding gloves against his palm. A long-suffering Martin
followed him.

"Mr. Elliott is here to see you, sir," Martin intoned,
determined as ever to observe propriety.

"Thank you, Martin. Show him in," Alec returned, with
the same degree of formality. If he didn't know better, he
would have imagined a twitch to Martin's lips before the
butler left the room.

One glance at Griffin told Alec that his friend had already somehow gleaned the turn of events taken in Alec's
fiasco of a marriage. Oh yes, the heavens had most likely
gone for centuries without so much to keep them amused.

"Mrs. Hawthorne and Mrs. Hawthorne." He seemed to
stress the name when he bowed toward Shaelyn. "May I
compliment the two of you on your loveliness this morning?"

"How kind of you, Mr. Elliott," Alec's mother said
with a smile.

Shaelyn merely gave him a distracted nod. Somehow her lack of interest pleased Alec. Women always threw themselves at Griffin, waxing poetic about his lovely blue eyes and shiny dark hair or some such twaddle. That Shaelyn hadn't fallen under his spell no doubt tweaked at his friend's self-confidence. Not that Griffin's confidence could be dented with anything less than a kick from a Clydesdale.

"Alec, I have some business to talk over, and there is no sense in boring the ladies." He bowed to the women, winked roguishly at Alec's mother, then strode toward the library.

Perhaps not even a Clydesdale's kick.

Alec excused himself and followed Griffin, trying to put Shaelyn from his mind. No doubt his friend had news of the next shipload of smuggled goods.

The moment the door closed behind him, Griffin dropped into a chair and cast a lazy gaze at Alec, but the look did little to hide his true concern.

"Your father will have your head over this if he ever finds out."

Alec lowered himself into the leather chair behind the desk.

"At this moment in time, I am not all together certain that he isn't welcome to it. What news have you?"

Griffin pulled a crisp piece of vellum from within his coat and unfolded it.

"The shipment is to be unloaded at the next dark of the moon. Really, Alec," he tossed the scrap of paper onto the desk and assumed his casual rogue façade, "are you not tiring of this little game? If you mean to continue, we should at the very least devise a name for you, so that you can gain a reputation. Let me see." Griffin tapped his temple with his forefinger. "Robin Hood has been taken. So has the Swamp Fox. I know!" He snapped his fingers. "The Black and White Puffin!"

Alec had to force the deadpan stare at Griffin's outrageous suggestion. But only Griffin would have the audacity to suggest he name himself after the silly looking bird that lived along the coast.

"Actually," he picked up the piece of paper from his desk and scanned the message, "if you even suggest that again, you shall be able to call *yourself* the Black and *Blue* Puffin, from the beating I will give you."

Griffin cocked an eyebrow at him. "Indeed? Which means that you would then have to settle for being known as the Severely Bruised ... Something-or-Other." He waved his hand like the dilettante he loved to pretend to be. Obviously tiring of the banter, he leaned forward and pointed at the message.

"You have less than a week to sail to Maryland and meet the shipment, then get back here in time for your parents' ball. You'll not be able to explain your way out of missing the event."

Alec rummaged in his desk for the almanac, found the date for the new moon, then calculated in his head.

"If we leave tonight, we should be back in time enough not to raise questions."

"And what of your new wife? Will she not find the disappearance of her dear husband suspicious, especially when he fails to slip between her sheets to warm away the chill?"

Alec resisted the urge to throw something at his friend.

"Do not play the fool with me, Elliott. It's obvious that you are well aware of the turn these events have taken. I would like to know, however, how you came by such knowledge."

Griffin leaned back in his chair and smiled.

"I could blame it on the servants' grapevine, but Ned's squeaky wife has been well-oiled. In this case your dear little sister has made the knowledge known. Of course, I'm sure she believed she was being discreet at the time."

Molly! The little troublemaker. He would strangle her with his bare hands.

"Tell me, Alec. If this wife of yours isn't Phillipa, who is she and where did she come from? I can understand the story about her finding the ring, perhaps even believe it. But why hasn't her family come to her rescue?"

Alec cringed on the inside at all the questions he'd meticulously avoided.

"I don't know, Griffin. I asked her on that first day, and she gave me a cock-and-bull story about being a journalist writing a story for a newspaper." He leaned back in his chair. "An obvious lie. Who ever heard of a female journalist? But I attributed her story to fear. She most certainly is not from the area. Her speech patterns are odd, and her voice holds the lilt of a Southerner. Indeed, she sounds quite a bit like you. Only more refined." He couldn't resist that last attempt at humor.

"You've not asked her?" Griffin ignored the goading comment and leaned forward, his shock evident.

Alec picked up a quill and busied himself with trimming the point.

"No, as a matter of fact, I've not." He looked up. "There is something about her, Grif. I find myself drawn to her, and at the same time I've avoided asking her questions. I fear I don't want to know the answers. She's not sent for relatives. She's not even sent for clothing. She's wearing a gown today from Phillipa's trunks."

Griffin listened with his mouth agape. "This is not like you, Alec. You never leave a stone unturned, a question unanswered."

Alec tossed aside the quill and rose from his chair to pace the length of the library.

"I know. But I have placed her in this untenable situation. I've not felt it right to pry, and I have assumed that she would tell me her history if she chose. I did ask her if she had anyone here she needed to contact; anyone who would worry."

"And her answer?"

The flicker of sadness that had passed across Shaelyn's

face danced through Alec's mind. A perfect picture of loneliness.

"No one. She had no one to notify."

"Do you not find it strange that she has no relatives, apparently no friends? No clothing, for that matter?"

Alec rubbed the back of his neck and wished Griffin were the lackwit he sometimes pretended to be.

"Yes, it's strange. Damned strange. But I put her in this position, and she has a right to her privacy. Besides, as soon as the marriage is annulled and she gets that ring off her finger, she shall be on her way and I will never see her again."

He refused to even begin to consider why that statement left him feeling so empty. He felt sorry for her. Of course. He simply felt sorry for her.

Griffin studied Alec for a moment, then started scratching at another sore spot.

"Molly tells me that Faith Almany is to be your next wife."

Alec stopped pacing. As much as he loved his baby sister, he would squeeze the life from her, and he would smile as she gasped her last breath.

"Oh, come now," Griffin said, reading Alec's mind. "She's but a child."

"Did she glean what I consumed for breakfast and pass that information to you as well?"

"Don't be ridiculous." Griffin smirked and made himself more comfortable. "Your eating habits are not nearly as interesting as your mating habits."

Alec glared at his cocky friend and continued pacing.

"Well, are you going to comment on this business with Faith? Is she to be the next Mrs. Alec Hawthorne?"

Alec fell back into his chair and massaged his eyes with thumb and forefinger. Oh, for the days when his life had been simple.

"I have not seen Faith in more than a decade. No doubt her husband left her with more money than she can spend in a lifetime, or a business that Father covets, else he would never have considered her. But Father is in for a rude awakening. When Faith arrives, we shall talk, and we will marry only if she and I agree. I have played the obedient son for thirty years, but I do not intend to allow my father to pick yet another wife for me, no matter who she may be, nor what my duties to my father are.''

Griffin stretched and yawned, then shoved himself from the chair.

''Can't say that I blame you, old man. But enough talk. If we are to set sail for Maryland tonight, we both have things to attend to. Not the least of which, no doubt, is your present wife.''

After Griffin left, Alec remained sequestered in the library until he could no longer deny he was putting off the inevitable. With a sigh, he rose and went in search of Shaelyn. He would decide what to say when he found her.

Shaelyn picked her way along the rocky beach, trying not to think about Alec's vague, stilted explanation of having to leave on a business trip the night before. The early-morning sun glistened off the crystal water as it curled across the pebbly sand before retreating. A gull squawked in the distance.

Even the most peaceful moment in her own time seemed hectic compared to the atmosphere now. It seemed that she and everyone she knew had been in a race to see who could burn out the quickest. Until a few days ago, she had certainly been in the lead. When she got this ring off her finger, would she go back to the same breakneck pace she'd left? Did she *want* to go back to that pace?

She tugged on the ring subconsciously, but it showed no sign of budging. Would it ever come off? Would she be stuck in the past forever? Would Alec ever let her go if the ring didn't come off? She wasn't ready to listen to the voice that said she hoped not.

She sank down onto a boulder and watched the morning

light dance on the water. The prospect of staying in 1830
terrified her, yet somehow beckoned her. Though Alec had
frightened the daylights out of her at first, she'd soon realized what a good and gentle man he was. But would he
want to spend the rest of his life with someone he'd married by mistake? If not, what would she do if the marriage
was annulled and she still couldn't get home?

And what of her family and friends in her own time?
Were they frantic? Did they know what had happened to
her? Her parents had loved her, raised her as if she were
a child of their blood. They would grieve for her no less
if they thought she was gone. And she would grieve at
losing them just as much. As for her friends . . . She had
only one true friend. The others were all acquaintances
collected during her travels on the job. But she and Brianne
had ended up in the same class together in second grade,
and they had been steady friends who had counted on each
other for the past twenty-three years. Bri would miss her.
Everyone else would probably just eventually wonder what
ever happened to Shaelyn Sumner.

One thing was certain. Aaron and Rachel would never
miss her. Just the thought of her so-called friend and her
fiancé eloping had her reliving the pain of their betrayal.
But she'd put that all behind her years ago. She no longer
hated them. She pitied them for their lack of humanity.

"Hello."

Shaelyn jerked, then slapped a hand over her racing
heart. A girl—or rather a young woman—strolled toward
her with a frilly yellow parasol matching her gown
propped against her shoulder.

"I'm sorry. I didn't mean to startle you. But I saw you
sitting there and I wanted to introduce myself. I'm Molly
Hawthorne. And you must be Shaelyn."

The girl, a female version of Alec, could have been anywhere from sixteen to twenty.

"Yes, I'm Shaelyn. And you've got to be Alec's sister."

The breeze lifted perfect dark curls to swirl about a long

ivory neck. The girl giggled and shook her head.

"His baby sister, according to both him and Charles. Has he not mentioned me?"

Shaelyn shook her head. "No, but then he hasn't really talked that much about himself."

Molly smiled and twirled her parasol. The girl would break a lot of hearts. "No, he wouldn't. Alec loves to be mysterious. And the rest of the family tries to forget me, I think. You see, I am what Mother calls 'a chore.' But, actually, I've simply learned from my brothers' mistakes."

Shaelyn felt an immediate rapport with this outspoken young woman of the 1830s. She scooted over on the rock and patted the warm stone beside her.

Molly picked her way across the rocks and settled her skirts around her as she seated herself next to Shaelyn.

"So, you are my new sister-in-law. It's not like Alec to bring home someone we've never met. Father is in a tither, of course. He cannot abide it when his children do not bow to his wishes."

Shaelyn had already pegged William Hawthorne as a dictator. She even thought of him as *Der Fuehrer*, when she bothered to think of him at all.

"Are you married?" Shae asked. The girl seemed much too cheerful for anyone living under *Der Fuehrer's* roof.

"Oh, heavens, no!" she laughed. "I do not intend to ever marry, though Father has not yet accepted the idea. He continues to promise my hand in marriage, and I continue to develop diseases or mental disorders or undesirable personality traits, until the weak-kneed sons of Father's business associates cannot withdraw their offers quickly enough. I can even chase away the fortune seekers, which is no small task."

Shaelyn smiled. She could well imagine this spirited young woman babbling like Dustin Hoffman in *Rain Man,* or languishing with a mystery disease that would do any soap opera proud.

"Are you and Alec truly having the marriage annulled?

You are so perfectly suited for each other.''

Shaelyn quirked a brow at Molly and studied her for a moment.

''You've just met me. How do you know I'm perfect for him?''

''I just know. I wouldn't like you if you weren't. And I liked you the moment I saw you.'' Her smile spread all the way to the golden-brown eyes so like her brother's— eyes fringed with inky black lashes that matched her hair.

''Well.'' Shaelyn smoothed a few wrinkles from the white gauzy skirts of the latest gown she'd borrowed from Phillipa's trunks. ''Marriages due to mistaken identities don't usually make the strongest relationships. Besides,'' she looked back at Molly, ''the whole thing was just one big mix-up. I have a life I need to get back to, and I'm sure Alec does too.''

''How very odd your speech is. Where do you come from? Certainly not from this area.'' Molly studied her, as if trying to place the accent. Shaelyn wondered if the sudden warmth she felt in her cheeks showed on her face. What would Molly say if Shaelyn told her *when* she'd come from, as well as where?

''I'm originally from a small town in southern Louisiana, near Baton Rouge. I guess I still have a hint of the Southern drawl.''

''Yes, most definitely. But I was referring to your speech patterns. You have a very . . . colorful way of expressing yourself.''

''Oh. That.'' She made a mental note to watch how she phrased things around people. The last thing she needed was to be carted off to the loony bin. ''I guess that's just my journalistic style coming out.'' She shot Molly a lame smile.

''A journalist? Truly?'' The young woman sighed and scanned the powder-blue sky above her. ''How I love to write. I would be most pleased to publish a book someday. I read Jane Austen's works at night when Father thinks I am asleep. He would fair have a fit if he knew I read such 'trash,' as he calls it. Or that Alec smuggles it to me.''

Too bad *Herr* William couldn't peek into the future and see what respect would be given to the classic ''trash'' he so disdained.

''Have you tried to write anything?'' Shaelyn asked, steering the conversation away from herself.

Molly shrugged and sighed. ''I have dabbled. I write *volumes* in my journal.'' Suddenly she brightened. ''Perhaps I shall write yours and Alec's story!''

Shaelyn stood and shook out her skirts, smiling to herself at this hopeless romantic. ''Then it's going to be a short story. The marriage was a mistake. An accident. It will be over as soon as I get this ring off and Alec sees his attorney.''

Molly scooted from the rock and strolled beside Shaelyn, ignoring her words.

''Perhaps I shall write how he will sweep you off your feet at the masquerade ball. You cannot help but swoon when you see him in costume. And balls are so romantic, especially when everyone's identity is hidden.''

Shaelyn rolled her eyes while Molly blissfully wove a fairy tale. Had *she* ever been that naïve?

''I'm not going to the ball, Molly.''

''Not going to the ball? But you must!''

''Why? I don't know anyone. No one will know me. I'll just be an embarrassment to your father and mother.''

''But if you do not—'' Molly turned and grabbed Shaelyn's hands. ''Please say you'll come! No one will know you anyway. You'll have on a mask. I shall procure a costume for you. You can be the mystery woman who never removes her mask!''

Shaelyn couldn't help but smile at such enthusiasm. And, heaven help her, she was actually considering it. What a chapter it would make when she made it home to write down her experiences. Alec wouldn't be there anyway. When he'd informed her yesterday evening of his

business trip, he hadn't sounded like he would be home
any time soon. Although, she thought to herself, the ball
might be eminently more entertaining if he did get back
in time.

Molly sensed her weakening. "Please say you'll
come!"

She thought about it for a moment more, picturing the
article. A firsthand account of a nineteenth-century ball!

With a grimace, and a prayer that she wasn't making
one more harebrained mistake, she nodded.

Alec stood on the bridge of the three-masted ship while
the deck beneath his feet rolled and pitched, swelled and
ebbed, soared and fell. As always, his queasy stomach
matched the movements, and once again he turned to the
varnished wooden rail and emptied that stomach over the
side. The night sea looked more like a black abyss than
an expanse of ocean.

Jimmy, the slip of a cabin boy, appeared beside him
with a ladle of fresh water. While the towheaded youth
rose and fell with the deck, Alec growled a thank you,
rinsed his mouth, then spit the water into the dark rolling
waves. With the back of his sleeve, he wiped the sweat
and salt water from his face.

"The Puking Puffin, perhaps." Griffin strolled up,
whipped a linen handkerchief from his pocket, then presented it with all the finesse of Beau Brummel before his
fall from grace.

Alec turned and glared, knowing his face, undoubtedly
a sickly green hue, looked only slightly more healthy than
a corpse.

"One more comment about *any* kind of puffin, and I
will beat you to within an inch of your life."

"Ah. The Pugilistic Puffin."

With a strangled roar, Alec grabbed two fistfuls of Griffin's pristine white shirt and hauled him up onto his toes.

"Mr. Hawthorne, sir, the cap'n says there be a ship sighted off the port bow."

Alec cursed at his smirking friend. "Lucky bastard," he growled, before shoving him away and stalking to the helm. On his way, his roiling stomach forced him to make another deposit over the heaving side of the ship.

"Ah, laddie. In the light of day, I'd wager you're as green as the coat of a wee leprechaun." The captain slapped Alec on the back when he finally arrived at the wheel.

Though his tendency toward *mal de mer* was well known to all of the crew, Alec was in no mood to trade witticisms about his malady.

"Where's the ship?"

Captain Finley handed him the spyglass and pointed due east. The faintest pale shadow of ghostly gray sails skimmed across the black waters.

"She be the one we're looking for, laddie. Do we take her now or wait till she drops anchor?"

Alec raised the glass to his eye, then handed it back to the captain. His stomach tightened, but this time the sensation had nothing to do with the peaks and valleys of the waves.

"We wait."

Chapter 6

SHAELYN STOOD IN the shadow of a huge potted plant, trying to make herself invisible while she watched dozens of kings and queens, fools and fairies, Caesars and Cleopatras circling the room in one of the intricate dances of the nineteenth century. Chandeliers threw rainbows of light around the room, reflected a thousand times in the matching mirrors on opposite walls.

She had already given more lame excuses to potential dance partners than she could count, and now she just wanted to avoid being asked at all. No way was she going to venture onto that dance floor. Her specialties ranged more with the Texas two-step or the latest line dance. Or *maybe* a leftover disco step from the eighties.

What she wouldn't give for her mini-recorder or note-pad. She'd have even settled for a piece of vellum and a quill pen, if she could have figured out where to hide them in that costume. The minute she got back to her rooms, she would write every electrifying moment down on what-ever paper she could find. Imagine! Attending a true nineteenth-century masquerade ball! She planned to absorb

every detail, every color, every movement, every moment.
If only Alec were here to—

She stopped the thought before it had a chance to be
fully born. Any involvement with Alec would only complicate matters when she finally managed to coax the ring
from her finger. No sense letting a few overactive hor-
mones make life harder on her when it came time to return
to the future. She shook away the memory of his kiss—
the one she'd all but forced on him when he thought he
was marrying Phillipa Morgan. The way his lips had slid
over hers. The taste of his tongue. The way she fit perfectly
against his—

"I've not seen you dance once! Did I sneak you in here
so that you could hide behind the potted palms?" A raven-
haired gypsy with Alec's eyes pirouetted up to her as if
on a cloud. Gauzy scarves draped over the lower half of
her face lent Molly the perfect air of mystery.

"Better to not dance than to go out there and make a
fool of myself." For the hundredth time that evening,
Shaelyn tried to sigh, and for the hundredth time she failed
to expand her lungs enough within the confines of the
tightly laced torture chamber. "And why did *you* get to be
the gypsy and I have to wear this iron maiden?" She
tugged at the squared-off décolletage on the seventeenth-
century gown of a French aristocrat . . . or courtesan. It
was hard to tell the difference. One more time, she tried
to stuff her overflowing breasts back into the scant bodice,
but the prehistoric push-up bra kept shoving all that skin
right back out. Even if she did manage to take a deep
breath, Shaelyn feared the unthinkable might happen.

"Stop that." Molly moved Shae's hands away and readjusted her neckline. "You're going to make your skin
all red. One would think you'd never shown your cleavage.
And why do you not know these dances?"

Shaelyn gave one final, futile yank to her bodice, then
eyed Molly's comfortable gypsy costume with envy.

"Where I come from, the dances are . . . quite a bit different."

"The dances are that much different in Louisiana?"

Before Shae could come up with a suitable half-truth, masculine voices broke into her thoughts.

William Hawthorne, dressed ironically as Henry VIII, rounded the corner of the room, deep in conversation with a rather tall leprechaun with limp blond hair combed in thin yellow stands across his balding head.

"She's nearly eighteen. Past time to be wed. If we can come to an agreement—"

He glanced up and stopped dead in his tracks. He nailed Shaelyn with a glare, then raked his angry gaze to his daughter. Molly's eyes grew innocently round above the scarves. Even in the dim light in the corner, Shaelyn could see his face darken in anger and the veins pulse at his temples.

"Hello, Father, Mr. Crimmer." Molly acknowledged the second man with a slight shudder. "I just came to fetch Shaelyn to . . ." She searched the ballroom and adjoining dining room. "Oh, there he is! Come along, Shaelyn. He wants to dance with you."

The girl grabbed Shaelyn's hand and pulled her toward the vacant dining room and out of sight before William could do more than sputter. Both girls staggered, giggling and out of breath, into the shadows of a deserted alcove.

"He's going to kill you, you know," Shaelyn laughed, gasping for air.

"He shall have to find me first." Molly shrugged with unconcern and flicked at her scarves. Her eyes danced with humor.

The sound of someone approaching caught their attention and they sank even deeper into the shadows.

"Ah. Two fair damsels, hopefully in distress." The voice belonged to a knight in chain mail with a helmet for a mask. "Are either of you in need of rescuing?"

Though he spoke to them both, his eyes never left

Molly's. And Molly's never left his. It didn't take a genius
to figure out that he had come in search of his gypsy, and
he'd zeroed in on her even when they'd been hiding.

Molly's gaze flickered to Shaelyn with a hint of apology
before turning back to her fairy-tale hero.

"Oh, yes, kind sir. Even now, the evil dragon stalks
me." She glanced toward the ballroom. "Pray, save me
from the clutches of such a monster!"

The knight presented his arm to Molly as he bowed to
Shaelyn. "With your permission . . . Your Highness?"

Shaelyn snapped open her fan and waved them away.
"Be gone, peasant."

When the two melted into the throng of dancers, Shaelyn left her hiding place and wandered onto the brick terrace of Alec's parents' huge home. Perhaps she would find
a dark corner and remove the emerald-and-black feather
domino that covered the top half of her face.

The cool night air caressed her skin like a lover's kiss
when she stepped through the diamond-paned doors and
into the star-sprinkled night. The thumbnail moon lent just
enough light to glitter off the inky waters below. Forgetting her plan to remove the domino, she leaned against the
stone balustrade and drank in the beauty of the night; the
scents of sea and subtle perfumes and fragrant summer
flowers. How nice it would be to have someone to share
it with.

"Would my lady care to dance?"

"Alec!" She spun around to face a towering pirate who
might have just stepped off his ship. He was dressed all
in black. Black boots. Black trousers. Black silk shirt
stretched across a broad chest. Even the mask that framed
his familiar brown eyes blended with the night. A small
golden hoop dangled from his left ear. Without thinking,
she reached up and touched the tip of his earlobe.

"It's really pierced," she said, almost to herself.

He inclined his head. "A ring for every shipwreck survived, my lady. And now I would have this dance."

Without waiting for her consent, he pulled her into his arms and spun her into a waltz, right there on the terrace of his parents' home.

She stared up into his eyes—eyes so intense they melted her bones. While she matched his steps, a flock of tiny birds took flight in her chest.

"Forgive me for deceiving you into marrying me," he whispered.

She swallowed hard against the fist that now gripped her heart. At that moment she would have forgiven him anything, had there been anything to forgive.

"I'd not have a friend think ill of me," he teased.

She swallowed again and willed her knees not to buckle, mirroring his steps as they swept around the terrace.

"There's nothing to forgive."

A smile curved the lips she'd been dreaming of earlier. Lips that any woman in her right mind would want pressed to her own.

"Would my lady care to give a token, to show that there is truly no ill will?"

A token? Translated as a kiss. Shaelyn looked away, forcing her racing heart to slow, fighting the laser heat that shot through her being. It would be a stupid, stupid thing to do, to kiss this man and complicate her life.

She looked back up at him, lost herself in the golden magic of his eyes. Her gaze dropped to lips that moved closer, and closer still. The sweet warmth of his breath fanned across her face, and then her body nearly convulsed when his mouth settled on hers.

"Shaelyn? Are you out here?"

The two jumped apart at the sound of Molly's whispered call. Alec with an oath. Shaelyn stifling one.

"Oh, there you are . . . Alec? Is that you?" His sister tiptoed up to the couple. "What in the world are you wearing? That is not the costume—"

"What do you want, brat?" Alec demanded, with all

the frustration in his voice that Shaelyn felt. Molly's eyes widened, then a smile teased her lips.

"Only to tell you that Father is on his way out for a breath of air. You see, he doesn't know that Shaelyn—"

"Yes, yes. Thank you, pest." He brushed a distracted kiss atop Molly's forehead, then took Shaelyn's arm and guided her to the granite steps that led to the gardens below. She managed to take three running steps before tripping over the hem of her skirts. Alec took no time to steady her. He simply scooped her into his arms in a flurry of lace and petticoats, and they disappeared into the shadows of the garden.

"Why, Alec," she teased as the night engulfed them, as her heart rose in her chest, "if I were a bystander, I'd swear you were running from your father."

"Merely removing myself from a nasty situation, my dear. I've no desire to be present when my brother announces that he and Mary Templeton have been wed these past several days."

Just the thought of *Der Fuehrer*'s reaction would have put wings on Shaelyn's feet.

"You can put me down now," she reminded Alec, who had carried her through the gardens and down toward the beach.

His steps slowed, and finally, almost reluctantly, he lowered her to the ground.

She stood there for a moment, looking up at him, toying with the idea of resuming the kiss, fighting down the butterflies that swarmed beneath her ribs.

He toyed with the same idea. She could tell by the way his head slowly tilted; the way he stared at her mouth.

The earlier brief, interrupted brush of his lips had nearly devastated her. She didn't need to know what the full force of his kisses would do. She knew enough to realize that she could become addicted to them with not much more than a taste.

"How did you know it was me?" She broke the spell

deliberately, reluctantly, and turned to stroll along the edge of the water. "I mean, I have on this mask," she pulled off the feathered domino, "and my back was to you. I wasn't even supposed to be—"

"Your scent."

Those two little words stopped her in her tracks. Stopped her breath. Turned her blood to warm, thick honey. She turned back to him with a teasing grin.

"But I'm not wearing perfume."

"I know."

Every nerve ending on every square inch of her body came alive with a fiery surge at his simple, honest statement. He wasn't playing fair. How could she remain immune to such words, uttered with such intoxicating sensuality? And was he playing? Or was he simply being complimentary? A friend trying to right a wrong he'd committed?

He answered her unspoken question when his silhouette blocked the thin silver line of the moon and slowly moved ever closer to her upturned face.

"Hawthorne?"

Another curse burst from his lips, and this time Shaelyn donated a hundred charitable dollars under her breath as well. Would she *ever* get to taste his kiss again?

"Griffin," Alec ground through clenched teeth as he yanked off his mask, "if you plan to make a comment about a Puckering Puf—"

"Florence has lost the baby, Alec. I leave for Baton Rouge with the tide."

Shaelyn gasped, both to hear about a miscarriage, and to learn that Alec's friend had connections so near her home.

Alec strode to the dark shadow that was Griffin Elliott. A shadow dressed in very similar attire to Alec's.

"Grif, I am truly sorry. Is Florence well? Other than the disappointment?"

The night hid Griffin's face, but nothing could mask the grief in his voice.

"The message said she is well. But I fear what this might do to her spirit. We have lost so many babies."

So Florence was his wife. And the baby would have been his child. Shaelyn had not even imagined this laid-back flirt to be a married man, let alone a father-to-be. But, when she thought of what little she'd known of him, he had always been a perfect gentleman, if a tad confident of his charm. Now she saw the act for what it was.

By the time she managed to form words of condolence, Alec had murmured something to his friend and Griffin had disappeared into the night.

Shae shook her head, at a loss when Alec turned back to her.

"I . . . I didn't even know he was married," she said. She'd never been good at finding comforting words.

Alec took her arm and led her back along the beach. All of the mystery and romance from that sliver of moon had fled with Griffin's announcement.

"He has been married for several years now. Another case of joining fortunes and businesses through family. But he's fond enough of Florence, and she is everything sweet and kind. A beautiful woman, both inside and out." They walked on in silence for a moment, her slippers and his boots crunching companionably against small shells and rocks. "Beautiful and boring," he muttered under his breath. Then he raised his head. "And now she has lost a sixth babe, and a child is all she has yearned for from the moment of their marriage."

She could well imagine the emotions tearing at poor Florence. All her life, Shae had heard how her own mother, Louisa, had suffered each month when she realized she wasn't pregnant. How she'd grown more desperate with each passing year, until Jack Sumner had feared for his wife's sanity. And then there had been the years of waiting to adopt. Even after Shaelyn had become their child, they had agonized over whether or not the birth parents would show up and snatch her from their arms. But whoever had left her in that busy airport terminal had never come looking to reclaim her.

She shook off those musings. They only made her worry about what her poor parents might be going through now. Just the thought of them tore at her.

"I'd assumed Griffin was from Maine," she ventured, changing the subject. "But after hearing him tonight, I guess he *does* have a Southern accent."

"As do you," Alec countered, but he didn't wait for her to comment. "His home is in Baton Rouge. He has been helping me with . . . some business dealings."

"But he hasn't been staying at Windward Cottage. Does he have a summer home here?"

"He stays in the guest house. Sometimes his visits are quite lengthy, and he prefers the solitude Harbor Mist affords him."

"Oh." Shaelyn hadn't even known there *was* a guest cottage.

She wondered if Florence ever got lonely during those lengthy visits. What would it be like to be trapped in a marriage of convenience? Did they feel trapped, or were they happy?

"And what part of the South are *you* from?" Alec's voice sounded almost hesitant, pulling her thoughts back to his question. Truthfully, she'd been a little surprised that he hadn't grilled her for answers long before now. He most certainly wasn't the timid type. But there was no getting around giving at least *some* answers now.

"Why, suh! What makes you think Ah'm not a Nawthener, bawn and bred?"

He threw back his head and laughed at the sky. The sound did funny little things to Shaelyn's insides, made her ache to touch him.

"If you are a Northerner, madam, then I am a Chinaman." He reached up and dragged a blowing tendril of hair away from her cheek. "And I know nothing of China, save that some of my ships sail there."

His touch sent a delicious ripple through her blood, and she shivered as it left a trail of heat in its wake.

"Are you chilled?" He reached for the lapels of his nonexistent jacket, then sighed. "The night has grown cool. We must get you back to the ball before you catch a chill." He slipped his arm around her shoulders, which nearly caused another shiver, then guided her back toward the golden rectangles of light pouring from the windows of the house.

The warmth of his body, the feel of his arm around her, the scent that belonged to him alone, all swirled in her senses. All felt so *right*. She fought the feeling. Moments like these would come back to haunt her when she was back in her own time.

They climbed the steps together from the beach to the garden. Music still drifted on the wind, and several costumed guests strolled the torchlit paths that wound through the summer foliage. He stopped her just beyond a pool of light, took the feather domino from her hand, then slid it back into place on her face. With a teasing flourish he tied his own mask back on, then took her hand and kissed the back of it.

"Many thanks to my lady for the waltz, interrupted though it was. Could this poor, undeserving peasant persuade yet another dance from madame?"

"Alec?" a husky, decidedly male voice called from the lighted path beyond.

Alec's head dropped to his chest, then he raised his face to the heavens and muttered, "I beg You, find someone else with whom to amuse Yourself." He took Shaelyn's arm and guided her into the light. "What is it, Charles? If Father has not killed you, I very well might."

After Alec had seen Shaelyn home—never having gotten a second dance—he rode to the docks to see Griffin off.

On his way, he allowed Irish, his gelding, to pick his own pace while Alec lost himself in thought.

Not until after he'd left her did he realize Shaelyn had never given him an answer about where she came from. His conversation with Griffin before their trip to Maryland had made him realize how lax he'd been in researching who she was or why she was in Maine. It was as if she held him in some sort of spell. Just this evening proved that. While he'd toyed with kissing her—tried his best to, as a matter of fact—his mind had shoved thoughts of Faith to its darkest recesses. Faith, the woman he'd first loved; the woman he could now marry with no tantrums from his father.

He shuddered at the very thought. After Charles's ill-timed arrival in the garden, he and Alec had sought out their father in the library to break the news of Charles and Mary's marriage before making the announcement at midnight. Alec had truly feared William might burst something in his brain. Veins had popped out at his temples and forehead; his face and neck had flared to an alarming red and bulged out over the starched white of his collar. The effort of holding in his roars of rage had left him sputtering incoherently.

Charles, surprisingly, had stood up to his father and insisted that even had he not wed Mary, he would not have bowed to William's choice of another wife for him. Their mother had made little noises of alarm, then fluttered around William in a vain attempt to calm him. She might have been a gnat, buzzing around his head, for all the calming she did. In fact, her efforts, coupled with Charles's stand, had turned their father's face from alarming red to explosive burgundy.

Not until he had ordered them all from the room, then smashed everything breakable, did William Hawthorne even begin to calm himself. Jane had hovered beyond the doors, wringing her hands and giving prayerful thanks that the ballroom was so far removed from the library. When

the massive grandfather clock in the foyer had chimed
twelve o'clock, William had somehow collected himself
enough to suffer through the festive, happy toasts, giving
every impression that the whole idea had been his. Even
when Charles mentioned their plans for an extended wedding trip to the continent, their father's color had barely
heightened at all as he clenched his teeth.

Sounds and smells from the docks pulled Alec's
thoughts back to the present. The *Rising Star* bobbed in
her moorings while the crew swarmed like insects over
her, preparing to set sail. The mere smell of fish, wet hemp,
tar, and wood set his stomach to churning, and the sight
of the gently swaying ship sent bile climbing in his throat
like mercury in a thermometer. He swallowed hard and
cursed himself for his weakness.

Griffin stood at the rail, smoking a cheroot and blowing
out the gray plume with studied contemplation. He was
still dressed—as was Alec—in the black garb they wore
when on a "trip." Alec had barely made it back to Cape
Helm in time for the ball, and rather than take time to
fetch his costume and explain his tardiness, he'd simply
cut holes in a black silk cravat and went dressed in his
"uniform." Only Molly, his bright, incorrigible, infuriating baby sister, had seemed to notice that he was not in
the costume he'd ordered.

When Griffin turned and saw Alec approaching, he mo-
tioned for him to stay on the dock, then trotted down the
gangplank to meet him.

"No sense in you coming on board to see me off," he
called. The glowing orange tip of the cheroot arced
through the air as it flew toward the water. "Wouldn't
want to have to think of you as the Pea-Green Puffin while
I'm away."

Alec pasted on a tolerant smile and nodded his head
with studied patience. He would make allowances for his
irreverent friend. Griffin suffered more from this latest loss
than he would have anyone know.

"You needn't have come, you know," Griffin continued. "I'm reasonably sure I'm on the right ship."

Alec leaned against a stack of wooden crates and turned
away from the rocking ship.

"Remember who you're talking to, Grif. I've known
you since I bailed you out of that pub brawl on my grand
tour."

Griffin massaged his eyes, then dragged his hand down
his face to scrub at the stubble on his jaw.

"Oh, yes. You bailed me out right after I pulled those
three toughs from your supine body and rendered them
unconscious. And it was *my* grand tour, as well."

The truth of the matter, which neither would ever admit,
was that they both had been fighting a losing battle with
a half-dozen drunken Englishmen when the constables arrived and saved their skins.

Alec bit back a grin, but he didn't pursue the endless
argument.

"Send a message when you arrive home and let me
know how Florence fares."

Griffin's smile disappeared when he nodded.

"Will the doctors insist she not try again?"

Griffin shrugged, but the torment showed in his eyes.
"They insisted after the last one, but she is so desperate.
She is a good wife, Alec, and when she comes to me, begs
me, my conscience cannot tell her no."

Alec nodded, hearing Griffin's unspoken words. His
longtime friend reminded himself quite often of what a
good wife he had. And he could not deny at least trying
to give her the baby for which she so desperately yearned,
since he could not give her love. Not the kind of love she
wanted, anyway. He could only love her as a friend. But
to Griffin's never-ending credit, he was as faithful to her
as the most devoted husband.

"Speaking of wives," Griffin changed the subject that
always made him uncomfortable, "have you learned more
about yours, or are you still woefully ignorant?"

Alec reached up and patted Irish's muzzle when the horse whickered restlessly.

"I broached the subject, but we were distracted."

Griffin arched a leering brow but said nothing.

"She was chilled—"

"And you had to warm her?"

"Damn it, Griffin, you would try a saint's patience." *Especially when so close to the truth.*

His friend shrugged. "I was only in hopes that *some* husbands are distracted by wives who want warming, and not just a baby."

Griffin's rare declaration, the opening of his soul, effectively silenced further words from Alec.

The ship thumped against the dock. Sailors shouted orders to each other. A dark pearly gray crept over the horizon, replacing the velvet black of the sky and fading the brilliance of the stars.

"Well." Griffin cleared his throat. "Captain Pruitt is staying behind with my second ship, in case you have need of her before I return." He glanced at his other vessel. "She looks ready to sail." He clasped Alec's hand and pumped it once. "I'll return when Florence is recovered. In the meanwhile, try not to accumulate any more wives."

Alec's farewell pat to his friend's shoulder sent Griffin stumbling several feet up the gangplank.

"May your journey be as agreeable as your personality," he called to his infuriating friend.

"Anything *that* agreeable would be boring." Griffin flashed the smile that women seemed to find so charming. "Kiss the wife for me."

Alec chose to ignore the last words. He cupped his ear and shrugged, then swung atop Irish and threw up his hand in a wave as he trotted away from the dock. But Griffin's words echoed in his thoughts.

Kiss the wife . . .

Chapter 7

"FATHER HAS PUT it about that you are the sister of one of Alec's old classmates, here to meet your brother. He has spoken to all of the servants, as well as Ned's wife. He threatened them, but did not specify the consequences, which is infinitely more frightening for them, since their imaginations are much better than Father's could ever be." Molly giggled and popped the last bite of shortbread cookie into her mouth, then daintily dusted off her fingers. "And for smuggling you into the ball, he has sent me here to pretend that I am chaperone to you and Alec. He actually believes that to be a punishment! Need I say I have not disabused him of his notion?"

Her laughter shimmered in the quiet of the parlor, and Shaelyn couldn't help but laugh, too. Obviously, when it came to his children, *Der Fuehrer* didn't have a clue.

"Well, don't act too happy when you see him, or he's liable to realize his mistake."

"Oh! I will be misery incarnate."

Molly had arrived after lunch, bubbling with excitement and commandeering a bedroom on the opposite end of the house from Alec's. *Not* a coincidence, Shaelyn was sure, since her own room adjoined Alec's.

"Here," Molly handed Shaelyn the plate of cookies and gestured for her to eat.

"No, thanks." Shae shook her head. "I've had my cookie quota for the week."

"Oh, but you *must* eat! To get your finger nice and plump so the ring will never come off."

Shaelyn rolled her eyes and automatically tugged on the stubborn piece of jewelry. It showed no more sign of coming off than it had on that first day. How in the world could something that had slid so easily over her knuckle be so impossible to remove? It fit her finger perfectly, yet when she tried to take the thing off, it almost seemed to shrink with each attempt.

"You know," she gave up her efforts, "Alec won't wait forever for me to give back the ring. Sooner or later he'll decide to get on with his life and have a jeweler cut it off. It's not like he'd stay married to someone because she had the engagement ring stuck on her finger." In the back of her mind she wondered, with more than a little panic, if she would return home if the ring were cut off instead of slipping over her knuckle. She tugged again, harder.

"But by then he'll realize how much he loves you and he won't want it back. He'll want *you!*"

Shaelyn shook her head and tried to remember ever being such a starry-eyed romantic.

"For someone who declares she'll never marry, you're certainly set on keeping others in that condition."

"Only those who are perfect for each other," Molly declared with the self-assurance of youth.

Just wait until she's in her thirties, Shaelyn thought, *and has racked up a few major errors in character judgment.*

The front door swung open at that moment and Alec strode into the foyer. He tossed his hat, which looked like a stunted version of a top hat, onto the mirrored hall tree, then yanked off his gloves, one finger at a time. With a glance into the parlor, his steps slowed. Was it her imagination that his gaze softened when he looked at her?

"Hello," he said, that single, softly spoken word curling into a warm little glow in the center of her chest.

"Hello," she breathed back, reliving certain moments of the night before, aware of the avid audience of one looking on with smug interest.

"Alec, dear brother! You are looking unusually agreeable." Molly rose with a rustle of skirts, drawing his attention to her for the first time. She nearly skipped to his side to give him a sisterly peck on each cheek. He sighed dramatically but couldn't hide the obvious affection he held for his baby sister.

"Up so early after the ball, pest? I'd have wagered you to be just now rising."

"Oh, Father routed me from my bed early to dole out my punishment for smuggling Shaelyn into the ball."

Alec held her at arm's length and narrowed his eyes at her.

"Somehow I fear your cheerfulness does not bode well for me. He has disowned you, and you have come to live at Windward."

"Very nearly."

Alec moaned.

"He has sent me to chaperone you and your classmate's sister."

"My classmate's . . . *that* is what he is telling?"

Molly gave him a megawatt smile. "Yes! Here to join her brother, who has been delayed in Europe. Rather creative for Father, I thought. And now I am here to keep everything proper."

Alec groaned again and plowed his fingers through the black silk of his hair, displacing the indentation his hat had left.

"Ah, yes. Two punishments with one action," he muttered.

Molly flounced back to her seat, unaffected by the brotherly insult.

"I'm sure that was his intention," she said as she happily munched on another cookie. "He actually believes your transparent act that you can barely tolerate me."

"Ah, yes. My *act*." He tossed his gloves on a nearby table and plucked a cookie from the heaping plate. "Has Martin put you in a room, or do you expect me to give up mine?"

Molly tapped her lips with her finger as if considering that option.

"No. I believe the room overlooking the front lawn will do nicely. Actually I am quite settled, but I'll need Ned to drive me home this afternoon. I've forgotten my riding gloves, and I'm certain Bridget will never find them on her own." She all but leered at them when she paused and arched a brow. "The two of you *will* behave while I am gone. Father would have my head if—"

"One more word out of you," Alec interrupted, "and Father will have you back in his lap, with details of your choice of conversation topics."

Shaelyn blinked in surprise at the faint flush creeping up Alec's neck. She expected Molly to gleefully point out the near-blush, but for once the young girl held her tongue. She did, however, look up at him with wide-eyed innocence.

"I am only trying to do Father's bidding, Alec. I would not be accused of shirking—"

With a growl that rose from deep within his chest, Alec chomped a bite from the cookie, as if it were possibly Molly's head, then turned on his heel and stalked from the room.

Shaelyn tried her best not to laugh, but when Molly turned that mischievous grin to her, the giggles started. Within seconds, the two sounded like a couple of teenage girls at a slumber party.

*   *   *

Shaelyn spread a patchwork quilt over the tiny section of beach she'd just spent thirty minutes clearing. She'd never realized how convenient those folding aluminum beach chairs could be. Or how rocky the Maine coast was.

After settling herself with a sigh onto the quilt, she rummaged in the small basket she'd brought, pulling out a sheaf of papers, a quill pen, and a bottle of ink. With Molly on her errand and Alec wherever he'd stalked off to, she looked forward to having a little time alone to collect her thoughts and put them into a journal of sorts. She might not be able to take the papers with her when she went home, but she wanted to solidify them in her mind by writing them down.

Which proved easier said than done.

She fought with the stupid feather pen, dipping and writing, getting as much ink on her fingers as on the pen. By the time she got the knack of scratching out a few words, her first two pages looked as if someone had cried black tears all over them. The following pages came out a little neater, then once she got the hang of it, she lost herself in finding the perfect words to describe the unbelievable experience she was living. The sun moved across the sky, warming her until she flopped her skirts back off her legs, kicked off her slippers, and opened the top buttons of her bodice. She vaguely wondered if Phillipa had any kind of swimsuit in her clothes, something Shaelyn could wear on the beach without scandalizing anyone who might see her. Not that a single soul had passed by.

"Hello."

"Holy sh—" Shaelyn jerked, knocking over the bottle of ink, stifling her charitable donation just in time. She scrambled to grab the bottle she'd been using as a paperweight before the ink could spread across the blank paper to the quilt.

The highly polished toes of Alec's boots stopped at the edge of the quilt. She crooked her neck to look up at him, then took a moment to savor the acrobatics her heart did at the sight of his dark good looks and broad shoulders framed by the blue of the sky.

"Ever hear of knocking?"

He didn't appear to have heard her. She followed his gaze to the expanse of bare, lightly tanned legs protruding from a thigh-high froth of gauzy skirts. Without thinking, she curled her legs around and flipped her skirts down. His gaze then traveled to the gaping V of her unbuttoned bodice.

For some unaccountable reason the display embarrassed her, though in a hundred and seventy years she would think nothing of uncovering all but a few inches of skin.

"Well, it got hot out here!" she defended as she fastened the half-dozen tiny buttons. "Where I come from, it's so darned hot we don't layer on . . ." Too late, she realized she'd just given him the perfect opening to grill her.

He swallowed hard, then nodded toward her.

"When you missed tea, Molly insisted I come looking for you." He knelt on the quilt, then settled himself with his back against a boulder. "Where *do* you come from, Shaelyn?"

He looked prepared to stay as long as it took, and Shaelyn could have kicked herself for once again speaking before thinking. She'd told him things on that first day when she still thought she was in 1999. How much did he remember from that first conversation? How much should she tell and what should she leave out?

Think before blurting, stupid, she chanted. *Think before blurting.*

"Actually, I'm from Louisiana, near Baton Rouge."

He nodded, as if he'd expected that answer. Had she told him that in the carriage?

"Then I am somewhat surprised you weren't acquainted with Griffin."

She squirmed a little while her mind raced. "Well, several miles can make a big difference. And I travel a lot.''

Alec nodded again. "As does he." He shifted position, drew up a knee, and propped his forearm on it. "How did you come to be in Cape Helm? That's an extraordinary distance from Louisiana. For one so young. Alone."

She smiled at the comment about her youth. More than a few years ago she had made that overnight transition from being offended to being flattered when someone assumed her to be younger than she was—something that happened quite often.

"Thirty-one isn't so young. And I travel alone all the time."

He looked genuinely surprised when she mentioned her age, but she already knew that nineteenth-century manners wouldn't allow him to pursue the topic.

"You mentioned before that you are a journalist. I cannot recall ever having read an article written by a woman."

She shrugged and tried to look innocent. "Maybe you're reading the wrong newspapers. Has Molly gotten back yet?" she asked, trying to change the subject.

"Yes. She insisted I come find you when you missed—"

"Oh, yeah. You told me that. Did she find her gloves?"

"I didn't ask. Do you have family in Louisiana?"

Shaelyn opened the basket and started putting away her writing paraphernalia.

"Yes. My mom and dad live there. Is your father still angry with Molly?"

"He's always angry with everyone. Does your family own a plantation? Slaves?"

The man had tunnel vision. She sighed and sat back on her heels.

"No, they don't own a plantation. They live in New Orleans. And no, they don't own slaves. Neither do I."

Good grief! Had she ever in her life even *dreamed* someone would ask her that question?

"You don't live with your parents? You don't even live

in the same town?'' A sudden look of horror crossed his face. ''Have you a husband?''

She gave him a deadpan stare.

''Yes. I do.''

The color drained from his face.

''And he's sitting here, crumpling the papers I've worked on all afternoon.'' She pulled several creased sheets from beneath his boot. He lifted his foot while a healthy hue returned to his face.

''Then your father supports you—''

That did it.

''Look, bubba.'' She leaned toward him and pointed the papers at his face. ''I'm not married. My dad doesn't support me. I don't have a sugar daddy paying the bills for me. I support myself by writing for newspapers.'' She tossed the handful of papers toward the basket. ''And I make a darned good living at it because I'm a darned good journalist.'' While she read him the riot act, she moved closer and closer until they were almost nose to nose, then she poked him in the chest. ''And if you'd pull that male chauvinist head of yours out of the Middle Ages, you'd know that women are actually capable of doing more than taking care of a house and cranking out babies.''

As the last word drifted on the air, the rest of her tirade died on her lips.

He seemed intrigued rather than affronted.

Her face hovered inches away from his. His golden-brown eyes held her gaze, searched her soul, ignited a smoldering heat that spiraled through her blood to the center of her being. Her breath caught in her lungs and she could feel his own, shallow and warm, ghosting across her mouth. Her gaze dropped to his lips: perfect lips. Lips meant to be kissed. But that would be a stupid move right now.

Her face inched closer as a voice in her head said, ''Who cares?''

''Helloooo!''

They jerked apart. Alec banged his head on the boulder while Shaelyn found an errant rock under the quilt with her knee.

"Ow! Damn!"

"Sh . . . oot!"

"There you are!" Molly approached them by playfully hopping from one large rock to another. "I was beginning to fear you'd both drowned! What in heaven's name have you been doing?"

Alec sat behind his desk in the library, toying with the rainbow-shaped letter opener, trying his best to break the spell Shaelyn Sumner . . . Shaelyn *Hawthorne* held on him.

The first woman, the *only* woman he'd ever loved would arrive from Boston within the month. The annulment, according to Lawrence Sheffield, his attorney, would be granted before Faith's arrival. Surely the ring would slip from Shaelyn's finger by then. If not, he'd decided to have a jeweler cut the piece from her hand. It could be easily done, with no danger of injury to Shaelyn, and then the ring could be repaired. Had the jewelry been given to him instead of to his mother, he'd have gladly told Shaelyn to keep it, in some small recompense for what he'd put her through.

But though he impatiently anticipated Faith's arrival, anticipated marriage to the beautiful, precious angel of a woman, in spite of his desire to defy his father, every time he spent more than a fleeting moment with Shaelyn, he found himself plotting ways to kiss her—dreaming about more than kissing her. Damn it to hell, he felt like a mischievous schoolboy torn between the forbidden fruit and the righteous path. Why, just that afternoon he'd been determined to get some answers from her. But before he had asked even a fraction of his questions, he'd had the devil's own time keeping his gaze from wandering to her lips, remembering the taste of her kiss after their ill-fated wedding ceremony. Reveling in the jolt of pure, unadulterated lust that had slammed through his body when he'd stepped around the boulder and seen the expanse of shapely thighs and calves, the open bodice framing a feminine collarbone and shadowed hint of cleavage.

Hell, even her tirade in that odd speech of hers hadn't cooled his want to feel her lips on his. But she was a mistake of Fate, and he owed her her freedom without taking advantage of her first.

He planted both elbows on the desk and plowed his fingers through his hair. Once she was gone, his life would return to normal. The annulment should be granted within a matter of days, and then—

"Ahem."

He released two fistfuls of hair and raised his head. Martin stood just inside the door, stiff and formal as usual, but clearly uncomfortable.

"What is it, Martin?"

The man hesitated for a moment, then closed the door with a deliberate click before turning back to Alec.

"A . . . situation . . . has arisen, sir, which needs your immediate attention."

Excellent! A diversion was just what he needed to get his mind off his wife.

"And what would that be?"

Martin hesitantly stepped forward, his gaze studiously directed toward the ceiling.

Alec had never seen his unflappable butler lose his composure. What on earth could have the man so uncomfortable?

"What is it, Martin?" he prodded.

"You see, sir, there has been talk, ever since your father . . . that is to say . . . well, I have done my best to quell the gossip, but . . ."

"Martin," Alec interrupted, "what has you so concerned?"

The butler's face bloomed to a rosy pink as he visibly

stiffened his spine and squared his shoulders. He stared straight into Alec's eyes.

"It is your annulment, sir. It appears Margaret has stated that the marriage was consummated, and unfortunately Ned's wife heard the declaration, and in her usual manner—"

"My marriage was *what*?"

"Consummated, sir."

"I heard you the first time! Where would Margaret get such a notion? Why would she tell such a blatant lie?"

Martin's gaze wandered back to the ceiling.

"She has said, sir, that the sheets . . ." The pink in his cheeks bloomed to scarlet. ". . . were stained, sir."

"St . . ." Alec couldn't find his voice. Couldn't even *think*.

"Ned's wife does cleaning for your solicitor, sir. And the woman hasn't an ounce of wit. She prattled the allegation to Mr. Sheffield, and he queried her to some extent, him being a minister as well as solicitor."

Alec fell back into his chair, speechless.

"Sir?"

He groaned. "Saint's blood, Martin. There's more?"

"Mr. Sheffield is on his way here to speak with you. Ned's wife ran straight here and told Ned, who came to me, begging me to warn you. If there is anything I might do . . ."

Alec resisted the urge to pound his head against the desk.

"You can send in Lawrence Sheffield when he arrives. Then find Margaret and . . . my wife, and send them in as well."

When Martin left, Alec stared at the closed door. What had possessed Margaret to fabricate such a story? Up until now she'd been a faithful, reliable servant, if a bit on the frivolous side.

A despicable thought occurred to him. What if Shaelyn had made it appear as if they'd . . . But she'd wanted the annulment as much as he. Had that been an act?

A knock preceded Martin's re-entry into the room, followed by the attorney.

"Sheffield, come in." Alec rose and gestured toward a chair. "I understand there is a question we need to clear up. Martin, have you sent for Shaelyn and the maid?"

Martin nodded. "Yes, sir. They should be here presently. Shall I bring tea?"

"Yes, unless you'd prefer something stronger, Lawrence?" Personally, Alec wouldn't have minded a stiff shot of whiskey, but the jolly, round-faced attorney shook his head.

"Tea is fine, son. The wife frowns on any imbibing, and the woman has a nose like a bloodhound." The leather squeaked and the chair groaned when Lawrence settled himself comfortably. "Never saw anything wrong with a medicinal snort now and then, but Lori maintains temperance in the household. And I'll admit, she wears the pants in the family. I am afraid of the woman."

Alec grinned despite himself and shook his head. Sheffield was unlike anyone he'd ever met. An Episcopal minister, he'd taken up law as well, running a scrupulous practice. He would charge around the courtroom like a huge, angry bear, argue a legal point until every head in the room swam, yet he bowed to the slightest whim of a wife who stood barely five feet tall and wouldn't weigh a hundred pounds soaking wet.

"How is Lori? We missed you at the masquerade ball."

"Tyrannical as ever. The oldest daughter had her baby that night. A girl. Couldn't miss it. That makes six grandchildren now."

"Congratulations, then." Alec couldn't help but wonder if his own father had been present for any of his children's births, let alone if he would bother to attend the birth of a grandchild, no matter how much he harped for one.

Shaelyn rounded the doorway just then, her head lowered as she shook out her skirts.

"Yes, master. You sent for me?" She raised her head just before bumping into Sheffield's chair. "Well, crap. Oh!" She cringed a little, but smiled and held out her hand to Lawrence, who had risen with a smile of his own. "Sorry. Didn't see you there."

"I am easy to miss," the bear of a man said as he took Shaelyn's ink-smudged fingers. Their hands waggled for a moment, then she let out a nervous giggle when he managed to bow over her knuckles.

"Well." She cleared her throat, then retrieved her hand and fiddled with a button at her neck.

"Shaelyn, may I present my attorney, Lawrence Sheffield. Lawrence, my . . . wife, Shaelyn Sumner . . . Hawthorne."

"Is this about the annulment?"

Alec gestured for her to sit while he composed what he would say.

"Yes, there seems to be—"

A knock on the door frame drew everyone's attention. Margaret hesitated outside the door, looking as if she were on her way to the gallows.

"Margaret, come in." Alec waved her in, and Lawrence moved to stand behind the desk. "Please sit. We need to ask you some questions."

While it was clear that Margaret already knew the reason for her presence, Shaelyn obviously did not.

"Alec, is there a problem with the annulment? And what does Margaret have to do with it?"

"That's what I am attempting to find out." He coughed, then took a deep breath. "Now, Margaret, Ned's wife has babbled to Mr. Sheffield that you claim the marriage was . . . uhh . . . was consummated."

Shaelyn gasped as Margaret's cheeks mottled with deep patches of crimson. He hadn't realized how embarrassing this conversation would be. The maid squirmed in the leather chair and looked as if she might burst into tears at any moment.

"Oh, sir, I wasn't gossiping. At least I didn't mean to gossip. It's just that after Mr. William threat . . . spoke to us all, well, later in the laundry room I mentioned to Mrs. Smithers—she's the new laundress, sir—that I didn't see how a body could annul a marriage that had been . . . well . . . that the deed had been done. And being new, Mrs. Smithers didn't know better than to say anything in front of Ned's wife, and—"

Alec jumped from his chair. "Where on earth . . ." He stopped and forced himself to calm down after Margaret cringed. "Where on earth did you get the notion that the marriage has been consummated?"

"Yeah!" Shaelyn challenged with a glare.

Margaret wadded her starched apron into a tight ball. "Because of the . . ." She stared at her lap, her cheeks flushing to an alarming shade of puce that clashed with her hair. "The stain on the sheets, sir."

"*What* stain?" Alec bellowed. Lawrence put a calming hand on his shoulder and pressed him back into his seat.

The glare left Shaelyn's face and her hand came up to cover her mouth. Her shoulders dropped with a sigh of relief.

"Margaret, that stain was from one of the scratches I got when I jumped from the carriage after the wedding. It must have bled during the night."

Alec went limp with relief too, until Lawrence rubbed at the back of his neck and took on his courtroom pose.

"You jumped from the carriage after your wedding? Why did you not wait until someone helped you down?"

Shaelyn slid a quick glance toward Alec, then looked at the ceiling.

"Because the carriage was moving."

Lawrence tossed his own glance at Alec, then lowered his head and paced with hands clasped behind his back.

"The carriage was moving. You leapt from a moving carriage after your wedding."

She could have told her side of the story and made Alec

out to be the cad that he was, but instead she simply shrugged.

"Yes." Finally she shot the maid and Sheffield a challenging stare. "The marriage wasn't consummated. That's all I need to tell you. Alec's never come anywhere near my bed."

A quickly muffled gasp swiveled everyone's head toward Margaret. Lawrence spoke first.

"What is it now, dear?"

She twisted her apron and rocked back and forth in the chair, looking up at Alec in abject misery.

"Speak up, Margaret. I've nothing to hide."

"Oh, sir. I saw you there. That first night. I brought the dinner you'd ordered for the missus. When I opened the door, you were there on the bed, half dressed, holding Mrs. Hawthorne, and she . . ." The apron suffered more abuse as her voice trailed off.

"Go ahead, dear," Lawrence encouraged.

Alec closed his eyes and wanted to bang his head against the desk again.

"She was undressed, sir."

"Well, I'd had a nightmare!" Shaelyn jumped from her chair and paced the floor. "Alec just came in to check on me. It was totally innocent!"

"Do you make a habit of sleeping without your nightclothes, Mrs. Hawthorne?" Lawrence asked gently.

Shaelyn spun around and stared at him with an arched brow.

"As a matter of fact, I do."

The attorney studied her face for a moment, then turned to Margaret.

"You may go, dear, unless Mr. Hawthorne has further questions."

Alec shook his head and waved her toward the door. Margaret fled the room as if fleeing a burning building.

Shaelyn flopped back into the chair, her fingers worrying the ring against her knuckle.

"Mrs. Hawthorne, do you mind if I have a word in private with Alec?"

Her hands stopped fidgeting.

"Does this concern me?"

"Well, yes—"

"Then, yes, I *do* mind! I'm not going to toddle off to the parlor and embroider a slipcover while you big strong men smoke cigars and sip brandy and decide things without me." She leaned back into the chair with defiance.

Lawrence nodded slowly and looked at Alec.

Alec stared at Shaelyn and wondered how he could change so quickly from wanting to kiss her to wanting to choke her. At that particular moment, he was sorely tempted to do both.

"I suppose she is entitled to be here, Lawrence, after all—"

"You suppose!" She jumped from the chair. "You *suppose*!" She leaned across the desk, her weight on her fists. "We're talking about my life here! I'm entitled to be in on any discussions concerning me or this marriage. If there's a problem with this annulment, let me assure you that this little woman isn't going to have the vapors over it."

Alec rose from his chair and towered over her, glaring her into silence, but she didn't give an inch. She stared him down, their noses nearly touching.

"And furthermore . . ." she said, raising a finger.

"Don't even *think* about poking me with that pointy little finger of yours," he growled. "I'll not be poked twice in the same day."

She looked at her hovering finger, poised to strike, then looked back at him.

"I'll poke you whenever I darn well feel like it."

She hesitated only a moment. His hand whipped up to encircle her wrist before she could move more than a fraction of an inch toward her target. Her other hand came up. He grasped that wrist as well.

She glared at him, her moss-colored eyes sparking with green fire.

"Let go of my hands," she demanded, her voice calm, civil, threatening.

"Make me," he challenged with equal civility.

A wisp of silky mahogany caressed her cheek and curled down her neck. His fingers itched to push the tendril away, and the all-too-familiar urge swung from wanting to choke her to wanting to kiss her.

Her mouth twitched once as they locked stares, but she narrowed her eyes and readjusted her glare. He had to bite the inside of his cheek to keep from smiling. When the second twitch came, he bit harder. Amusement, sudden, unexpected, replaced the anger in her eyes, then heated to something more than amusement. More than a truce.

The look seared Alec to the depths of his being. His gaze dropped to lips no longer set in a firm, defiant line. While he stared, those lips parted slightly and her sweet, ragged breath warmed his cheek. He moved closer, his head tilting to one side. She raised her face to his and her eyes drifted closed.

"Well, then."

They jerked apart so violently, had there been another boulder behind his head, he surely would have suffered a concussion. How in the name of heaven had she made him so completely forget Sheffield's presence?

Lawrence clapped his hands together and avoided looking at them. Instead, he sank into a chair and gave them time to find their own seats and collect themselves.

"This is a ticklish situation, Alec," he finally said before the silence could grow even more embarrassing. "The annulment was to be granted because the marriage had not been consummated. But there seems to be a witness who insists she saw you together in a compromising position, then removed stained sheets from the bed the next morning." He leaned back, and the chair groaned as if in agony. "Under those circumstances, it might be difficult to convince the court that a consummation did not take place. And seeing the two of you together . . .''

"Bloody hell, Sheffield! Nothing happened!"

"It would not be the first time a couple unintentionally—"

"Mr. Sheffield, are you questioning our integrity?" Shaelyn finally spoke.

"Not at all, my dear. But when this comes before the court, we can do no less than answer truthfully."

"Well, I assure you, if we say the marriage wasn't consummated, we will be answering truthfully."

Lawrence nodded. Alec daydreamed about inflicting medieval tortures upon Ned's wife.

"Be that as it may, I fear the hope for a swift annulment has died. My suggestion is that I submit a petition for divorce—"

"Divorce!" Alec jumped up and slammed his hand on the desk. "Absolutely not!"

"Alec, there are questions surrounding the validity for an annulment. I've no doubt your entire staff has heard the allegations by now. Even if they have not, there are Margaret, the laundress, and Ned's wife who know. The burden of proof now lies with you. Now, if Mrs. Hawthorne would be willing to submit to an examination . . .''

His words trailed off. Understanding slowly dawned in Shaelyn's eyes and her brows shot skyward. She leveled a glare at both men in turn.

"Not a snowball's chance in . . . Hades."

"It would simplify matters, Mrs. Hawthorne. We have several qualified physicians—"

Shaelyn rose from her chair, her face stoic, her spine stiff.

"No examination. No way. You can go for the divorce or pursue the annulment, but either way, when this ring comes off, I'm outta here."

"But you cannot—"

"I can, and I will. End of conversation." She walked toward the door, her spine stiff.

"Shaelyn!" Alec called.

She ignored him as if she were deaf, but before stepping into the hall and out of sight, she turned and cast one miserably sad glance at him.

He looked at Sheffield, searching for something to say.

The attorney stared at the empty doorway, a half-smile amazingly curving his lips.

"Reminds me of my Lori." He turned back to Alec. "God help you, son."

Chapter 8

SHAELYN TOSSED AND whimpered, caught in the throes of her nightmare—the nightmare she'd had for as long as she could remember. She never knew what disturbed her so about the dream. She never retained any details. But she would always awaken with an overwhelming, devastating sense of loneliness. The loneliness would plague her for days. She never knew why. She'd always assumed it was some psychological throwback from being adopted.

She'd never really cared about looking for her birth parents, partly because there were no clues or paper trails to follow, and partly because she had no desire to meet anyone who would abandon a three-day-old baby in an airport terminal, but mostly because her adoptive parents had given her so much love and support that she couldn't imagine biological parents doing more. She loved her parents every bit as much as, if not more than, her friends loved theirs. As far as she was concerned, Louisa and Jack Sumner were the best mom and dad anyone could ever ask for.

How many of *those* parents had agonized for years over having a baby? Filled out reams of paperwork? Had their lives and lifestyles scrutinized under a microscope until the agency knew more about them and their families than they knew themselves? And that was just to *get* a baby. Then came the social workers, showing up at a moment's notice, inspecting the house and the child, checking off every item the courts deemed necessary for a baby to have, even though parents with their own babies were left to their own devices.

Jack and Louisa Sumner had never begrudged the stiff requirements. They had even taken up for Shae's birth mother, reasoning that she had probably been a young teenager, confused and desperate. She'd probably left Shae in that infant carrier in the airport because she'd known the baby would be found quickly and taken care of. Besides, they'd always pointed out with a hug and a smile, if the girl hadn't left Shaelyn there, then who would they be hugging right then? More than once, Louisa had puddled up and told Shaelyn how grateful she was to that young mother and the sacrifice she'd made; how she'd like to thank the woman for giving her a child. And Shaelyn had come to thank that mother herself.

The whimpers increased as she fought her way out of the nightmare. Finally her mind surfaced enough from the swirling images to wake herself. She opened her eyes and stared into the darkness, then rolled over, trying to escape the oppressive loneliness already settling in. As always, not a hint of the dream lingered. Just the loneliness.

She tossed the light quilt aside and swung her feet to the floor. Had Alec heard her this time? Would he burst through those doors and scoop her into those strong, safe arms of his?

She listened for him, hoping, but she could hear no sounds in the other room.

With a sigh, she rose from the bed, turned up the low-burning lamp, pulled on one of Phillipa's looser gowns, then slid her feet into a pair of leather slippers. What she wouldn't give for her jeans and tee shirt she'd left draped across the bunk on the ship.

She closed her burning eyes in defeat. She had more to worry about than the fate of a pair of jeans.

No doubt the conversation with Alec and his attorney had triggered her nightmare. Nothing like having a guy desperately deny sleeping with you, even if he actually didn't, to make a girl feel wanted. Especially when his goal was an annulment for a marriage that never should have happened.

She fumbled with the buttons on the gown and stared at her reflection in the night-blackened glass of the window. If she was honest with herself, she would admit that she'd wanted Alec to beg her to stay married to him and to leave the ring on her finger. Whether or not she could do that—stay in 1830 and never see her parents again, never see her native time—she didn't know.

But she knew beyond a shadow of a doubt that when she went back to 1999, she would miss Alec for the rest of her life.

With the last button fastened, she tiptoed to his adjoining door and listened one more time. When she still didn't hear any signs of activity, she fought down the stab of disappointment, then coughed delicately, but loudly enough to be heard. Still nothing. She gave some thought to dropping a book or "helping" a window slam shut, but decided maybe it was best if she just walked off her nightmare in the gardens.

She crept down the stairs and made her way outside, tripping over the hem of her gown twice before collecting the skirts and throwing them over her arm. The darned things were cumbersome enough with petticoats, but without them the hem dragged the ground by a good two inches.

When she stepped into the gardens, the cool night air swept away the last remnants of the nightmare. She combed her fingers through her hair and let the flower-

and salt-scented breeze sweep the strands behind her. How she loved summers in Maine, with nights so cool one could curl up comfortably in front of a fire. So different from the oppressive, smothering heat of Louisiana. Even at this time of night, the air there would be thick with moisture and still heavy from the heat of the day. But the winters at home were wonderful. Sunny days. Christmas shopping in shirtsleeves.

She sighed.

Caught between two worlds. Would she ever feel like she belonged in one place over another? And now one *time* over another? With every day she spent there, every moment she spent with Alec, she felt more and more comfortable in the nineteenth century than in her own time. Even with all the stuffy, unwritten rules and lack of conveniences.

Small rocks and shells crunched quietly beneath her feet as she roamed aimlessly through the paths of the garden, the peacefulness reminding her of her all-too-brief vacations there in the future. Amazing, how little this 1830 part of Maine had changed from its 1999 counterpart.

An assortment of fragrances wafted on the breeze—roses, petunias, several unnamed flowers that thrived in the cool summers of the North but would never survive the enervating heat of the South. She plucked a waning rose and idly pulled off the petals as she walked.

He loves me. He loves me not.

The soft, golden lights of a ship bobbed in the Stygian waters fifty yards off shore as it slowly made its way up the coast.

She found herself at the steps overlooking the water, and as always, she was drawn to the beach as the tide is drawn to the moon.

The damp berm muffled her footsteps along the water's edge. Gazing at the star-spattered sky and sorting through a myriad of emotions, she leaned against a huge boulder and stared up at the heavens, the remnants of the rose still in her hand.

How could it be that one moment all that separated their lips was a ragged, warm breath, and the next Alec was facing her across a desk with an attorney, raking desperate fingers through his hair and searching for a way to get rid of her?

The sound of oars slapping against water pulled her attention from her contemplative thoughts. She squinted, scanning the gently rolling waves, then finally caught sight of a rowboat when it scraped to shore. A man jumped out, dragged the boat onto the beach, then tied it off as two other silhouettes staggered from the boat. Had they come from the ship headed north?

A frisson of twentieth-century panic froze her. She was alone on a deserted beach in the middle of the night, and the three passengers of the dark rowboat were dressed in black, as camouflaged as a guerrilla in jungle warfare.

Shaelyn pressed herself against the rock and dropped the dark, heavy skirts to cover her legs. If she didn't move, would they see her?

Murmuring male voices drifted to her but she couldn't make out the words. One of the three silhouettes, Shaelyn realized with a start, was a woman who'd fallen from the small boat onto her knees, the unmistakable sound of retching mingling with the men's voices. One of the men helped her to her feet, and the two followed the one who had tied off the boat.

As they drew closer, Shaelyn inched her way around the boulder, trying not to step on crunchy shells, praying that they would pass by her and disappear down the beach. She caught snatches of a deep voice distorted by lapping waves and three sets of feet scuffling across the rocky shore.

". . . stay in the cave . . . authorities looking for you . . ."

She held her breath and willed herself invisible. They drew nearer. The woman moaned occasionally. Shaelyn planned what she would do if she were caught. Three against one. But the woman was obviously sick. Could she escape two men?

She could hear their footsteps on the other side of the boulder now. Would they pass by? Could they see the edge of her skirts? She took one more tiny step to the left and breathed a sigh of relief . . . until the tiny shell beneath her slipper crunched. To her it sounded like the crack of a gunshot inside a church.

The footsteps halted. Shaelyn held her breath. She pressed against the rock, then slumped in relief when the footsteps resumed.

"Who are you?"

She yelped when a hand grabbed her left arm and yanked her away from the boulder. Without benefit of thought, her knee came up and plowed into the groin of her attacker, making contact a split second before she gasped his name.

"Alec!"

His breath whooshed from his lungs like air wheezing from a bellows as he curled forward, gagging.

"Alec! Are you all right? What are you doing out here?"

He stayed doubled over, his knees together, his hands cupping that so dear to all men, dry heaving. She tried to help him upright, but he shrugged off her hands and crab-walked several feet away. Undaunted, she followed him.

"I'm sorry, Alec! I didn't know who you were! For all I knew—"

"Don't!" he managed to gasp. He moved away from her again, but she followed, tripped, tossed her skirts over her arm, and trailed after him as he tried to walk off the pain. A massive, gentle hand touched her arm before she reached him.

"Ain't nothin' you can do to help him." Shaelyn looked up into the face of a huge black man, his eyes gentle yet wide with fear. "You needs to let him be, so's he can lay down."

Her gaze swung back to Alec, who'd staggered to a relatively smooth patch of beach and dropped to his knees. He fell to his side and continued to gag. She looked back at the man, then moved her gaze to the woman beside him.

Runners, she thought, her mind automatically thinking in the Southern vernacular. Even in the twentieth century, in the stories of long-ago runaway slaves, they'd been called runners. The bayous of Louisiana were filled with such stories. Where had these two come from, and why were they with Alec?

Was he part of the underground railroad?

"Shaelyn." The raspy, pain-filled voice made her cringe.

"Yes, Alec?" she answered, her voice about as meek as it had ever been in her life.

He writhed on the ground several more seconds, visibly forcing himself to regulate his breathing and to stop moaning. Finally he rolled onto his knees, then staggered to his feet, still bent at the waist, his hands on his thighs now as he tried unsuccessfully to straighten.

When he glared up at her, the glittering gold of his eyes nearly visible in the colorless shades of night gray, Shae mentally squirmed at having done this to him a second time.

"Saint's blood, Shaelyn," he finally gasped, "what are you doing on . . ." He stopped and cringed for a moment. ". . . on the beach at this hour?"

She took a step toward him, but he stopped her with a glare.

"I . . . I couldn't sleep. I always walk on the beach when I can't sleep."

He cursed under his breath and took a few more crouching steps.

His attitude irritated her more than a little. She had a right to walk on the beach whenever she darn well felt like it. All she'd done was protect herself. He'd more or less asked for her knee to his groin both times she'd delivered it. Would he rather she make it a habit of swooning or getting the vapors whenever she felt threatened?

"What are *you* doing on the beach at this hour?" She threw his question back at him, with enough defiance in her voice to gain herself another glare. She ignored him and turned to the couple witnessing this whole exchange.

"Hi." She offered her hand to the enormous black man. He stared at it suspiciously. "I'm Shaelyn Sumner... Hawthorne." She flicked a glance at Alec, then went on, undaunted. "I'm Alec's wife. And you are...?"

Neither of the frightened slaves answered nor made a move to take her hand.

"Who they are is not important." Alec limped up to the little group, grabbed Shaelyn by the arm, and dragged her toward the steps back up to the gardens. "Go back to the house. We'll discuss this later."

She jerked her arm free and snatched up her skirts to keep from tripping. "Let me help you, Alec. Women worked on the underground railroad all the time."

She had to hand it to him. He didn't bat an eyelash. Instead, he laughed a humorless laugh.

"Don't be ludicrous, Shaelyn. I know nothing of the underground railroad, other than it is a myth concocted by journalists to sell newspapers, or politicians to stir the slavery issue on both sides. I took this couple off one of my ships bound for Nova Scotia because Naomi was seasick and the physician feared she would lose the baby. This couple is free. Robert is a blacksmith. He's going to work there."

Shaelyn nodded and rolled her eyes. "That's why they're scared to death. And why you said something about the authorities looking for them."

He stared her down. She didn't blink. She wanted to help, darn it. Imagine helping someone escape to freedom.

Imagine a twentieth-century woman working on the underground railroad. And a journalist at that!

As they waged their battle of wills, Robert and Naomi fidgeted, staring down the beach with worried looks. Finally, Robert crushed his hat between his beefy hands and cleared his throat.

"Mistah Hawthorne, suh. They's somebody comin'."

Alec jerked his head around, then hustled the couple behind the boulder.

"There's a narrow cave back there. Get into it, then pull the bushes back across the opening."

Once the couple had disappeared, Alec turned back to Shaelyn and yanked her toward the steps.

"Get back to the house and call for Martin. I'll try—"

"Don't be ridiculous. They'll see me go up the steps. How will you explain what you're doing out here?" What was the penalty for helping slaves to freedom thirty years before the Civil War?

"Shaelyn," he hissed as the voices grew louder, "I said go back—"

Without thinking, she threw herself into his arms, locked her mouth to his, then pulled his shirt free from his trousers. When he recovered from his shock, he wrapped his arms around her and did a very convincing job of thoroughly kissing her. She took a moment to loosen the top buttons of her bodice and drag one side slightly off her shoulder, their lips never parting. He deepened the kiss and she rose to meet him as he turned and pressed her against the boulder, every inch of his body now contoured to hers. Their tongues met, and Shae nearly convulsed at the heat that arrowed through her. She melted against him, slid her hands under his shirt, shivered at the indescribable feel of hard muscle under warm skin. The air was so cool, the wind off the ocean chilling, but inside his shirt rose the heat of a Louisiana night. She traced the outline of his muscles while his hands worked their own magic, working their way up her bodice and down to her hips, pressing her ever closer to him. A tiny sigh escaped her throat as the heat of his hands burned through the thin fabric of her gown.

"Well, what have we here?"

When Alec jerked away, Shaelyn didn't have to fake her gasp of surprise. His touch, his kiss, had wiped the existence of these men from her mind. He'd reduced her to a weak-kneed, aching mass of lust.

"Be on your way!" Alec ordered, his voice as raspy as Shaelyn's knees were weak. He glared at the two men while he tucked in his flapping shirttails. Shaelyn made a halfhearted attempt to drag her gown back over her exposed shoulder, more to get the men's minds off looking for Robert and Naomi than from a sense of modesty. After all, she showed a heck of a lot more than a shoulder every time she went to the beach in her own time.

Her gesture drew their attention, and their leering gazes evaporated the last lingering effects of Alec's melting kiss.

"I said be on your way," Alec repeated, more threatening this time, "or explain why you are trespassing on my property."

The two men dragged their gazes from Shaelyn's exposed flesh to glare at Alec. One of the men, the smaller of the two, sniffed constantly, as if he had a bad cold. The other man, tall and thin and harsh, stared at Alec. Shaelyn could see from the look in the man's eyes that he was not one who would be easily tricked.

"Did a small rowboat come ashore near here?" he asked, ignoring Alec's demand. Though it shouldn't have, the man's heavy Southern accent surprised Shaelyn.

"I will not ask again," Alec growled. "Either leave now or explain yourselves."

The man stared Alec down, then finally nodded in acquiescence.

"Franklin Tilburn, suh, of Georgia. I am chasin' a shipload of runners."

"Overland?" Alec snorted.

"We were on the ship followin' them." Alec's body stiffened beneath Shaelyn's fingers, but he showed no outward signs of concern. "We saw a rowboat meet the ship, so Riggs here and I followed. We lost sight of where they came ashore."

Shaelyn watched the three men, certain that any moment they would start circling each other like dogs. The side bulges beneath the two Southerner's coats were undoubtedly guns. She gasped, deliberately getting the attention of all three men.

"Why, Alec, darlin'." She drew out her thickest Southern accent, which always seemed to surface anyway whenever she got nervous. "Do you suppose those men in the boat . . ." She turned to Tilburn, hoping her eyes were wide with shock. "Why, suh, you mean to tell us those men were slaves?"

Tilburn's hand moved to rest on the bulge at his side.

"You saw them? Where? Where did they go?"

Alec stepped in front of Shaelyn protectively. "If that is a weapon you're holding, Tilburn, I'll warn you not to use it on my property." He turned to the perpetually sniffing Riggs. "You, either."

"I have the authority to apprehend those slaves and return them to their masters," Tilburn argued. "If you attempt to interfere—"

"I am not interfering. I am protecting my property and my loved ones. The men came ashore where that boat is." Alec pointed toward the shadow of the rowboat further up the beach. "Before I could get to them to question them about their business, they were met by a man with three horses. They rode north up the cliff path nearly a quarter of an hour ago."

Tilburn slid his gaze west, then brought it back to study Alec's face.

"It is quite late for strollin' on the beach. May I ask what you and the lady are doin' down here?"

Alec's body tightened under Shaelyn's fingers.

"No, you may not."

Shaelyn cuddled up to Alec like a besotted lover. *Not much of a stretch*, she thought when their bodies made contact and her blood pumped harder.

"Why, Alec, darlin', I don't mind tellin' him," Shae put in before Tilburn could respond. She turned to the man glaring at them. "I don't mean to be rude, suh, but you are interruptin' our honeymoon." Did they even use that word in 1830? No matter. She snuggled closer to get the point across, then stifled a shiver when Alec slid his arm around her waist possessively, almost automatically.

Tilburn studied them. Alec bent his head to brush a kiss against Shaelyn's upturned face. It didn't take any acting skill at all to look up at him as though she wanted more. She had to keep reminding herself that their goal was to keep Robert and Naomi safe.

"Do you think we are out here helping slaves to freedom?" Alec asked as he continued to gaze at Shaelyn. He flicked a glance at Tilburn with a couldn't-care-less attitude, then settled his gaze back on Shaelyn's face. "Look around. Search the beach. But be quick about it and leave my wife and me alone."

Alec dismissed them then, as if they no longer existed. His head lowered to nuzzle against her neck and the skin along her left shoulder. Shaelyn concentrated on breathing evenly and keeping her knees from buckling while he played havoc with her senses. She heard the crunch of the men's boots when they finally stopped staring at them and started their search. They crunched around the boulder. She felt Alec tense. The moon cast that side of the boulder into pitch black shadows. If the fugitives stayed absolutely quiet, they should be safe.

Alec nuzzled her hair, sifted his fingers through the disheveled strands to cup the back of her head.

"Saint's blood, you smell good," he murmured, but loud enough to be heard by the men.

Shaelyn's mind spun, her senses alive. Her blood heated

and cartwheeled through her veins, coiling and spiraling to the center of all that made her a woman. Never in her life had a man's touch come so close to bringing her to her knees.

He continued to work his magic, trailing kisses along her neck, his lips never quite coming back to hers. When the men's footsteps rounded the boulder, his body relaxed but his kisses continued.

"I apologize for intrudin'," Tilburn said from behind them.

Alec didn't even raise his head. With an unconcerned wave of his hand he dismissed the existence of the two men, then brought his lips back to Shaelyn's, settling into a long, languid kiss that shot a trail of fire to the core of her being. Her body molded with his, ground into his as she encircled his waist beneath his shirt and pulled him closer. But still, she couldn't get close enough. She wanted to crawl right into his skin, into his mind.

The kiss went on for an eternity and she lost herself in the play of their tongues, the sweet taste of him, the feel of his heated hands against her bare skin and through her thin gown.

Finally he raised his head and pulled her toward the steps. She followed him like an addict after her fix. As they climbed each step, his arm at her waist holding her close, he dropped light, butterfly kisses on her forehead, her cheeks, the tip of her nose. Every now and then they would stop and he would settle his mouth over hers again, his tongue sending delicious shivers through her body with the finesse of a master lover.

When they reached the top step and he pulled her to him once again, she wasn't sure her legs would carry her any further. She wanted to sink with him into the cool, dew-kissed grass at the edge of the garden and let him put out the fire he'd kindled in her.

He raised his head and stared at the beach. Anyone watching them would have just seen two lovers embracing.

Shaelyn looked up at him, her mind still drugged with his kisses. He guided her through the gate, and once the rose-covered arbor hid them, he took her head in both hands and delivered a quick, brotherly kiss to her forehead.

"Excellent job, dear wife. I think they believed our act. Now, go to the house and tell Martin what has happened while I take the south path back to the cave."

"B . . . but," Shaelyn stammered, her body screaming, her mind numb with disbelief as he disappeared into the garden amid the dark shadows of tall, fragrant bushes, "I wasn't acting."

Chapter 9

ALEC'S BODY STILL burned with the fire of Shae-lyn's kisses, nearly twelve hours after the last one had all but consumed him. Leaving her standing there with tousled hair, all soft and open and freshly kissed, had quite possibly been the hardest thing he'd ever done in his life. But he'd had a mission to finish.

He and Martin dismounted and wearily handed their reins over to Ned. After retrieving a terrified Robert and Naomi from the shallow depths of the cave, they had worked their way inland to meet Martin, who had arrived with horses and food. The four had then ridden as hard as they dared, considering Naomi's condition, and had finally arrived at a farm on the underground network where the two slaves would be safe with the conductor until they could be sent further north.

Alec had had only one other foray with the newly formed, highly secret underground railroad. He much preferred his smuggling endeavors at sea, where, even though plagued with seasickness, he didn't have to be concerned about what lurked behind each bush or tree or bend in the road.

And now, all he wanted to do was go plunge his exhausted, still-burning body into the icy waves of the ocean and try to extinguish the flames that Shaelyn's kisses and warm, willing body had ignited so many hours ago.

Then he would finally have a talk with her.

His swim in the frigid waters off shore had revived his energy, cleared his mind, but only smothered the smoking fire of Shaelyn's kisses. Hot little embers still danced in his blood, just beneath the surface, threatening to burst back into flame at any moment.

But too many disconcerting thoughts and questions plagued him for him to pay much heed to the embers. Too many unanswered questions haunted him. He was determined to uncover some answers.

He'd sent Molly on several errands to get her out from underfoot, and now Shaelyn sat across from him on the silk brocade love seat, the delicate peach of one of her new gowns accentuating the color in her cheeks.

She was angry with him, and hurt. Alec had enough experience with women to recognize the signs. Her gaze scanned the room, very deliberately avoiding looking anywhere near him. She relaxed into the love seat, as if she hadn't a care in the world, but he could hear the muffled, rhythmic tap of her foot beneath her skirts.

Oh, yes, she was angry. But he wasn't sure if it was because he hadn't allowed her to go with him, because he'd kissed her, or because he'd stopped. For all he knew, it could be all three.

"Ahem," he began. She blinked slowly and finally directed her gaze toward him. The usual good humor and life in her odd, moss-colored eyes had been replaced with total disinterest and just a hint of irritation. Surprising, how empty that made him feel.

"Shaelyn, in light of what occurred last night, I feel we must talk. I have been hesitant to pry into your life, considering I wrongly forced you into marriage. But you have now been involved in an illegal activity, one of which you seem to know quite a bit about for a genteel woman, or for any woman, and I must ask you some questions to protect both you and myself.''

He awaited her reaction. He didn't know if she would deny everything, become angry, play innocent. All he knew was that she was entirely too well-informed about the underground railroad.

She merely arched a well-defined brow and asked with anger dripping from her voice, ''Such as?''

He hadn't quite expected that reaction.

''Such as what you were doing in Cape Helm? On that ship? Why have you not contacted any relatives? Where are your own clothes? Why is your speech so odd? Why are you not like any other woman I have ever met in my life?'' He stopped and took a breath. ''And why did you say women *worked* on the underground railroad? Why do you know so much about a covert operation that is so newly in existence?''

With her Southern accent and her unusual self-confidence, he could not help but fear that she worked as a spy for the Southern states, to arrest and prosecute those working for the cause. Could she not contact anyone, or retrieve her own clothing, for fear of discovery?

The anger seemed to drain from her with each question he posed. Uncertainty entered her eyes. She looked away and visibly searched within herself for answers to his questions. Was she testing out lies? She stared at the floor for so long, he feared she would refuse to answer.

Finally she raised her eyes to meet his, the anger now replaced with something akin to resignation. A ripple of dread spread up his spine at that look. Whatever followed could not possibly be something he wanted to hear.

''I don't know how to tell you this,'' she began, and his dread increased. ''I . . . I'm . . . not from here.''

He blinked at such an obvious statement.

She clasped her hands, swallowed, and looked at her

lap. After several seconds she raised her head and sighed. Her head shook in denial as she spoke.

"I don't know how to tell you this so that you'll believe me. You've . . ." She looked down at her lap again and then back at him. "You've been very good to me, and I wouldn't repay your kindness with lies. Besides," she gave him somewhat of a pained smile, "I can't think up any lies that would answer all your questions."

The dread nearly smothered him now, but she seemed genuinely distressed. He forced patience into his voice while he tried to relax the muscles knotting at the base of his neck.

"What is it, Shaelyn? I can be an understanding man."

She gave him a doubtful look, chewed on her lower lip, then finally locked her gaze with his.

"I got on the ship," she began, "to do an article."

Oh, no. Not the journalist story. He struggled to keep the disbelief from his eyes and nodded for her to go on.

"I went to the cabin that Pete sent me to. Pete was one of the sailors on board. Anyway, in the companionway I dropped my pen and paper. The hallway was dark, so I had to sort of feel around for them. That's when I found the ring." Her hand went automatically to tug on the band. "Just as I put the ring on, the ship lurched. I bounced off the bulkheads and banged my head. I thought that's why the room spun and I got so dizzy."

She searched his face and he nodded, trying to keep his expression open. She looked miserable, as if the words wouldn't come. Her mouth opened to speak a couple of times, but then she dropped her gaze back to her lap. She quite obviously was struggling for words. He forced himself to remain quiet while she worked through it, though the effort was nearly impossible.

She looked back up at him, her eyes pained, begging apology, begging to be believed.

"The story I was writing was about . . ." She hesitated, as if she wouldn't finish, but then she rushed on. ". . . was about the turn of the millennium.'' She swallowed hard, her gaze locked with his.

The millennium? The turn of the millennium? The year 1000? What had that to do with 1830, or why she was on the ship? Why had she been so hesitant to tell him that? He continued to look at her, the questions forming on his lips, but she stopped him from speaking.

''I put the ring on . . .'' she began, the same plea for belief in her eyes, but with a sense of resignation now instead of misery, ''. . . when I put the ring on . . . it was in 1999.''

His initial reaction was an uncontrollable arching of his eyebrows. Total silence filled the room, save for the faint heartbeat that drummed ever louder in his ears.

Nineteen ninety-nine? What a very foreign-sounding number. What could she possibly mean by that? Surely not the *year* 1999. That was what . . . one hundred and seventy years in the future? *Why, that was just before* . . . A shiver snaked up his spine. . . . *The turn of the millennium!*

His gaze focused back on Shaelyn, who obviously knew exactly what he was thinking, and who stared at him, affirming what she'd said and what he thought with her direct gaze. Almost challenging him with it.

''You cannot possibly mean . . .'' he began, but the words refused to come.

She lifted her chin and finally glanced away.

''That's why I don't have any clothes to send for. Why I don't have any family or friends to contact.''

Alec massaged his eyes, then dragged the palm of his hand down his face to rasp against his freshly shaved chin.

1999? Did she honestly expect him to believe her? Was she insane? Did she think him that ignorant? He kept his voice calm, fighting anger and confusion at such blatant lies.

''So you are from 1999,'' he said. ''And what manner of transportation brought you to 1830?''

She bristled at his patronizing tone but said nothing.

Instead she held up her left hand and displayed the emerald-and-diamond ring.

"The ring?" He kept his voice steady. "You think the ring brought you here?"

She dropped her hand back into her lap and challenged him with her stare.

"Yes, I do. You said yourself there were rumors about the ring having powers. The last person I saw in 1999 was Pete, and that was right before I put the ring on. The next thing I knew I was bouncing off the walls of a lurching ship, my head spinning and my mind fuzzy. The ship seemed newer, the cabin had two trunks filled with clothing. I dug through them until I found something appropriate for a wedding, then—"

"A wedding? How did you know about the wedding?"

Shaelyn sighed and rubbed her temples with her fingers. When she spoke, she told an unbelievable story about something called a living history, where the participants dressed in historical costume and took on roles of different people, acting out everyday life and special occasions, somewhat like a play but not necessarily with a script. She told how she'd thought he was the actor portraying her betrothed, and why she'd panicked and behaved as she had when she'd realized he wasn't taking her back to the ship.

It all made sense. Her story was flawless, explaining everything from the wedding to why she knew so much about the underground railroad. Of course she would study such a thing in school. It explained her foreign behavior and odd speech. It explained everything flawlessly. Except why in the world she thought him dull-witted enough to believe she was from a hundred and seventy years in the future.

Throughout the telling of her tale he remained calm. He also remained numb. He could not believe she had told him such outlandish things, yet he could not decide if she was insane and truly believed what she said, or if she merely acted the part in hopes of turning away suspicion.

His heart fell, and the last glowing embers coursing through his blood faded and flickered out. He shoved away the memory of her kisses, the fiery passion she'd ignited within him, relegating those memories to the coldest, darkest part of his mind. As for his heart, he swept away even the tiniest ache to touch her.

She saw it on his face. The defeated look in her eyes told him that. Surprisingly, she didn't try to convince him. With a sigh of resignation she stood, smoothed the wrinkles from her skirts with studied control, then turned to leave the room.

"Shaelyn."

She stopped but didn't turn around.

"I have contacted a master jeweler to remove the ring. When he returns from settling his brother's affairs in South Carolina, you will be free to leave."

She drew in a breath but said nothing. After several seconds she took a step, and then another, toward the hall. With her hand on the door, her glance came around to meet his, just for an instant, as if she could not stop herself. Her eyes glittered with unshed tears, her brow creased with unspeakable pain. Their gazes locked, as if time had stopped, and then she turned and quietly shut the door.

Shaelyn spent two days in her room, sending word of a headache to Molly, sending no word at all to Alec.

She had never dreamed anything could ever hurt her as much as Alec's declaration of her freedom had.

She hadn't expected him to believe her. She'd have been shocked if he'd said he did. But of all the scenarios that played through her mind while she decided whether or not to tell him the truth, his telling her he was having the ring cut off and then kicking her out never once entered her mind.

Perhaps it should have. What else could he have done? He didn't believe her. He probably thought she was a few bricks shy of a load. Did she expect to tell him a farfetched story and then have him invite her to spend the rest of her life there?

She rolled over and hugged the pillow closer to her.

In the last few days she had fallen in love with a man who belonged in the past. A man she should never have met. She didn't try to deny the fact anymore. She'd tried to ignore the feelings, tried to remind herself that she was a twentieth-century woman, almost a twenty-first-century woman, and she had family and friends there, a job she loved, a life of conveniences and luxuries beyond the most pampered lifestyle here.

But she didn't have a man there who could stop her heart with a smile, who could fire her blood with a brush of his lips across her hair, who could bring her to her knees just by telling her she smelled good. What would he do to her if he ever did more than just kiss her? She would probably melt into a pool of hot, thick honey, or ignite in a burst of flames and be reduced to a crumbling pile of ashes. Either way would be a wonderful way to go.

But she didn't have to wonder about that anymore. She already knew Alec well enough to know he would never seduce the lunatic in his home, even if she *was* his lawfully wedded wife. Even if she wanted it so much she ached.

Damn, what a fool she'd been. A dreamy, fairy-tale-weaving fool. She'd even toyed with ideas about how she could have the best of both worlds. If the ring came off and she returned to her time, if she took the ring with her, then why couldn't she put it back on and return to Alec? She could see her parents, explain what had happened. Maybe even go back a couple of times a year to visit. She'd only managed to see them once or twice a year anyway, with her scheduling and all her traveling. Of course, there wouldn't be the weekly Saturday morning phone calls, but they'd have peace of mind. And she'd have Alec.

One lone tear cut a path from the corner of her eye to trickle over her temple and into her hair. No need to plan her trips to her parents now. Soon she would either be back in 1999, or homeless, fending for herself in a time she might be stuck in when the ring was cut from her finger.

Alec would surely be there when the jeweler removed the ring. Would he finally believe her if he witnessed her body fading into nothingness, back to its own century?

But by then it would be too late.

She closed her eyes, willing away tears. She was too stubborn to cry. How long did it take to travel from South Carolina in 1830? How long did she have left before the jeweler showed up on the doorstep?

A quiet knock sounded at her door. She ignored it until the footsteps faded down the hall. No doubt it was Molly again. The girl had already become a dear friend, but right now Shaelyn couldn't deal with talking to anyone or answering any more questions.

Hours later she still lay in the bed, staring up at the pitch-black ceiling. The quiet sounds of Alec preparing for bed drifted through the double pocket doors adjoining their rooms. The pain twisted like a knife in her heart as she imagined the masculine ritual, as she ached to share it with him.

Unable to bear the sounds a moment longer, she flung the covers from the bed and yanked on the first gown she came to. She couldn't lie there and listen to Alec prepare for bed. She'd wallowed in enough self-pity. She had to get out of the house, breathe the brisk sea air to clear her mind, walk off her frustrations and disappointments. She had to go where she always went for peace. She had to go to the beach.

"You big bully! What have you done to her?" Molly stormed into the library, a female William Hawthorne if ever there was one. "And don't you dare bother to deny it, you great dumb lummox."

Her voice echoed off the walls and banged around in Alec's already throbbing head. He cringed and rubbed his aching temples, regretting again the bottle of whiskey he'd polished off in the hours after midnight when sleep had eluded him for a second night.

"And don't try to fob me off," she yelled, "by telling me it's none of my business or that I wouldn't understand, you . . . you . . . you *man*!"

She'd obviously struggled for the worst possible slur she could fling at him and decided that *man* was the height of all insults. He wasn't sure he would argue with her at that moment.

"Would you mind slandering me in a tone somewhat softer than a bellow?"

"I am not bellowing!" she bellowed. "What did you do to Shaelyn, Alec Christopher, that would make her leave?"

He jerked his head up to stare at his sister while a sick knot formed in the pit of his stomach. He ignored the hammers banging in his temples.

"What do you mean, 'leave'?"

Molly glared. "Leave! As in go away! To depart! I just left her room. Her dinner tray was untouched. Her breakfast tray is still outside her door. Her room is empty. She's gone, Alec, and it's all your fault!"

The hammering increased as the knot in his stomach turned to a chunk of heavy, jagged ice.

He knocked the chair against the wall when he stood, then he marched from the room and up the stairs. He had to force himself not to run.

The door banged against the wall when he strode into her bedchamber. The bed linens looked as if a fight had taken place amid them, but the dinner tray from the night before was truly untouched. The silverware still lay in place beside the china, the napkin still lay in intricate folds, a red ring of evaporation stained the top of the wineglass, and the beef and vegetables had a dry, crusty look about them.

The sight of that untouched food shamed him more than

a slap in the face. More than Molly's bellowing.

A great bubble of emptiness welled in his chest. He fought it off and opened the doors to the armoire. The new dresses he'd ordered for her, along with some of Phillipa's, lined the interior. He would never know if any were missing.

With a sudden jolt of instinct, he dashed to his room and dug into a drawer at the bottom of a chest. The odd blue trousers, white shirt, and boots were still there. He didn't know why that comforted him, but it did. He picked up the shirt and breathed in the scent that was forever branded in his mind. Oh, yes. These were hers. He had no doubt these were hers.

A rustle of skirts in the door brought his head around, but it was only Molly, shooting accusatory daggers at him.

"What did you say to her, Alec, to make her spend two days in this room and then run away?"

How could he tell her the ridiculous story? His little sister thought Shaelyn hung the moon. He didn't want to dash her illusions.

"You cannot be certain she ran away, Moll. She may have simply gone for a walk."

"It is barely past dawn, Alec. I came in to check on her before daylight, worried that more than a headache drove her to bed. I doubt she makes a habit of walking in the middle of the night."

Alec lifted a brow. "As a matter of fact—"

"Alec!" Shaelyn's cry for help came from the gardens. He and Molly dashed to the window. "Alec, help us," Shaelyn yelled up at them. She walked, supporting a man with his arm around her shoulder, another man supporting his other side.

Molly followed Alec at a run as he thundered down the stairs toward the back of the house. His heart soared at the knowledge that Shaelyn had not left. He burst through the back door and immediately took her place beneath the man's arm.

"What is it, Shaelyn? What happened?"

"Sir, Cap'n Finley sent this man ashore. He came aboard as a passenger after we dropped off the . . . our cargo in Canada. Said it was just a nasty bout of the ague, but the cap'n thinks it's pneumonia."

Alec recognized Jake Welford, Captain Finley's first mate.

"Where was the ship's doctor? Couldn't he help him?"

"Doc Payne got drunk and got himself hitched at the last port. Cap'n planned to pick up another doc in Boston. But Mr. Smythe here is too sick for a ship's sawbones. He's out of his head with fever now."

Alec could feel the heat of the fever through the man's clothing. He was barely conscious enough to move one foot in front of the other. Alec doubted the man could stand on his own if they were to release him.

"I was out walking," Shaelyn offered, "and I saw the ship drop anchor and the rowboat lowered. I hung around to see if . . ." she glanced at the sick man dangling between Alec and Jake, "if anyone needed help. Jake said Captain Finley feared for Mr. Smythe's life and the quickest way he knew to get him help was to bring him to you. He was afraid he wouldn't make it to Cape Helm."

The man erupted in a series of deep, hacking coughs that left him gasping for breath and moaning in pain. What little weight he had borne earlier now weighed on Alec's and Jake's shoulders.

"Let's get him into a bed. Martin!" Alec called just as the butler rushed onto the back terrace. "Send Ned to fetch the doctor, then come help us get . . . what is his name again, Jake?"

"Smythe, sir. Samuel Smythe."

"Help us get Mr. Smythe settled."

Martin disappeared as Jake and Alec all but dragged the nearly unconscious man into the house. Shaelyn sped up the stairs, followed by Molly. The two of them turned back the bedcovers in the center guest room. Molly rang for fresh water while Shaelyn guided the men's efforts to get the patient into bed. She pulled off expensive, handmade boots that probably could have fed a family for a year. Without hesitation she peeled off his socks, then tugged to remove his coat of navy superfine.

Jake hitched his trousers at the waist and cleared his throat. "The ship's waiting for me, sir. If you have no further need . . ."

"No, no." Alec waved him off. "You have done all that you can. Tell Finley that he did the right thing."

"Aye, sir." With a touch to his cap, the first mate disappeared.

Shaelyn had pulled off Smythe's perfectly tailored coat, removed his silk tie, unbuttoned the pearl buttons of his fine lawn shirt, but when her fingers moved to the trim waistband of his trousers, Alec grabbed her hands.

"I will do it."

She looked up at him in shock.

"I *am* a married woman, Alec," she said with a completely unreadable expression.

"Not in the biblical sense," he reminded her quietly, then realized he'd only assumed she had no experience with men. Could she have . . . ? Unreasonable jealousy raked at him with jagged claws.

She tried to move his hands away and continue her progress, but Alec grasped her upper arms and set her away from the man.

"Leave the room, Shaelyn. I will tend to him until the doctor arrives." He glanced up at Molly, who stood wide-eyed, taking in their exchange and the undressing of a stranger. "What are you doing in here, Molly? You've no business here. Go wait for the doctor."

Amazingly, Molly scurried from the room, but Shaelyn stood, her arms crossed, defiance in her very stance.

"Do I have to remove you forcibly?" he queried calmly.

"Just try, and you'll be nursing your crotch again." She

stepped away from him. "I may be able to help this man more than your archaic doctor."

He glared at her. She glared back. The same hurt look from two days before flickered in her eyes for just an instant. It proved to be his undoing.

"Fine," he barked. "Do as you please. Go or stay. But I will finish undressing him." He turned back to Smythe.

Shaelyn sat stiff as a poker on a chair by the door while Alec used his body to shield her from seeing more of this man than she should. Removing trousers damp with sweat and salt water from an unconscious body took more effort than he would have imagined.

Margaret arrived with a bowl and a pitcher of steaming water. Shaelyn sent her back for cool water and several cloths. By the time she returned, Alec had wrestled the trousers from Smythe's body and finally had him decently covered, all the way to his chin.

Shaelyn poured cool water into the bowl, then carried it to the bedside. She threw both windows open before settling herself by the bed, dipping a cloth into the water, then wringing it out. With a worried look carving twin creases between her brows, she tossed the sheet to Smythe's waist and began bathing his face and shoulders with the damp cloth. She glanced up at Alec.

"I'll do his head and arms, you do his chest and legs. We need to get his fever down."

"Will cold water not aggravate his illness and make him sicker?" Alec argued.

She stopped long enough to lock her gaze with his.

"I know what I'm doing."

She went back to bathing Smythe's fevered skin.

After several seconds of debate, Alec picked up a cloth and plunged it into the pitcher.

They worked together in silence for three quarters of an hour, Alec making sure the sheet never crept too low or too high on the man's abdomen. After what seemed an eternity, Martin ushered Dr. Maxwell into the room and

Alec and Shaelyn handed the care of the patient over to the doctor.

Shaelyn hovered at the foot of the bed while Alec roamed around the room. Maxwell grunted to himself with each procedure of the examination, thumping and listening, poking and prodding. Smythe was either unconscious or too weak to protest. Several minutes passed before the doctor straightened and tugged on his waistcoat.

"Bad case of pneumonia, Alec. Bad. Be surprised if the man survives. Any relatives around?"

Alec shook his head. "I don't even remember his first name."

"Samuel," Shaelyn supplied quietly. "They said his name is Samuel."

Alec turned to her, saw her staring at the man in bed, then turned back to the doctor.

"Nor do I know where he's from." He expected Shaelyn to supply that information as well, but she remained silent. "Is there nothing you can do for him?"

The doctor hooked his thumbs into the pockets of his waistcoat and bowed his head.

"I don't like to do it. Don't think it helps that much, if at all, but I could try leeching him."

"No way!" Shaelyn nearly yelled before the words had died in Maxwell's throat. "That's the worst thing you could do! I know what to do for him."

"Shaelyn, now is not the time to spin your—"

"Our neighbor had a child with cystic fibrosis. I used to help her—"

"What the devil is a cystic fibrosis?" Alec could barely disguise his frustration.

Shaelyn sent him a withering glare. "It's a genetic disorder that causes the lungs to fill up with—"

"I shudder to ask, but what is a genetic disorder?" he asked through clenched teeth, then wished he hadn't called notice to her comment. All she needed was to start babbling her strange story for Dr. Maxwell to examine *her* as well as Smythe.

"I can't explain it." She threw up her hands. "There's an extra chromosome in the genes that make up the DNA, or something like that. It doesn't matter what causes it. What matters is that I can probably help this man."

He turned his gaze to Maxwell, who listened with eyebrows drawn into one straight line across his brow.

"She fancies herself a writer of sorts," Alec offered, trying to keep her out of an asylum. He speared her with a silencing look. "One must have quite an imagination to write such fiction."

She stared at Alec, then turned her attention to the doctor.

"Fiction or not, I *did* have a neighbor with a child whose lungs filled with fluid. Surely you've come across that condition in your practice. The treatment we used on Allison should help Mr. Smythe, as well."

Alec stifled a sigh of relief when Maxwell cocked his head in interest.

"I have come across that particular illness. What method of care did you administer, Miss . . ." He glanced at Alec.

"Shaelyn," Alec offered, not sure which last name to give. "Shaelyn Sumner Ha—"

"Yes. Shaelyn Sumner, Doctor. An old friend of the family. Nice to meet you." She marched forward, took the doctor's hand, and shook it. "The first thing we have to do is loosen the mucus in his lungs so that he can cough it up."

"And how do we go about that?" Maxwell remained interested, but a hint of doubt entered his voice.

"It's easier to show you than to tell you." Shaelyn shoved up her sleeves, tossed her hair behind her shoulder, then moved to the edge of Smythe's bed. She grabbed his right shoulder and rolled him onto his left side. After tucking pillows around him to balance him, she looked back at the men.

"Now hold your hands like this." She held up slightly cupped hands, her fingers straight and her thumbs tight against the knuckle of her forefinger. The doctor raised his hands in imitation. Alec's fingers automatically cupped at his side, but he didn't bother to show them.

"Okay, now you just sort of firmly pop him all along here. It doesn't hurt," she added when the doctor opened his mouth to speak. "Try it against your leg. You don't beat him, you pop him with a cushion of air cupped in your hand."

Maxwell tested the method against his upraised thigh, following Shaelyn's example as she worked with confidence along the sick man's back. Alec and Maxwell watched for several minutes, then Shaelyn straightened and moved to the other side of the bed.

Without the slightest hesitation or sign of embarrassment, she hitched her skirt to her knees and crawled to the center of the mattress.

"Shaelyn," Alec warned in his best no-nonsense voice.

She glanced up at him with total unconcern before setting back to work.

"Don't be a prude, Alec," she mumbled distractedly while she removed the pillows, rolled Smythe onto his other side, then began the slapping process all over again.

"I don't remember all the details about this kind of therapy, but the popping helps to jar the mucus loose. We roll him back and forth, jarring it loose, and he'll cough it up. We also need to get lots of water in him, and steam in the room would help, too."

She continued to work while Maxwell and Alec watched. When she finished that side, she went back to the other and started over again.

"Dr. Maxwell, I apologize for this," Alec murmured under his breath, certain Shaelyn couldn't hear above the popping of flesh against flesh. "She's odd. Extremely odd," he added, more to himself.

"No, no." Maxwell shook his head, still watching Shaelyn. "Her theory has some credence." He watched a few more seconds with interest, then turned his attention back to Alec. "As I said, I can do nothing more for him but leeching. Let her try this for a while. And, as she said, it causes no pain. If he shows no improvement, then I will do what I can."

He collected his bag and moved to Shaelyn's side.

"A pleasure to make your acquaintance, Miss Sumner. I will stop by tomorrow to check on his progress."

Shaelyn raised her head as if she'd forgotten the men's presence. She tossed a straggling strand of curly auburn silk back over her shoulder and smiled at the doctor as she continued to work.

"The pleasure is mine, Doctor. I look forward to seeing you again."

Alec walked Dr. Maxwell to the door, then climbed the stairs back to the guest room.

He stood in the doorway and watched. The morning sun poured through the windows and exploded off her hair in sparkles of red and brown and gold. She didn't seem to notice him as she finished that side, rounded the bed, then crawled across the mattress again to roll him over.

A dog barked in the distance, the sound carried in on the breeze that billowed the summer draperies. She tossed her thick, wavy curtain of hair over her shoulder again, and when it slipped back in her way, she muttered, gathered it in her hands, and stuffed it down the back of her dress.

Who *was* this woman? Where had she really come from? He shoved his hands into his pockets and leaned against the door frame. When she finished on that side, she rolled him to his back, scrambled off the bed, then picked up the cloth and started bathing him again.

Alec jerked his hands from his pockets and shoved away

from the door. He crossed the room in four strides, plucked another cloth from the nightstand, then shouldered Shaelyn out of the way.

He ignored her one simple word.

''Prude.''

Chapter 10

SHAELYN'S GRITTY EYES burned from lack of sleep. She'd dozed off and on in a chair fit for a torture chamber, but never for more than a few minutes before Samuel's hacking cough woke her. Then she would go back to work gently pounding on his back.

The fever had finally come down somewhat. Not from their efforts with bathing him, though. Shaelyn had gotten tired of Alec's self-righteously refusing to allow her to touch more than Samuel's head and shoulders, and in a fit of impatience she called for a bath of cool water to be drawn. Once Alec and Martin had gotten him submerged in the water, the high fever seemed to release its hold on him.

Shaelyn reached over and felt his forehead. She pushed a lock of his wheat- and platinum-colored hair back to rest her palm against the still-warm skin. Even with his sickly pallor, the man was extremely easy to look at. While she studied the classic features with more than a little admiration, his eyes slowly came open to watch her.

"Will I live?" His voice sounded weak and rusty from disuse, and his question was a serious one.

She smiled and fussed with the covers. His accent surprised her. Was the entire North filled with Southerners?

"I'm not a doctor," she said as she tucked the sheet around his shoulders, "but you're a heck of a lot better than you were when they brought you in here."

He studied her face with weary hazel eyes and reached for her hand. When he seemed satisfied with what he saw, he allowed his lids to close and his body relaxed into sleep.

She worked throughout the day, taking a break only when Margaret came in to feed him. She'd tried to show the little maid how to work on Samuel's back, but her attempts always ended up more like slaps than the cupping necessary to help. So Shaelyn continued to do it herself.

In the late afternoon her head swam with fatigue and her eyes burned with lack of sleep. She crawled across the bed for the umpteenth time to roll him over and work on his other side. When she finished she sank back on her heels and looked at the fluffy white pillow next to him, so soft, so inviting. Without really thinking about it, she pulled the pillow to her and lowered her head until she sank into the soft, fluffy down. Pure heaven. She hugged the bottom half to her chest, curled into a little ball, and relaxed into the deep, dreamless sleep of the exhausted.

She never knew when Alec stepped into the room to check on her, didn't see the fire of jealousy light his eyes. She never felt him scoop her into his arms and carry her to her own bed, or lay her gently on the counterpane and cover her with a light quilt. And she didn't feel his fingers as they smoothed a strand of hair from her cheek, even when they lingered seconds longer than need be. And she didn't see him when he walked from the room with his shoulders slumped.

She waited until Alec was alone in the library and Margaret was taking care of Samuel before she slipped through the library doors and closed them with a click behind her. She couldn't go on with this tension between them, and the only way she knew how to deal with it was to face it head-on.

"Put the tray on the table, Martin. Thank you." His voice sounded as weary as she felt.

"I'm not Martin."

He raised his head from his paperwork and just looked at her until she squirmed.

"Do I have you to thank for getting me into my bed?"

He looked away and scratched the back of his head before answering. "You were asleep on his bed. It wasn't proper."

"And we wouldn't want to do anything that wasn't proper," she agreed. *Like tricking someone into marrying you,* she wanted to add.

He simply looked at her, as if he expected her to go on.

"Alec," she walked to his desk and sank into the chair opposite him, "I know you don't believe my story. I don't blame you. I wouldn't either if I were in your place. And I'm not asking you to believe me now. But you offered to be my friend once, and now I'm asking you to be. I've done nothing wrong, except be in the wrong place at the wrong time." *Literally.*

He continued to stare at her, but his eyes flickered away for a moment.

"I'm not crazy," she went on. "You don't have to believe me, but until the jeweler gets back or the marriage is annulled, at least be my friend."

The sound of a carriage rolling up the drive drifted through the open window as his face softened and an apology entered his eyes.

"Friends?" she asked hesitantly as she held out her hand.

He looked her in the eyes, then his lips curved in a reluctant grin.

"Friends," he agreed as he curled his fingers around hers. The very warmth of his hand raced up her arm and spread through her body, drugging her with his touch, making her dream of impossible lives with fairy-tale endings.

They sat there, connected by more than just their hands, their smiles of friendship turning to something deeper.

"Alec Christopher!" William Hawthorne's dictator voice boomed even through the thick closed doors of the library. The doors flew open and he stood there, framed by them, as he took in the picture of his son holding Shaelyn's hand across the desk.

Martin advanced around him to announce blandly, "Your father, sir."

Shaelyn released Alec's hand and turned in her seat to see what doom *Der Fuehrer* brought with him today.

"Alec, my boy." He ignored Shaelyn's presence completely. "Look who I have brought."

He turned and held out his hand. An absolutely stunning angel of a woman stepped through the door. Blond, gorgeous, ethereal; Shaelyn wouldn't have been surprised if a halo had wreathed her head. A light of anticipation lit her eyes when she smiled a brilliant smile at Alec.

Please let this be a cousin.

"Faith," Alec rasped, then glanced at Shaelyn and back to the blond angel. He rose from his seat and moved around the desk like a man in a trance. Shaelyn watched, wondering who in the world this woman was.

"Alec, you look wonderful. You've only gotten more handsome." She glided to him, took both his hands in hers and pressed a chaste kiss against his cheek.

"And you are more beautiful, if that is possible."

He stood there, holding her hands and dragging his gaze up and down her body. She wore an exquisitely tailored traveling suit, her hair twined to perfection beneath a frilly scooped bonnet.

Shaelyn watched, feeling like a frumpy schoolmarm in her rather plain yellow dress and hair hanging loose down her back.

The room fell silent while Alec and the woman stared

at each other, then the woman turned to Shaelyn with a smile.

Alec snapped out of his worshipful trance and turned his attention to Shaelyn.

"Forgive me. Faith, may I introduce Shaelyn Sumner." He didn't even stumble over leaving out the Hawthorne, she noticed. "Shaelyn, this is Faith Almany."

"Alec's betrothed," William added with a smirk.

Shaelyn had stood, but now her hand stopped in midair. Her gaze shot to Alec while William's words screamed in her mind. Betrothed. *Betrothed.* Alec had the decency to look uncomfortable, but he could have fallen on his knees and begged forgiveness right then and she wouldn't have felt less betrayed.

She forced herself to extend her hand. Faith took it, obviously not quite sure what to do with it.

"Nice to meet you," Shaelyn managed, toying with the idea of introducing herself as Alec's wife. But she wouldn't sink to William's level. "If you'll excuse me, I have to get back to our patient."

"Patient?" Faith asked, but Shaelyn was already making her escape, her only thought to get away.

When she stepped into the hall she turned and gave Alec a look that told him exactly how she felt. He apologized with his eyes, sincerely, clearly torn over what to do. She kept her voice light and chatty when she spoke.

"Alec, when you have a minute, would you mind coming upstairs? I'll be with Samuel."

As she walked away she heard Faith ask, "Samuel? Is that her husband?"

She was too numb to stay and hear Alec's answer.

Hours later she heard the carriage wheels on the drive as the carriage pulled away. Margaret had brought her dinner on a tray and Shaelyn had picked at her food in Samuel's room. Even though he'd improved enough for her to leave him for short periods, she knew she could never sit through a meal with William and Alec and his future wife.

Just the thought set the nausea churning in her stomach.

She heard his steps in the hallway just as she finished working on Samuel. The door had remained properly open and Alec now stood in the frame, all trace of his usual good humor replaced with a dead-serious expression.

She straightened and massaged the small of her back, staring at him, not giving an inch when he started looking uncomfortable. Finally she walked toward him until he moved out of the way.

"Let's go into my room," she said, her voice weary, dead. "I don't want to disturb Samuel."

She led the way. Alec followed her in and shut the door behind him.

"Shaelyn . . ."

She turned and stopped him with an upraised hand. She'd had plenty of time to think about this.

"You don't owe me any explanations, Alec. I'm a mistake that should never have happened. All I ask is that you let me live in Harbor Mist until I can leave."

"There's no need to move to the cottage, Shaelyn."

"Yes, Alec. There is." She looked at him and felt as if the light in her life had died.

He bowed his head and nodded. "Whatever you wish."

"She has a right to know who I am, Alec."

He nodded again and looked back up at her.

"I told her. Against Father's wishes, but I told her."

"Why didn't you tell me?" The minute the words left her mouth, she regretted them. "No. Never mind. You don't owe me anything." She wished he owed her the world.

"Shaelyn . . ." He started to take her by the shoulders, but let his hands drop to his sides when she stepped back. "I didn't know myself until after we were married. This is Father's doing."

"But you care for her. I can see it in your eyes. There's history between you two."

"Yes," he said, the word telling her what she already knew. "She was my first love. Twelve years ago. But I was eighteen and Father had other plans."

She was his first love. He loved her. The thought ripped through Shaelyn like a jagged, red-hot dagger. She clenched her jaw, refusing to let him see what pain his words caused. His knowing would serve no purpose, and she wouldn't have him pitying her for being such a hopeless sap.

"Well," she said, lifting her chin and looking him in the eye, "I figured it was something like that. So, how did she take finding out you have a wife?" Did her unconcern sound as false to Alec as it did to her?

He took a deep breath and released it.

"Faith is an unusual woman."

Oh, of course, she would be the salt of the earth.

"Once she heard the entire story, she understood."

Well, of course, she would understand. "How fortunate for you that she is an open-minded person." Shae tried her best to sound sincere, but her words might as well have been a meow. When Alec looked at her she forced an innocent smile. "Really. Most women would not have been so accepting. I know I wouldn't."

"Shaelyn, I did not purposely keep this from you. It just never occurred to me to tell you. After all, we're not truly married. It is only a matter of time before the union is legally dissolved and you go back to . . ." His voice trailed off, avoiding the subject looming between them like a concrete wall.

"You're right, Alec." Defeat settled over her like a heavy, suffocating fog. Amazing, how quickly he forgot the power of those kisses on the beach, the energy-charged air at the masquerade ball. Had it all been an act? Pity for her and her dreamy thoughts? A convincing display for a couple of slave catchers? She didn't know which would be worse, that he could turn off the feelings so easily, or that she was so gullible.

"Shaelyn, I believed this fiasco would be over with before Faith arrived. She should not have been here until—"

"It's all right, Alec. No more explanation necessary." She didn't know if she could handle much more of his explaining. Nice to know she was just a fiasco to him. "As soon as Samuel no longer needs my attention, I want to move to the cottage."

"I told you, that isn't necessary."

She rounded on him. "It's the least you can do," she snapped.

He looked as if she'd slapped him, but she'd choke before she'd apologize. She couldn't stay in that house and bump into him day and night. She couldn't watch Faith come and go, staking her claim on him and preparing to move in for good.

She grabbed the ring on her finger and yanked with a vengeance. Tears burned in her eyes. Before they could gather she stepped around Alec and moved for the door. "Just let me do this my way," she said, then escaped to the safety of the sickroom.

Alec knotted his tie, still plagued with guilt from the look on Shaelyn's face. That look haunted him now, while he finished dressing to dine with Faith.

Good Lord, how ludicrous. Dressing to dine with one's betrothed while feeling guilty over one's wife. When had he lost control of his life?

He yanked the lopsided knot loose and started over again, cursing himself for his lack of concentration.

If he'd just left her alone. But he'd had to try to make amends, and then be her friend. And then he'd given in to the urge to kiss her. If only he hadn't kissed her.

Blast it! His damn silk tie refused to knot properly. He yanked it loose again and strode from the room. He didn't even hesitate outside the sickroom door, but his peripheral vision caught a glimpse of Shaelyn spooning broth into

Smythe's mouth. A spike of unreasonable jealousy bit into him.

Saint's blood, why didn't he just knot his tie into a hangman's noose and put himself out of his misery?

Ned waited with the carriage on the front drive. Alec leapt into the seat and slammed the door, closing himself into a nice, dark cocoon where he wouldn't see flashes of Shaelyn, where he could fumble with his blasted defective tie, and where he could calm himself and look forward to a soothing evening with Faith.

When he stepped from the carriage a half-hour later, his mood had improved a degree or two. Ned's eyes strayed to the hopelessly wrinkled tie, the final knot a creation that fashion had yet to see, but the coachman wisely kept his own counsel.

Faith's father, Caleb Almany, met Alec at the door. The man had not changed much in all the years Alec had known him. The smell of expensive cigars still clung to him like a child clinging to its mother. His portly frame had perhaps grown a bit in girth, and his thinning hair grown thinner, but his affable smile beamed out from a weathered, seaman's face that had not aged a day in nearly thirty years.

"Alec, it's been too long, son. Come in, come in." He waved Alec into the cheery interior of the house, then led the way into the parlor.

"It's good to see you, sir. The shipping business isn't the same since you retired."

"A man has to give up the sea sooner or later," Caleb said, gesturing to a decanter of port and quirking a brow. At Alec's nod he poured two glasses. "Better to give it up for dry land than to wear the sea as a coffin." He handed the wine to Alec. "You still get seasick, son?"

Alec grimaced while he sipped the heavy port. "Worse than ever, sir."

Caleb *tsk*ed. "What a shame. Well, I'm happy enough being a landlubber. Two shipwrecks in a career are two too many. Didn't want to press my luck. You still wear your ring?"

Alec knew he referred to the earring a sailor got for each shipwreck survived. Caleb had been the captain of the *Hampton Cross* when Alec was fifteen and a crew member for the first time. The ship had gone down when a storm blew them off course and they hit a reef near the Philippine Islands. Fortunately another ship saw their distress and picked them up before any lives were lost. Each sailor on the wrecked ship came away from the voyage with a gold hoop in his ear for his troubles.

"I still wear it when I sail, sir, which isn't very often." He sailed only when relieving certain ships of their special cargo. But Caleb would know nothing of that. "How is Mrs. Almany?" he asked, changing the subject.

"Hester is fussing like a mother hen, now that the youngest is back in the nest. And where the devil are they?" It seemed to just then occur to him that they were missing. "Hester! Faith!" he bellowed toward the ceiling. "All hands on deck!"

"Captain Almany, I have asked you not to yodel in the house." Faith's mother calmly entered the parlor from the dining room.

"I was not yodeling, my dear. I was issuing an order."

"There would have been no need if you had sent word that Alec had arrived. How are you, Alec, dear?"

Alec took Hester's hand and brushed the back of it with his lips.

"I am well, ma'am. And there is no need to ask that question of you. You are fairly glowing."

She allowed herself a small smile. "My baby, Faith, is home."

A movement on the stairs caught Alec's attention, and he turned to watch Faith descend like an angel gliding down from heaven.

"Alec, no one told me you'd arrived." She took his hands and offered a cheek for his kiss.

Touching her was like stepping back in time. He was a youth of eighteen again, and she a sweet, serene girl of seventeen, so different from all the other giddy females of his acquaintance. He had loved her with the passion of first love. He would have moved mountains for her, but he could not budge his father's will. How different their lives would have been if William had not imposed his business dealings upon them.

All through dinner he marveled at how she had not changed one whit. Approaching thirty years of age, her porcelain skin looked as fresh and young as twelve years earlier. Her figure was as lithe and trim as Shaelyn's.

Just that fleeting thought of his wife sent an image of her flashing through his mind. The guilt that had quieted returned. He shoved it away and focused his attention on Faith, but for the remainder of the evening, when he least expected it, thoughts of his wife crept into his mind and he found himself wondering what she was doing.

Chapter 11

SHAELYN KEPT HER distance from Alec, which wasn't all that hard to do. When he wasn't working with Charles and *Der Fuehrer* in the Hawthorne Shipping offices, he was dancing attendance on Faith.

Shae sighed and glanced at the clock on the marble mantel. She'd promised to have lunch with Molly on the back terrace, and it was almost noon. She rose and checked the sleeping Samuel one more time. He'd improved dramatically since falling out of that rowboat at Shaelyn's feet. Another day should see him well enough for her to move into the cottage. She needed to get away so she wouldn't be constantly on guard to avoid Alec. And if she never saw Faith again it would be too soon.

As if that hope had conjured her, the woman stood at the front door when Shaelyn came down the stairs. At the sight of her, Shaelyn made another contribution to her favorite charity under her breath. Her first instinct was to turn and retreat, but she had never been a coward and she wasn't going to start now. She lifted her chin and continued down the stairs.

Faith turned at the sound, obviously expecting Alec.

When their eyes met, Shaelyn braced herself for a smug smile of triumph, but instead Faith seemed as uncomfortable as Shae. Hesitating at the bottom of the steps, she searched for something to say.

"Well, isn't this awkward," she blurted, then gave herself a mental whack on the head.

"Yes, isn't it, though," Faith agreed after an embarrassed pause.

Shaelyn told herself to leave it alone. To excuse herself and go meet Molly on the terrace. But for some unfathomable reason, she didn't.

In her journalistic way, she assessed the woman before her in a matter of seconds.

Dressed again in the height of fashion, Faith made Shaelyn feel as if she were garbed in a feed sack compared to the form-fitting, corset-hugging contours of Faith's navy riding habit. Surprisingly, Shae realized that Faith's attitude had nothing to do with Shae feeling frumpy.

Indeed, if anything, the woman facing her exuded an apology for any unpleasantness she might be causing.

"There's no need to feel awkward," Shae found herself saying. "After all, I'm just a case of mistaken identity who means nothing to Alec." When had she decided to be so magnanimous? Especially when just saying those words caused dull pinpricks to her heart. "And I thought he was an actor of sorts, playing a part." Much like she was doing at the moment.

Faith visibly relaxed and relief replaced the apology in her eyes.

"Yes, Alec told me. But, truly, men are not always aware of a woman's feelings, and I feared he had been rather . . . well, dull-witted about how you might feel now. After all, he is a wonderful person. Women have always thrown themselves at him." Her eyes widened and the apology came back. "Not that I am inferring that you threw yourself at him. I only meant to say that he would be easy to fall in love with."

Shaelyn forced a smile and nodded. She knew exactly how easy it was to fall in love with him.

Faith let out a nervous little giggle.

"I am so very relieved because—"

"There you are." Molly appeared in the hall from the back terrace. "I feared Samuel had taken a turn for the . . . oh, hello, Faith. I didn't know you'd arrived." Molly appeared to be oblivious as to how strange it was to find the wife and the fiancée chatting, but Shaelyn knew the young girl was sharper than she would ever allow these people to see. She played the part of an innocent, obedient female well.

"Will you have lunch on the terrace with us? It is just too beautiful a day to stay inside," Molly invited. Shaelyn wanted to choke her, but Faith shook her head.

"I would love to, but Alec has invited me to go riding. We have so much to discuss, and I—"

Masculine footsteps thudded down the upstairs hall just before Alec appeared at the top of the stairs.

"I'm sorry, Faith. I found my watch, but then Martin had a message . . ."

His voice trailed off at the sight of Faith and Shaelyn facing each other. He looked as if he expected them to launch into a catfight at any moment. Shae didn't bother to disabuse him of the notion.

"Faith and I were just getting to know each other." She allowed just enough of a smile to make him nervous.

"Yes, Alec, we had just invited Faith to have lunch with us. Why do you not postpone your ride, and we can all have lunch together?"

If glares had been daggers, Molly would be lying in a pool of blood on the floor, and Shaelyn and Alec would be wiping their blades on her skirts.

"I think not, pest. We have plans to dine in town. But thank you for the invitation." He slid his pocket watch into his waistcoat and gave her a look that dared her to pursue the subject. She wisely remained silent.

"Faith." Alec offered her his arm, then guided her to
the door. "If you'll excuse us, ladies. Have a pleasant
lunch."

When the door closed behind them, Molly turned to
Shaelyn. A twinkle of mischief lit in the girl's eyes before
it disappeared into an innocent smile. Shaelyn wasn't sure
she wanted to know what was going on in that pretty little
head.

The guest "cottage" could have housed a family of four
comfortably. Shaelyn stood outside the house and stared,
thinking how much she would have enjoyed this little
place under different circumstances.

Built of snowy white clapboard, it sat atop a sloping
lawn overlooking the same panoramic view as Windward
Cottage, like a mascot to the mighty sentinel. The sun sparkled off windows, a swing hung on the porch, quiet in the
absence of a breeze, and twin chimneys jutted toward the
sky from the rust-colored roof like a jaunty, pointed hat.

She loved it before she ever stepped inside.

Molly led the way to the front door, grumbling the
whole time.

"I still insist you needn't do this, Shaelyn. There is no
reason why you cannot stay at Windward."

They had already had this discussion, once during their
lunch on the terrace, when Shaelyn announced she should
leave while Alec was gone, once while Martin fetched the
key, and again on the short walk to the cottage.

It touched Shaelyn to know that Molly didn't want her
to go. At least someone in that house would miss her.

"It will just be better this way. Trust me."

Molly didn't argue further, but Shaelyn was sure she
hadn't heard the last of it yet.

The inside of the cottage charmed Shaelyn the moment
she stepped through the doors. Sunlight tumbled through
sheer lacy curtains, and shades of green and blue pulled
the ocean and sky right into the parlor. She could see her-

self spending hours at the small secretary, writing down her thoughts, or curling up on the blue damask sofa and reading long into the night.

Molly marched through the room with little enthusiasm, obviously not wanting to say or do anything that would encourage Shaelyn to stay.

"The kitchen and dining room are back here, but of course you can either come to the house for meals or Margaret will bring them to you."

That was fine with Shaelyn. Kitchens of the 1830s and their odd contraptions looked just as foreign to her as microwaves, double ovens, and dishwashers would look to Molly.

They went back into the roomy parlor and up a stairway that hugged the back wall.

The upstairs opened into a huge bedroom that faced the water. Windows framed a view worthy of a seascape by a master artist. A door opened onto a small balcony over the porch.

A summery, white eyelet bedspread covered the massive bed, and Shaelyn smiled to herself at the thought of Alec's friend, Griffin, sleeping under something so feminine. A dark, heavily carved armoire matching the bed stood against the pale green walls. A shaving stand with its pitcher and bowl stood by the windows, and several peach-and-green throw rugs dotted the hardwood floor.

Two smaller bedrooms opened off the large one, furnished just as nicely, but with a view of the woods instead of the ocean.

"Molly, this is so wonderful. No wonder Griffin always stays here."

Her little sister-in-law gave her an unenthusiastic half-smile. "It can be terribly eerie here at night."

"Great." Shaelyn saw through Molly's ploy. "I love a good haunted house."

Molly plopped onto the bed, looking for all the world like a pouting six-year-old. The girl always seemed so wise beyond her years, Shaelyn had to remind herself that she was only seventeen.

"I don't know why you must move out. You and Alec were getting on so well. You were meant for each other. My blind Aunt Sophia could see that."

Shaelyn studied the view and tried to muster up a convincing voice to deny Molly's words, but the girl went on.

"What happened between you, Shaelyn? What happened before Samuel came?"

Shae watched the play of light on the water, watched the waves swell and ebb, mirroring what her emotions had done since the moment she'd arrived. Suddenly she was tired of denying who she was.

"I told him where I'm from." When she finally turned around, Molly just looked at her as if she'd uttered a non sequitur.

"You are from Louisiana. So is Griffin. Alec would not find fault with that. Or are you not truly from there?"

Shaelyn rounded the bed and sat opposite Molly on the eyelet cover. She looked her straight in the eye.

"I'm from Louisiana, just as I told Alec." She held Molly's gaze. "But I was born in the year 1968."

Molly cocked her head, a question in her eyes, obviously trying to make some sort of sense with that number. Shaelyn clarified it for her.

"One hundred and thirty-eight years in the future. When I left my time it was 1999."

Molly shook her head, still not understanding. Shaelyn couldn't blame her. The concept was beyond imagination, even in the year before the twenty-first century.

"I'm from the future, Molly. I don't know how or why, but somehow I traveled back through time. I'm from a world nearly a hundred and seventy years from now."

If Shaelyn gave her even the slightest hint of a smile, Molly might never believe that Shaelyn was serious. They stared at each other, and Shaelyn willed her to read the truth in her eyes.

"How?" Molly asked, still shaking her head. At least she hadn't lowered those terrible shutters over her eyes and shut her out like Alec had.

Shae held up her left hand and studied the sparkle of green-and-white fire.

"It sounds crazy. The whole thing sounds crazy, for that matter, but I think this ring had something to do with it."

"Great-Aunt Eleanor's ring? What has that to do with anything?" Molly still shook her head, looking more confused than ever.

"I found it on the floor of an old ship. It was wedged between the floorboards. When I put it on to remember to give it to the captain, just as it slipped over my knuckle the ship lurched really hard. I thought my dizziness was from banging my head on the bulkhead, but I believe now that that was when I traveled to 1830. Everything seemed newer then, and I haven't been dizzy since. And I can't get the darned thing off, even though it slid on without a problem."

Molly's head continued to shake slowly back and forth, but more in a way of trying to assimilate the information rather than to deny it. Shaelyn could tell that the girl was trying her best to believe her.

"If you are from the future, what is it like?" She sounded dreamy, like a child questioning a fairy tale, wanting to believe yet skeptical of its truth.

Shaelyn's first impulse was to tell her about all the obvious things, like airplanes, cars, TV, radio, men walking on the moon. But that would be more than even the most open-minded person could believe.

"Well, there are a lot more people. Everywhere. And, of course, we dress differently. We're a lot more casual. Women's dresses are comfortable, shorter, with a lot less fabric to haul around. We wear trousers as much as or more than dresses. In fact, I had on a pair when I was on the ship."

A little more interest sparked in Molly's eyes, but she said nothing.

"Several diseases have cures or vaccines. Smallpox has been eradicated. Measles, mumps, polio, typhus all have vaccines so most people never get those diseases. If Samuel had been sick in my time, they probably would have given him a shot and then started—"

"A shot! They would have killed him?" Molly's eyes widened in horror. Shaelyn smiled.

"No, they wouldn't have shot him. They would have given him a shot, or rather an injection, through his skin, of medication. Then they probably would have given him some medicine to swallow, and it would have cured the pneumonia. Hardly anyone dies of pneumonia anymore."

Molly nodded, obviously considering this information. Shaelyn searched for more believable things to tell her.

"Engineering has advanced so that buildings have gotten bigger and taller. We call the tall ones skyscrapers because they look like they're scraping the sky."

"What about transportation?" Molly asked. "Is it true that the steam engine will replace the horse and carriage?"

Shaelyn searched her mind for an elusive piece of trivia that tickled at her memory. What was it about a contest between a horse and a steam engine?

"Oh yes! I remember now. Sometime this year, in the autumn, I think, there will be a race between a horse and the first steam locomotive built in the United States. I think they call it the *Tom Thumb*. Anyway, they'll race to Baltimore, but the steam engine will have mechanical problems and never finish the race."

"Oh." Molly's face fell.

"But steam does replace the horse," Shaelyn assured her. "They use the locomotives anyway, and by the late 1800s they develop what they call a horseless carriage that people use for transportation. They even measure the engine's power in horsepower."

"Have you ridden in one of those carriages?" Molly's

eyes were as wide as a six-year-old's on Christmas morning. Shaelyn had to bite her cheek to keep from laughing at the question.

"By the 1950s nearly every family had a car. That's what we call them. Cars. They used to be called automobiles, but hardly anyone calls them that now. By the 1990s, in the U.S., nearly every working adult owns one. Except in the large cities, then they have mass transportation, like buses, which is a big version of a car that seats probably fifty or sixty people. They also have trains." She'd save the concept of subways for later.

Molly just stared at her in wonder.

Shaelyn searched for something else awe-inspiring yet conceivable.

"Shopping!" she blurted. "Shopping is really different. Hardly anyone has their clothes made. We have huge stores filled with racks of ready-made clothes. In fact, you can find nearly anything you can possibly think of in a store of one kind or another. And grocery shopping is different. We have what we call supermarkets, and they're filled with every kind of canned and fresh and boxed food you can think of. The meat is already butchered any way you want it. We have every kind of fresh fruit and vegetables all year long."

"How do you do that in the winter? Don't tell me you don't have winter anymore."

Shaelyn laughed. It felt so good to talk about it. "No, we still have winter, though some people think that they aren't as cold as they used to be. We get the fresh produce by importing it from areas that have a growing season opposite ours, or a tropical climate, like California or Hawaii."

"Hawaii?"

"The Sandwich Islands. They're called Hawaii now, short for the Hawaiian Islands. They're also one of the fifty United States."

"America has fifty states then?"

Shaelyn nodded. If she didn't watch out, every word out of her mouth could turn into another topic of discussion. Maybe she should stop while she had the chance.

"Anyway, Alec didn't believe me when I told him where I'm from and how I got here. I didn't really expect him to. It's just better that I stay here at the cottage, especially now that Faith is here."

"But did you tell Alec what you've told me? About the steam engine and the stores and the skyscrapers?"

Shaelyn shook her head, her chest tightening at the thought of Alec's shuttered gaze.

"He didn't ask. And there's no reason he should have. If someone came to me in 1999 and told me they were from the year 2170, I'd be making them an appointment with the nearest psychiatrist."

"The nearest what?"

Shaelyn cringed. She was definitely going to have to watch what she said.

"A doctor who specializes in mental illness. Like the insane."

"But you are not insane."

"Thank you." She reached out and patted Molly's hand. "I'm not asking you to believe me. I just got tired of avoiding the truth. Now," she stood, letting Molly off the hook from saying whether she believed her, "let's get me settled while your brother is still out of the house."

Chapter 12

ALEC KNOCKED ON the door, then banged when she didn't open it immediately. A shadow in the windows moved through the dim light of the oil lamps, then the knob turned and the door swung inward.

She stood there, her long loose hair haloed by the lights, her gown unbuttoned at the neck. She made no move to button it even though his gaze lingered longer than it should have.

"What do you want, Alec?"

The righteous anger that had vanished at the sight of her returned.

"Why did you leave while I was gone? I told you there was no need to move here."

She simply looked at him. "Is this going to be a long argument? Should I make myself comfortable?"

"Shaelyn, there is no need . . ."

She turned and strolled back into the parlor, then flopped onto the couch and propped her feet on an ottoman.

He followed her in and slammed the door.

"Shouldn't we leave the door open, for propriety's sake?" she questioned.

"Damn propriety!"

"Okay," she agreed pleasantly, using more of her damned odd verbiage.

"I insist you come back to the house, Shaelyn. You have no business here alone. And you left while I was gone, like some sort of . . . of . . ."

"I left while you were having lunch with your future wife. I left because I found myself caring for you, falling in love, wondering what would happen if you fell in love too and we lived happily ever after. I left because it was going to hurt too much to stay there and watch you and your first love make plans for the future."

Any argument that Alec had vanished like a mist in the breeze. Her words formed a fist that squeezed his heart.

"I thought when you kissed me like you did," she said, "that maybe you cared for me, too. That you felt a little of what I was feeling. Were you kissing a fool, Alec?"

She gazed up at him, waiting for an answer.

"No," he finally said. They stared at each other, separated by more than a few feet. Separated by more than a woman who was his first love.

Shaelyn sighed, then rose and walked to the door.

"I'm going to check on Samuel," she said. "Close the door on your way out."

"Well, you're looking perky." Shaelyn forced an upbeat tone when she walked into Samuel's room. He turned a weak smile on her.

"Then it is good that I don't look like I feel."

"Oh, c'mon. You've got to feel better than you did when we dragged you off the beach. And you're talking without coughing. Probably out of self-defense. You got tired of our one-sided conversations, didn't you?"

His chuckle turned into a cough. She poured a glass of water, but he got his breath under control.

"What little of your monologue I remember was very entertaining."

"What little you remember? That's no way to flatter a girl, Samuel."

She wanted to keep him talking. Wanted to keep her mind off what she'd told Alec. She'd known he wouldn't argue with her if she told him how she felt. What she hadn't bargained for was how much it would hurt to say the words aloud.

"Well, now tell me, have you been behaving yourself? No wild parties or anything while I've been out?"

He smiled indulgently.

"Did Molly stop in to check on you?"

"Yes. She insisted on feeding me some broth. A true treasure. Are the two of you related?"

"I'm a friend of the family." She'd already introduced herself as Shaelyn Sumner. Alec and everyone seemed to have adopted the story about her being a family friend, and she saw no reason to tell him differently. Personally, she found it hard to believe they'd contained the news of Alec's marriage. William must truly be a tyrant to be able to stop gossip.

"What part of the South are you from?" he asked.

Shaelyn smiled and shook her head. She'd never be able to pass for a Northerner.

"I'm from near Baton Rouge. But I spend several weeks each summer up here. And how about you? I'd guess that to be a Georgia accent."

Samuel's brows arched and he nodded, obviously surprised at her accuracy.

"I grew up near Atlanta, but I live in the city of New York now."

It was Shaelyn's turn to be surprised.

"What's an Atlanta boy doing in New York?"

He coughed, and she gave him a sip of water. When he caught his breath, he leaned back against the pillow.

"I am a third son, and my father believes in the eldest inheriting. I tried my hand at several things, but I have finally found what I love. I run a small newspaper in the city."

"You're kidding. I'm a journalist," she blurted without benefit of thought.

His lips curved into a smile and he closed his eyes.

"You have such a unique sense of humor."

Shae sighed at such a typical comment.

"Thank you, but that has nothing to do with my being a journalist."

Samuel's eyes opened to weary slits, but a bit of a smile lit his gaze.

"I didn't mean to offend you. I fear I never thought of someone writing for women's periodicals as a journalist."

She bit the proverbial tongue and gave him a sugary sweet smile.

"I write for newspapers. Mostly human-interest stories."

"Indeed?" he lay his head back on the pillow and closed his eyes. "Would I have read you?"

She clenched her teeth and stifled a healthy curse. Of course he'd never read her. And he'd never believe she had things published around the world. She doubted he'd buy her story about sending articles via e-mail, fax, telephone.

"Probably not."

He nodded, his eyes still closed, as if to say, "I thought not."

"Why don't you let me write an article for your paper?" If Alec had the ring cut off and she stayed in 1830, she would need some way to make a living. Maybe this was her chance to network a little.

Samuel pried open both of his eyes and looked at her, as if determining whether she was joking. She just stared at him.

"Miss Sumner, our publication is rather radical. We do not print ladies' recipes and household hints."

"Good, because I don't write recipes and household hints."

He sighed and his head sank back into the pillow.

"Very well," he said. "Write something and I will look at it."

She tried not to let her anger get the best of her. It didn't take a mind reader to know that he was humoring her because she'd saved his life. Her anger wouldn't put food on the table if she found herself stranded here.

She tucked the covers up to his chin, closed the window against the chilly evening air, then turned down the oil lamp.

"I'll have something for you tomorrow," she said, then shut the door when a gentle snore answered her.

She halfway hoped that Alec would be waiting for her when she went downstairs, waiting to smooth things over and put things right. But the only person who greeted her was Martin as he made his evening rounds.

"Good evening, miss," he said in his ever-formal tone.

She tossed a "Hi, Martin," over her shoulder, then escaped out the back door. She wasn't in the mood to talk to anyone but Alec, and she wasn't even sure she could have talked to him.

As she let herself into the cottage she noticed that he had obligingly shut the door behind him. Somehow that symbolized how he'd shut her out of his life. She was just an embarrassing mistake to be dealt with. A little legal snafu that would be ironed out quietly and then forgotten.

"Stop feeling sorry for yourself, Sumner," she chided as she shut the door behind her. "That'll get you nowhere, and you have a story to write. And stop talking to yourself."

She lit a lamp on the small desk, pulled out paper and ink from the drawer, then fumbled with the stupid quill pen, trying to remember how she'd dipped it into the ink.

What she wouldn't give for her trusty old fountain pen.

What had happened to it? She closed her eyes and tried to remember.

Had she dropped everything again when the ship lurched? Had she held on to it and left it in the cabin?

When a shiver rippled through her in the chilly room, she stoppered the ink and went upstairs to find a shawl. Margaret had draped one of beige cashmere across the back of the rocker. Phillipa's shawl.

Shaelyn wrapped the soft fabric around her and sank down on the bed with a sigh. She didn't even have her own clothes here. Suddenly everything hit her at once. Fear of staying in the past. Fear of going back and never seeing Alec again. But there was no reason to stay if he was married to someone else.

She missed her parents and her friends. How would her parents take it when they found out she was missing? Did they already know? Was time passing there at the same rate? They would be frantic. Devastated. Brianne would be worried sick.

The foreign feeling of tears burned at the back of her eyes. She blinked them away but they came right back until her eyes filled with them and spilled over onto her cheeks. She wiped them away but they continued to flow, hot trails that chilled against her skin. She finally let herself cry, let all the anguish and fear she'd been hiding finally come to the surface. She missed her parents, her friends, her job. She missed jumping into her car to go places. She missed her telephone and her laptop. She missed diet Coke and microwave popcorn. She wanted to run a hot bath and soak without turning it into a chore for three or four servants. She wanted her own clothes. She wanted to wear jeans again.

She curled into a little ball on the bed and let the tears flow. She cried for all she missed and for all she would miss if she went back. She cried at forever being torn between two worlds. The tears came, hot and free, until her chest heaved and her head ached. She searched her pocket for a handkerchief, then cried harder at not having Kleenex that she could throw away. She cried over everything reasonable and unreasonable, and when she ran out of things to cry about she fell asleep to live it all again in her dreams.

Alec leaned back in his chair at the shipping office and rubbed the back of his aching neck. He seldom used his office in town, preferring to work at home, but he'd taken the coward's way out this morning, not sure he could face Shaelyn if he ran into her.

Though it shouldn't have, her declaration of how she'd grown to care for him had shocked him. Left him speechless. His heart had soared, then tugged in two directions as he thought of Shaelyn and then of Faith. Shaelyn was all fire and fury and a wild ride on the waves of a nor'easter, while Faith was a gentle wind on a tranquil, smooth sea. To his utter amazement he found he sorely missed the roll and pitch of Shaelyn buffeting his life.

He'd taken a walk during the night, unable to sleep as her words tumbled in his mind. He'd found himself outside the cottage, staring at the lace-curtained windows, watching for her silhouette moving in the glow of the oil lamp, but nothing stirred within. He'd stood there a long time, thinking about marching up to the door, barging in, kissing her senseless. But then he'd thought of Faith. Sweet, serene Faith, who didn't tell outlandish stories of being from the future.

Where was Shaelyn truly from? Obviously the South. More than once it had occurred to him that she might be a spy working to put an end to the underground railroad. If that was the case, why had she helped him with Robert and Naomi? Why hadn't she turned him in? Was she biding her time to find out more information?

He sighed and scrubbed his eyes with the palm of his hand. He couldn't believe that she was a spy, yet he couldn't allow himself to ignore the possibility.

He focused his attention back on the line of numbers in the ledger. He had too much work to do to spend time dwelling on something he could do nothing about at the moment. He wanted to finish going over the books before he met Faith at Windward.

He ignored the little voice that pointed out how empty that left him feeling.

Shaelyn stayed sequestered in the cottage all day except to go and work on Samuel. She thought he sounded better, but to be on the safe side she still pounded on him three or four times a day. Until he could breathe easily and really showed improvement she thought it best not to stop.

Molly had left her alone, but made her promise she would have supper with her. Alec and Faith had plans, so Molly and Shaelyn would have the house to themselves.

Shae all but dragged herself up the path to Windward. She hadn't slept well the night before, she'd struggled all day with the article for Samuel, and her eyes were still puffy from crying all night. What she really wanted was to go to bed and sleep for a week. Working on Samuel was taking its toll on her.

When she stepped through the trees and into the clearing surrounding the house, she groaned and almost turned back.

Faith stepped down from her carriage, her gaze instantly finding Shaelyn. The perfectly gowned woman gave a hesitant smile and waved as the driver pulled the carriage to the back.

Shae couldn't very well ignore her. She waved back and trudged on toward the house.

"How are you?" she asked as she walked up to the waiting Faith.

"Oh, I am fine. And you?"

"Fine, fine. I'm on my way to check on Samuel. I'm running a little late, so if you'll excuse me . . ."

She headed up the steps, but Faith put her gloved hand on Shae's arm.

"Please don't take offense, but you look exhausted. Can Molly or one of the servants not help you?"

"I can't seem to find a servant who can get the knack of what I'm doing, plus they have so much of their own work. Molly checks in on Samuel all the time, but I'm afraid Alec would have a fit if she crawled around on the bed with him, pounding on his back."

Faith smiled and seemed to relax a little.

"I daresay he would. Would you like some help right now? I'm a bit early and I don't believe Alec has arrived yet."

Shae blinked in surprise, not quite certain of what to say.

"I nursed my husband for months during the illness that finally took him. I helped to care for my grandmother, as well. I'm not at all squeamish."

Shaelyn finally managed to utter the word, "Sure."

Faith nodded and they climbed the front steps and entered the house. While Faith took off her gloves and hat and left them on the hall tree, Shaelyn ventured a comment.

"I didn't realize you were a widow. I'm sorry about your husband's death."

As they climbed the steps to Samuel's room, Faith smiled calmly and shook her head.

"It was a blessing in the end. He suffered so. And though the marriage was arranged, I did learn to care for him."

Did no one marry for love in this day and age?

When they entered the bedroom Samuel lay propped on a stack of pillows, looking out the window.

"All right, troublemaker," Shaelyn teased, "You've been so much work, I had to bring in reinforcements to help. Samuel, this is—"

"Mrs. Baldwin!"

"Mr. Smythe!"

Shaelyn stopped and looked at the two of them.

"Mrs. Baldwin?"

"My married name," Faith explained.

"You two know each other?" Shaelyn asked, though obviously they did.

"I met Mrs. Baldwin and her husband on a business trip to Boston," Samuel said. "I was the recipient of their hospitality for . . . for . . ." He erupted in a bout of bone-jarring coughs. His face turned the color of fresh blood, and what little breath he could catch came in wheezes.

Faith calmly poured a glass of water and gave it to him in little sips.

"Mr. Smythe stayed with us a week while he inter-viewed Thomas for his newspaper." She tilted the glass with all the cool efficiency of a nurse. Obviously she'd dealt with sicker patients than one trying to cough up a lung.

Once Samuel regained control of his breathing, he sank back into the feather pillows, his face now as white as the linen surrounding him.

"How is Thomas?" he wheezed with some effort.

Faith fussed with the covers. "He passed away over a year ago. He became ill not long after your visit."

Samuel reached out his hand and touched Faith's.

"I am sorry. I had not heard."

Faith merely nodded with a sad little smile and contin-ued to straighten the covers.

"Well." Shaelyn drew their attention away from the awkward moment. "Faith has offered to help me beat you up tonight." Samuel gave her a weak smile. "So we'd better get busy before Alec shows up and Molly comes and drags me to the dining room."

Faith immediately grasped the knack of cupping her hands and percussing his back. Shaelyn let her do the work, helping only when Faith had a question. When she finished working on one side, the exquisite angel of a woman hiked up her skirts and crawled across the bed as if she'd been doing it all her life.

As much as she tried not to, Shaelyn found herself liking this woman.

By the time Faith finished, Samuel's eyes drooped with exhaustion. Faith fluffed his pillows, covered him, asked if he needed anything, then she and Shaelyn slipped from the room. Before she shut the door, Shae pulled the folded article from her pocket and left it on the bedside table.

"There you are. I was just coming to fetch you. Oh, hello, Faith." Molly waited at the top of the stairs, then the three of them descended together. "I didn't realize Alec had gotten home."

"I don't believe he has," Faith said. "He hasn't come looking for me."

"Then you must have supper with us. I vow the aromas are making my mouth water."

The delicious scents wafting from the kitchen reminded Shae that she'd worked through lunch. Her forehead throbbed with a dull hunger headache.

"He is more than an hour late, Faith. Something must have held him up, and he wouldn't want you to go hungry."

Faith insisted she would wait for Alec, but after fifteen minutes or so, she gave in to Molly's pleadings and they adjourned to the dining room.

Conversation lagged when the food arrived, but once the three of them dug into their food they all chatted like old friends.

Someone brought up the topic of children, and Shaelyn asked Faith if she and her husband had had any. She couldn't believe *Der Fuehrer* would condone a marriage to someone who had not had children in ten years of marriage.

Faith glanced down at her plate and patted her lips with her napkin.

"We had a son when we were first married. Little Thomas lived nine months before a fever took him.''

Shaelyn could have kicked herself for asking.

"Thomas was more devastated than I, if that is possible. He never got over the baby's death and he . . .'' Faith stared at her lap. ". . . he never wanted to take a chance on it happening again."

It took a few moments for the meaning of her words to sink into Shaelyn's brain. The blush on Faith's flawless cheeks assured Shaelyn she hadn't misunderstood.

"Did I tell you about the litter of coon cats in the stable?'' Molly passed a slice of blueberry pie to Shaelyn. Shae could have kissed the dear girl for changing the subject. "The kittens are nearly full-grown now, but they still want to nurse. Poor Dolly has to fight them off. She batted one away so hard that it fell out of the hayloft, onto Irish's back. Irish bucked so hard he kicked down the stall door, then Ned had to go chasing after him, all the while the cat clinging to Irish's back.''

By the time Molly finished describing the chase, her infectious laughter had all three of them giggling like teenagers. Shaelyn mopped tears from her eyes, then burst out in another fit of giggles.

"I used to have this dog that belched like a human. Honest. And every time my boyfriend came over, she would sit beside me and belch when he wasn't looking, and he thought it was me. I couldn't convince him I had a burping dog.''

The three of them howled at the story like slap-happy children.

"When . . . when Thomas and I were courting,'' Faith struggled to catch her breath, "we went to listen to chamber music, but I refused to eat dinner so my corset wouldn't pinch. Every time the music stopped, my stomach rumbled so loud it echoed through the room.''

Struggling for breath and wiping away tears, they found each other's stories unreasonably funny. With every quip and anecdote, they fell upon each other in fits of weeping mirth.

It was during one particularly raucous bout of laughter when Alec walked into the room. He eyed them as if they were a three-headed calf, and approached them as if he didn't want to catch what infected them.

"I apologize for my tardiness, Faith. A problem arose at the office."

The three of them stifled their giggles, then took one look at each other and burst into howls of laughter again. Just as they started to settle down, Molly snorted and sent them all into more fits.

Alec gave an indignant yank to his coat sleeves.

"If you ladies will excuse me, I shall go and change."

They found this declaration terribly funny as well. Not until he'd climbed the stairs did they even begin to get control of themselves. Faith dabbed at her eyes and fought for breath.

"Oh, I have so enjoyed this," she sighed when she could finally speak. "Thank you so much for inviting me." She scooted out her chair and rose reluctantly. "I suppose I should freshen up before Alec returns. Thank you, Molly." She leaned over and gave the young girl a hug. "And thank you, Miss Sumner." Before Shaelyn knew it, Faith hugged her with a little squeeze.

"Call me Shae," she said, somewhat stunned.

"Shae," Faith repeated. "Thank you." She gave them one last smile, then disappeared toward the back of the house.

Shaelyn turned and looked at Molly, who gave her an innocent smile before taking another bite of pie. Shae looked back toward the back of the house and shook her head.

One thing was certain. There was no way in the world she could ever bring herself to hate Alec's future wife.

Chapter 13

SHAELYN GRABBED MARTIN by the shirtfront.

"Martin! Where's Alec?"

For the first time since she'd known him, a moment of shock crossed the butler's face before he tucked his chin and stared down at her, his calm façade firmly back in place.

"I wouldn't know, miss."

She let go of his shirt with a little shove.

"Don't give me that bull. Nobody sneezes around here without you knowing about it."

He adopted an innocent look and spoke to the ceiling.

"I assure you, I haven't a clue—"

She grabbed his shirt again.

"Remember who you're talking to, Martin. I helped him out with Robert and Naomi. This could be worse."

In as few words as possible, Shaelyn told him what she'd discovered. Martin's brows shot skyward, then he marched toward the back door.

"He's at the ship. I'll take him the message."

Shae nearly stepped on his heels following him.

"I'm going with you."

She had the feeling Martin would have argued under different circumstances, but he knew now was not the time to fight a losing battle.

They ran to the stables, bursting in on Ned and startling him so badly that half the bucket of oats he carried exploded onto the stable floor.

"Saddle two horses, Ned. Quick!"

He sat down the bucket. "Well, what's the—"

"Do it!" Martin ordered.

The coachman grabbed a saddle blanket and slapped it onto the nearest horse's back, grumbling under his breath about all the emergencies and strange goings-on recently. Apparently he'd been kept in the dark about some of Alec's activities. Considering the mass communication system Ned was married to, Shaelyn wasn't surprised.

Once he'd settled the saddle into place, she nudged him aside and started tightening the cinch.

"I'll do this. You saddle the other one." She looked up moments later in time to see him hoist a sidesaddle onto a gorgeous mare's back.

"Not a sidesaddle. I ride astride."

"But, miss!" he and Martin both yelped.

"Astride!"

Muttering, he dragged the saddle off and hefted another one. Shae grabbed two bridles and fastened them into place, gave her horse's cinch a testing tug, then swung onto its back while Martin struggled into the other saddle. She thought she would scream before the formally dressed butler settled his rear onto the fidgeting horse's back.

"Let's go." She shot out of the stables in a cloud of dust, then turned south at the road. The other horse followed, the proper Martin holding on for dear life. His legs flailed in the stirrups, his body bounced inches off the saddle.

Shaelyn held back for a mile or two, stifling screams and a few choice curses. When she got her bearings and knew she could find her way to town, she let Martin bouncingly draw abreast of her.

"I'll meet you there!" she yelled over the sound of running hooves and Martin's squeaks.

"But, miss!" he squawked. By that time his voice was just a faint sound in the distance.

She kicked her horse to greater speed, trying to remember how long it had taken them to get from town to Windward on that other fateful day. But they'd been traveling at a leisurely clip in a carriage then.

Just as she started to worry that she'd missed a turn, the little harbor loomed into view.

She finally clattered up the wooden dock amidst the cacophony of shouts and noises of a ship getting ready to sail.

Racing up the gangplank, she scanned the deck and the busy sailors, all oblivious to her presence in their preparations to weigh anchor. When she saw no sign of Alec, she ran to the door leading belowdecks and stumbled down the stairs. Within seconds she burst into the captain's cabin and found Alec and another man leaning over a map on a highly polished desk.

"Shaelyn! What the devil—"

"Alec, Samuel was in Canada researching the—" She stopped and glanced at the other man, then looked back and waited until Alec nodded for her to go ahead. "He was researching the underground railroad!"

Alec straightened.

"He wanted to do an exposé on it. He said too many lives were lost on both sides, and the slaves should be freed through legal channels. He found out that Franklin Tilburn has set a trap for the next load of slaves."

Alec's face darkened. "Does Smythe know about—"

"No. We were just talking. I asked him what he was doing in Canada and he told me about the story. He doesn't suspect us."

Alec paced for a moment, then looked at the man across the desk.

"Captain Finley, we shall simply meet the ship farther out to sea. They will expect us to follow our old pattern. By the time they realize their error, we shall be well on our way north."

"Aye, Alec. 'Tis a good plan."

The men studied the map, oblivious to Shaelyn. Captain Finley pulled his pipe from between his teeth and stabbed a grid on the map with its stem.

"We take them here. They'll not be following us through these islands. Not a man alive can navigate those shoals better than Angus Finley."

"Let's weigh anchor then. Shaelyn." He grabbed her by her upper arms and squeezed. She wanted to close her eyes and savor the feel of his touch. "Thank you for coming. Now let's get you off the ship and—"

He and the captain raised their heads and looked about the room, as if it had suddenly changed.

"No!" Alec exploded.

"I'm afraid so, laddie."

"What?" Shaelyn squeaked.

"We're at sea!" Alec roared, then stormed out of the cabin in two strides.

"We're what?" she squeaked again.

The captain rushed out of the room behind Alec.

"Laddie, I told the first mate to weigh anchor when ready."

Shaelyn hiked her skirts to her knees and ran behind the two men. She burst onto the deck seconds after they did, then ran to the rail to gape at the disappearing dock. The tiny figure of Martin bobbing on the back of his horse could be seen just approaching the dock.

"Damn and blast!" Alec slammed his fist on the polished wooden rail. "Give the order to turn about, Finley."

The captain pointed at Alec with the stem of his pipe.

"You know as well as I that if we take the lassie back

we'll never meet that slaver in time to beat them at their own game.''

Alec sputtered for a minute, then pointed to the rowboat hanging from the ship.

''Lower the boat. We'll send a man to take her back.''

Captain Finley put his hand on Alec's shoulder and turned him away from the rail.

''Alec, son, you know we run these trips with a skeleton crew. The fewer hands, the fewer chances of injuries if we ever have to fight, and the fewer chances of information leaking to the undesirables. I hate to tell you this, lad, but you're the only hand we can spare.''

Alec glared at the captain, then dropped his chin to his chest and scrubbed his eyes with the palm of his hand. After a few unintelligible mutters under his breath, he finally turned to Shaelyn.

''You're forced to sail with us, I'm afraid. I won't ask the men to do this without me.''

''No problem,'' Shaelyn very nearly chirped, then she dropped her gaze and tried to look disconcerted. ''Umm . . . I'll . . . ah . . . I'll make do somehow.'' Surely Samuel was well enough for Molly and Faith to nurse back to health.

''That's a brave lassie.'' Captain Finley patted her on the head as if she were three years old. ''We've had nary a bit of trouble in all our confiscations. Not with Mr. Griffin's ship and ours flanking them with cannons pointed.''

Cannons? There would be cannons?

She jerked up her head and scanned the sea. Sure enough, another ship sailed on the port side, no more than half a mile away and closing.

''You should get belowdecks.'' Alec took her arm and guided her toward the passage. ''Go to my cabin and stay there. I'll bunk with one of the other men.''

Shaelyn yanked her arm away and stopped in her tracks.

''I don't think so,'' she said in her best nineties-woman voice.

''Do not choose now to be unreasonable. It is not safe—''

She snorted and raised both hands toward the ocean, turning a full circle and scanning 360 degrees of horizon.

"Excuse me, but I don't see any warships out there barreling down on us. When we get within cannonball range, you let me know and I'll go cower in your cabin like a good little girl."

Alec's head dropped back between his shoulder blades as he stared at a china-blue sky. He muttered something about a sense of humor and the fear of breaking a wing from the slaps, but Shaelyn couldn't make sense of it. Finally he simply walked away, waving his hand in dismissal.

The captain smiled around the stem of his pipe, winked at her, then strolled away toward the helm.

Alec stumbled into the cabin long past dark, his stomach roiling, his knees shaky. He had no fear of embarrassing himself by puking in front of Shaelyn. He'd emptied every bite of food his stomach contained over the rail. Indeed, at times he feared he would lose his stomach as well.

"Alec! Are you hurt? I didn't hear any cannon fire!" Shaelyn appeared at his side with a book in her hand.

He staggered to his bunk and fell across it. When he opened his eyes he saw the cheery, bright lantern swaying to and fro, to and fro, to and fro. He moaned.

"Where are you hurt? I don't see any blood." Shae jumped on the mattress, rocking his stomach. She yanked at his clothing and yelled at him. "Answer me, damn it! I can't help you if I don't know where you're hurt!"

He shoved her hands away and tried to rise, which only sent the hot bile creeping farther up his throat.

"I am not wounded, blast it! I'm seasick!"

The cabin fell silent except for the nauseating groan of the ship's timbers as they heaved through the waters. The lantern squeaked quietly on its hook as it swung to and fro, to and fro. He slammed his eyes shut.

After several quiet moments, he thought he heard a very suspicious noise.

There it was again.

He pried open one eye, then the other followed at the sight that met him.

Shaelyn sat back in the shadows of the bunk, her hand over her mouth, her eyes sparkling with mirth. Her shoulders shook in silent laughter.

There was that obnoxious snort again! Her eyes widened and her shoulders shook harder.

"What the hell is so amusing?" he roared, then swallowed again.

She gave up any pretense of trying to hide her mirth. Her laughter gilded the air of the cabin, bouncing off pitching walls and lurching ceilings. She fell back into the shadows and laughed until she snorted again, then grabbed a pillow and buried her face in it, doing little to muffle that irritating sound.

"I'm so very pleased to be such wonderful entertainment for you," he tried to snarl, but it came out more of a moan.

Her giggles crescendoed as she elbowed her way to a sitting position.

"You're seasick!" she gurgled, then fell back again, holding her side. "A pirate who gets seasick!"

"I am *not* a pirate," he growled, successfully this time.

It had no effect on her whatsoever. He closed his eyes and let her laugh, which went on longer than any sane, compassionate person would have allowed. Finally her mirth died to occasional, sporadic snickers.

"Why didn't you tell me you got seasick? So do I." She was quiet for several seconds. He heard a strange sort of ripping sound, then she fumbled with something. "Here. Take this."

He opened his eyes and looked at her outstretched hand. She held two tiny, flat yellow pellets in her palm. A leather pouch lay open next to her on the bunk.

He arched a suspicious brow and picked them up.

"What do you suggest I do with these?"

"Swallow them."

The last thing he wanted to do was swallow *anything*.

"And why, pray tell, would I want to do that?"

She sighed and looked at him as if he were a very dim-witted child.

"Because they will help you stop being seasick."

He sighed at her nonsense and pointedly glanced at the minuscule specks in his hand.

"These two little bits of nothing will relieve my nausea?"

"Yes."

He conveyed his degree of belief with one jaded look.

"Hey, I was right about Samuel, wasn't I? What have you got to lose? Aside from that attractive green tinge."

He cursed under his breath, then tossed the pellets into his mouth. The things stuck to his tongue and started dissolving with a nasty, bitter taste. He crunched one between his teeth and nearly spit the blasted thing out.

Shaelyn rolled her eyes, fetched a glass from the holder on the table, poured it full of water, then shoved it into his hands.

"You don't chew them. You swallow them whole."

He washed the pellets down but couldn't control the grimace from the taste they left behind. Any minute now he expected them to come back up, but through sheer will-power he managed to keep the contents in his stomach.

"Thank you," he said with little sincerity. "Just let me get a change of clothing and I will leave you in peace."

She shoved his weak, trembling body back onto the bunk as if he were no stronger than a newborn kitten.

"Don't be ridiculous. Lie down there and rest until the pills take effect."

He thought he detected a distinctly amused quaver in her voice, but he chose to ignore it. Truth be told, he was not at all certain he could collect his clothing and make his way to the first mate's cabin without disgracing himself, staggering and puking his way there.

With only token resistance, he leaned back into the heavenly, blessed pillow and tried to ignore the rolling of his stomach with each swell of the waves. He felt Shaelyn heft his booted feet onto the bunk. The last thing he remembered was hearing her hum an odd little tune, the likes of which he'd never heard.

He came slowly awake, his mind muzzy and reluctant, as if he'd consumed a potent drug or liquor. The vague notion occurred to him that perhaps she had, indeed, drugged him. After all, he had no idea what manner of ingredient she'd put in those pellets.

Though the thought should have been alarming, he found even more interesting the realization that his stomach no longer heaved. He lay there and tested it, noted the ever-constant rock of the ship, watched the lantern swing back and forth.

Saint's blood, he found the experience most relaxing.

He rolled to his back and drowsily considered a possible apology to his odd little wife.

Thinking of her, he wondered where the devil she'd gone. Through the porthole, stars still glittered in a black velvet sky. She'd damned well better not be cavorting on deck with the duty crew.

He threw aside a quilt that had not been covering him earlier, grumbling about the low-burning lamp left burning. When he moved to rise, he heard a sound that made him freeze. With part dread, part disbelief, he rolled over and looked behind him.

Oh, yes. He should have known.

He closed his eyes and forced air in and out of his lungs in a somewhat regular rhythm, while every square inch of him suddenly developed a fever that had nothing to do with illness.

Her lashes fanned across her cheeks in sleep, her hair tumbled in piles of rich, shiny curls on the pillow. One hand nestled under her jaw while the other rested on the edge of the quilt at her chin.

He had never seen anything so heart-stoppingly beautiful in his life.

He couldn't pry his gaze from the sweet tranquillity of her face. From the full, rose-colored lips. From the long, ivory column of her neck or the mounds of auburn curls begging to be crushed in masculine hands.

Or the slow, regular pulse in her throat begging for his lips to send it racing.

His own pulse raced out of control. His arms ached to scoop her up and nestle her close. His fingers tingled to trace the outline of her mouth and to explore every inch of her soft, satiny body.

A lone spiral curl lay across her cheek, gently caressing the skin he so desperately wanted to touch. Without consciously planning to, he reached up and smoothed away the errant lock. The moment his hand touched her skin, a lightning bolt of fire seared through his body, spearing him in his soul.

He closed his eyes and treasured the feeling. How long had it been since a woman fanned such an all-consuming flame? Never had he thought to savor such sweet, aching torment.

She sighed, and her warm, gentle breath ghosted across his face. The need to touch her grew in his chest until it became a physical pain.

He wished now, with all his heart, that he had taken her on their wedding night. Taken her then and a hundred times since. They were married, after all. Man and wife. There was no reason why he should not take her now. Indeed, it was unnatural to lie there and gaze at his wife, yearn to feel her in his arms, yet leave her untouched.

He gazed at her, drank in the sight of her as he drew nearer and nearer. Should he gently wake her first? Or let the heat of his kisses rouse her from her slumber? Perhaps a warm, slow caress across—

She drew in a deep, full breath, then released a yawn so forceful he vowed he could see her tonsils. She stretched until she quivered, yawned again, then opened her eyes.

Their noses all but touched.

A sleepy little smile curved her lips. "Hi," she said in her odd vernacular. "Feeling better?"

Feeling better? Was he *feeling better?* When his body still burned with a fever? Screamed for release? When his hand still hovered, poised beneath the covers to awaken her in the most pleasant of manners?

"Helllooo?" she said, raising her glorious, tousled head so that she was no longer a blur at the end of his nose. "Didn't the Dramamine help?"

He looked up at her, her hair haloed in the dim light of the lamp, and waited for his body to calm so his voice would not be husky with want.

"Maybe you need a couple more. You were pretty green."

She flung back the quilt and climbed over him, as if he were nothing more than a . . . a . . .

"Shaelyn!" he roared, leaping to his feet.

She yelped and bounced against the desk, sending papers fluttering to the floor and a tumbler of water exploding into the air.

"What the devil are you wearing?" he bellowed, marching to the oil lamp and turning up the wick.

She leaned against the desk, her chest heaving, her hands clutching her heart as she looked down at the billowy shirt and snug trousers clinging to her body.

She looked back at him as if he were insane.

"You gave me heart failure to ask me *that?*" she said, then shook water droplets from that ridiculous mass of hair.

"What the hell are you wearing?" he demanded again in a voice that would rattle windows.

"I'm wearing your shirt and your cabin boy's pants! What does it look like I'm wearing?" she bellowed back. "Or did you expect me to wear my one and only dress on this voyage, tripping over coils of rope and snagging it on every stupid thing I pass?" She yanked up a handful of the gown draped across the back of a chair and shook it at him. "This thirty yards of dress isn't exactly designed for schlepping around the decks of ships."

"Schlepping?" he sputtered. "*Schlepping?* What the hell does *schlepping* mean? And where in hell do you come from, Shaelyn, that you wear men's trousers, think nothing of falling asleep in any man's bed, and use words like *schlepping?*"

She sucked in her breath as if he'd slapped her, then flung away the handful of gown and advanced on him.

"I come from 1999, bubba. From a time when women can wear comfortable clothes without some prude gasping in puritanical shock, even though I have more skin covered than any evening gown your virginal women wear. I come from a time," she extended her index finger and poked him in the chest, "when an exhausted woman can fall asleep after caring for a sick male without some tight-assed, dirty-minded man who's probably had carnal knowledge with more women than he can count turning it into a cardinal sin."

"Do not poke me again," he warned.

She jabbed him that much harder. "Do not tell me what to do," she mimicked his tone.

He grabbed her hands and yanked her to his chest. She glared up at him, and he moved just in time to miss her upraised knee. Newly born anger mixed with the lust that had not yet died. He covered her mouth with his, searching for her tongue, kissing her in a way that made women whimper for more. The whimpers never came and the tongue that he found failed to respond. He increased his efforts, gentling, pulling her closer, cradling her with exquisite tenderness. His body pulsed with need, ached for release. He forgot about dominating her, forcing a reaction from her, and simply gave to her with unselfish abandon.

And still she did not respond. Finally he raised his head to gaze down at her, his mind mourning the loss of her mouth against his, an apology on his lips.

She slapped him with such force that he staggered backward. By the time the pinpricks of light had cleared from his sight, the cabin door had slammed behind her.

Chapter 14

SHAELYN STROLLED THE length of the deck, pointedly ignoring the existence of Alec Hawthorne. The absolute nerve of the man! Yanking her to him and forcing his kisses, like some kind of Cro-Magnon. Even if she did have to use every ounce of willpower not to respond. It was the principle. And where had he neatly tucked his thoughts of Faith while he was practicing his caveman tactics on Shaelyn?

Every now and then she would catch a glimpse of him out of the corner of her eye. He seemed to be oblivious of her, but she had a feeling he was as studiously ignoring her as she was him. When he'd appeared on deck a good thirty minutes after she'd slapped him, when the dim gray light of dawn crept over the horizon, a faint, rosy hue still colored his cheek.

"Well, lassie, you're looking hale and hearty this glorious morn. The sea air has brought a bloom to your fair skin." Captain Finley strolled up to her and they both paused at the rail.

She smiled up at the burly, weathered seaman. The ocean breeze lifted her hair and tossed it about as she stared out at the endless expanse of rolling blue.

"I apologize for our setting sail and trapping you on board, lass. I know the ladies prefer a little time to plan for a voyage."

Shae smiled and turned to the captain.

"Oh, I'm a lot more resilient than the average lady today."

His gaze flickered past her clothing before he smiled around the stem of his pipe.

"I daresay, lassie. I daresay."

"Miss Shaelyn, ma'am." Jimmy, the cabin boy whose britches she wore, came trotting up to her and the captain. "Mr. Harker sent me to fetch you if you want him to show you how he mends the sails."

"Here now, Master Jim," Captain Finley barked. "How dare you be calling the lady by her Christian name? You address her properly or I'll have ye—"

"It's all right, Captain. I've asked all the men to call me Shaelyn." She patted him on the arm. "I'm not one to stand on formalities."

"Well, then," he grumbled. "If you wish it so."

She gave him her best innocent smile and he softened his glare toward Jimmy. The young boy shifted back and forth, obviously anxious to lead her away and remove himself from the captain's scrutiny.

"Would you excuse us, sir?" she asked. "I believe I'm late for a sail-mending lesson."

Jimmy led her to the grizzled old sailor who'd promised to let her watch him. She'd spent the evening before and all of that morning roaming the decks, making friends, asking questions, doing what she did best . . . collecting information. She had promises from half a dozen crew members to show her all they knew.

An hour sped by as Mr. Harker instructed her in 1830 sail mending. His gravelly voice encouraged her in her endeavors even as he sprinkled his speech with profanities, which he apparently viewed as polite conversation. Several times she had to turn a giggle into a cough to hide her amusement at the colorful old salt.

It seemed like no time at all before Jimmy returned to collect her for the noon meal.

"Mr. Ort sets a fine table for the crew," the boy jabbered happily as he led her across the deck. "He can take flour with more bugs than an anthill and still bake—"

"Oh, criminy, Jimmy," she groaned. "That's *way* more information than I want to hear."

Jimmy blushed and gulped, his eyes wide with apology.

"Oh, we ain't got no meal bugs in the flour yet. We always got fresh food on these short little trips. It's the longun's that'll have you sniffing your meat before you—"

"Okay, okay." She clamped a hand over his mouth. "I get the picture."

Just as she thought it might be time for a couple more Dramamine, she caught sight of Alec hovering near the rail at the helm. That lovely pale shade of green suffused his face again. Captain Finley called to him, motioning him toward the wheel. Alec cast a look back toward the rail, then straightened his shoulders and marched toward the captain just as Jimmy led her into the depths of the ship.

The ship's bow rose several feet with the swelling wave, then dropped like a stone only to rise again. Alec's stomach mirrored the movements. He wondered which was worse, seeing the horizon bob up and down in the daylight, or simply feeling the deck heave beneath him in the dark of night.

The earlier calm seas had given way to roiling turbulence. They'd sighted the approaching storm before sundown, and Alec's stomach had grown queasier with each passing moment.

He leaned over the stern's rail and dry-heaved again until his chest ached and his knees threatened to buckle.

When he straightened, it was all he could do not to shake like a quivering infant.

That did it. Humbling himself and asking Shaelyn for more of those pellets couldn't possibly be worse than what he was going through at the moment. And from the toss of the sea, he would get worse before he got better.

He made his way belowdecks, clinging to the stair rail for dear life, then staggering the last few feet to his cabin door. A cheery, yellow light seeped from the crack beneath the door, but he heard no sounds from within. Had she fallen asleep with the lamp burning again? Did the woman never extinguish a light before retiring?

He raised his fist to knock just as the lurching ship threw him against the door with a solid *thud*. As he bounced off the thick wood and tried to regain his footing, he heard her cheerful, perky voice call, "Come in."

For just the briefest of moments he considered going back up on deck and suffering the storm in his usual manner, but a well-timed, sickening roll of his stomach convinced him otherwise. He lifted the latch and shoved his way through the door.

She sat—or rather sprawled—in his leather chair, bathed in the golden light of the oil lamp, one britches-clad leg draped most indelicately over the arm, a book propped against her knee. How the devil did the woman read with the ship rolling over ever-growing waves? And did she have no sense of decency?

She looked up at him, an expectant smile on her face, then the smile disappeared.

"Oh. It's you."

She went back to reading her book.

He tried to roll with the ship when he walked into the cabin. The effort only rocked his stomach and erased any lingering thoughts he had of not asking for her help. He propped a hip atop his desk and tried to look casual.

"Do you have any more of those pellets?" he asked in his best conversational voice.

She raised her eyes to his, conveying her irritation at having her reading interrupted. After pointedly glaring at him for several seconds, she reached behind her and plucked the black leather pouch attached to a belt from the reading table. Seconds later, a small rectangular box flew through the air and bounced off his chest.

Bending to retrieve it from the floor nearly proved to be his undoing. He swallowed hard.

The word *DRAMAMINE* was emblazoned in orange across the lightweight paper box, along with all manner of words and instructions in print so small he could barely read them. He'd never seen the likes of such print. Or such packaging. He opened the box and slid a silver card from it. The little yellow tablets lay in perfect rows inside tiny, clear bubbles on the card. He shook it, but nothing happened. He emptied the contents of the box, but more of the silver cards with the sealed-away pellets fell out.

"What the devil?" he grumbled to himself.

Shaelyn sighed and swung her leg from the chair arm to stand. She slapped her book on the desk and snatched one of the cards from his hands.

"Here." She pressed two of the little bubbles with her thumbs. The pellets shot through the other side, landing neatly in his palm. "Use water this time."

She stuffed the cards back into the box, picked up her book, then flopped back into the chair, both legs draping the arm this time.

He swallowed the nasty-tasting specks with plenty of water, then picked up the box and examined it again. He pulled out the cards and studied the paper-thin silver backing. He pressed on the glasslike bubbles, amazed that the substance seemed flexible rather than breakable. A little yellow pellet clattered onto the desk.

"If you lose those, bubba, you're out of luck. I guarantee the local apothecary doesn't carry them."

He chased the errant medication across his desk, then tried to put it back in its bubble.

"Where did you obtain these, if not from an apothecary?"

She turned the page of her book, never looking up.

"At a Stop-N-Shop in 1999."

He should have known better than to ask. Watching her ignore him, he decided to humor her.

"And what, pray tell, is a stopenshop?"

She lowered her book and stared at him.

"It's a store," she said with exaggerated patience, "where you stop, and then you shop."

He stared back at her and clenched his jaw.

"Thank you for such an eloquent explanation."

She threw down her book and jumped to her feet.

"Well, hell. Don't expect me to play along with your patronizing games. You don't believe I'm from 1999, so don't ask me to be understanding while you have a good laugh at my expense."

She yanked the box of medicine from his hand and waved it under his nose.

"Where does this *look* like it came from? Have you ever seen anything like it?" She pulled a silver card from the box and shoved it so close to his face all he could see was a silver blur. "Have you ever seen one of these? They're called blister packs." She turned the card over and held it out so he could focus.

"This silver stuff is called foil." She flipped it over. "These clear blisters are made of plastic. And these—" She shot two of the pellets from their bubbles. "—are called *pills*, not *pellets!*"

She tossed the two *pills* into her mouth and washed them down with his tumbler of water.

"And look! Look!" She flipped the box on its side and pointed to letters and numbers engraved in the thick paper that made up the box.

EXP. 06/01

"That means the shelf life, the effectiveness, of these pills expires in June of 2001."

He just looked at her.

She grabbed the leather pouch and dumped its contents on the desk.

"Look. Look at all of this. Have you ever seen *anything* like any of this?" She held up a gold cylinder. "Lipstick. It's makeup. Watch." She slid the top off the cylinder, unscrewed a peach-colored stick, then ran the stick across her lips, leaving behind the color and a very attractive moistness. "And this!" She picked up a red-and-white rectangle with *Dentyne* printed across it, which she ripped open and pulled out a smaller paper-covered rectangle. She peeled off the paper and shoved the contents into his mouth.

"Chew it," she ordered, then put one in her own mouth. "It's called chewing gum."

While he tried to chew and swallow the tasty morsel, she picked up another silver card, but this one had no blisters. Instead, the word *Mastercard* was printed boldly across it, with a series of raised numbers across its width.

"It's a credit card. It's like money. Oh! And here!" She snatched up two folded pieces of grayish-green paper. "*This* is money. Five-dollar bills. Here. Look at the date."

She pointed to a minuscule number. 1995. The word "Series" was printed above it. The number on the second one read 1997.

She fumbled through the few things left, muttering, "Damn. I left my license at the condo. Why did I have to walk to the ship?"

While she babbled, Alec studied the "money." The number five was printed or spelled out in all four corners on both sides. A picture of a homely, bearded man with enormous ears sat in the center, beneath the words "The United States of America." The other side had a picture of a temple or building that looked like something from ancient Greece. The "money" felt more like stiff fabric than paper. He could see more printing but couldn't make out the words in the dim light of the oil lamp.

He tossed them on the desk. None of this proved anything except that she had a penchant for carrying odd things in her reticule.

"What is this in my mouth?" he asked as he tried once more to swallow the sweet, tangy glob. "It refuses to go away."

"It's not supposed to go away. It's chewing gum. You chew it, and then you spit it out when you're done with it."

What a revolting thing to do, even if he did enjoy the flavor.

He continued to chew while he perused what was left on the desk. He picked up two white paper-covered sticks with the word *Tampax* printed in blue.

"What are these? Do they taste as good as—"

They disappeared from his hand and back into the pouch before he even saw her move.

"Those are nothing," she said, her cheeks rosy in the lamplight. "They're just personal things. They don't prove anything."

He had a feeling they were much more interesting than a silver card with numbers, but he chose not to pursue the matter.

"Quite frankly, none of this proves anything. This is simply a collection of oddities with numbers that happen to be printed on them. True, none of it is familiar to me, but I don't profess to be acquainted with every unusual item that exists in the world."

She took a deep, angry breath and stuffed everything back into the pouch.

"Of course, you're not familiar with these things, because they don't exist yet." She looked up at him, poised to speak, then closed her mouth and dropped into the chair. "Oh, hell. What's the use? I'll be history before long anyway, and you'll be married to Faith." She raised an accusing brow at him. "You do remember Faith, don't you?"

He felt the sting of Shaelyn's predawn slap as if she'd just delivered it. He also relived the sweet taste of her mouth, unresponsive though it had been, and felt the guilt that had plagued him once he'd finally conjured Faith's image in his mind hours later.

"Yes, I remember Faith." Though he had to admit his excitement over the prospect of marriage to her had dulled somewhat over the last several days. She was everything he remembered her to be . . . sweet, beautiful, serene. Why, then, did he find himself so often daydreaming about the impossible woman glaring up at him, dressed in boys' britches and one of his best lawn shirts?

Saint's blood, he envied that shirt.

"Would you stop staring at my breasts?"

He jerked his gaze upward. She continued to sit there with a look of defiance.

"I was merely contemplating how you'd managed to appropriate my costliest shirt."

"Yeah, right."

Suddenly the ship pitched with such violence it threw Shaelyn from the chair. Alec caught her before she hit the floor, but her book and the water glass went flying. As they scrambled to pick up papers and other careening flotsam and jetsam, another wave hit. Alec grabbed the pitcher and stowed it in the chest while Shaelyn grabbed Alec.

"What the heck did we hit?" she yelled over the groan of straining timbers.

"It's what hit *us*," he yelled back. "It's the storm." He extinguished all the lamps but one, then pushed her back into the chair. "I'm going on deck to see how bad it is. You stay here." He turned on his heel and strode toward the door. Before he stepped into the companionway he turned back.

"I mean it, Shaelyn. Stay belowdecks."

She sat in the thin, meager light of the single lamp and looked at him as if he were insane.

"Oh, yeah, like I plan to go up there and get washed overboard."

She *seemed* sincere in her words, but one could never tell about her.

"Alec," she called before he closed the door. "Be careful."

Chapter 15

IF HE WASN'T dead, she'd kill him.

Shaelyn had moved from the chair onto the bunk after being pitched to the floor for the third time. She wedged herself in the corner, propped pillows between herself and every hard surface, then tried to decide whether to shoot him through the heart or slit his throat.

He'd been gone for hours, and for all she knew he'd been swept over the side while everyone on deck thought he was nice and cozy in his plush cabin. She'd expected him to at least send someone to tell her to batten down the hatches or whatever sailors did in a storm. But no. She just got to sit there and wonder if he was shark food while her body thought it was on the most nauseating amusement-park ride in the world.

Even as she thought it, another roller-coaster wave sent her stomach back into her throat for the umpteenth time. Not for the first time, she sent up a prayer of thanks that she'd taken that last dose of Dramamine. She wondered how Alec was faring, if he was even still on board.

That thought, more than all the Big Dipper waves put together, sickened her in the pit of her stomach.

Should she go looking for him? She hadn't lied when she told him she wouldn't go on deck. She was no sailor. She had no idea what was going on up there other than a struggle to keep the ship upright under the barrage of waves. The extent of her sailing experience, besides the small boats on summer vacation, was the huge floating hotels they called cruise ships, where a storm could barely be felt, and then with only a gentle rocking.

But what if he'd gone overboard? Could they turn around and find him in a storm at night? Could she even make her way to someone to tell them about him?

"Oh, for Pete's sake, Sumner." She massaged her forehead with the heels of her hands. "You've got him floundering in the water miles away, when he's probably up there doing man stuff and having the time of his life."

The cabin door burst open and the object of her worries lurched in with the pitch of the ship.

Well, maybe not the time of his life.

He stayed on his feet only by using the heavy furniture to hold himself up, leaving huge puddles of water with every step. She scrambled from her corner, then flew from the bunk with the upward heave of the ship, landing on his dripping body with a loud "Ooph!" They hit the rolling deck as one, Alec neatly cushioning her fall. Under different, drier circumstances, she thought, the experience would be quite pleasurable.

Alec groaned.

"Saint's blood, Shaelyn. Please remove your knee from my groin. You are far too close for comfort."

It occurred to her that she wouldn't have to slit his throat. That with just a little shift of her knee . . . But then she changed her mind and decided to be merciful. With only a token upward nudge, she rolled off him. He wasted no time in sitting up and removing the target from within her reach.

"I thought you'd been swept overboard." She lifted herself off the now-soggy Persian carpet and slapped at the wet spots on her trousers. "Thanks for keeping me informed of what was going on. I would have hated to huddle in the corner of that bunk all night long, not knowing."

"Overboard would have been preferable." He ignored her sarcastic remarks. "Two sails ripped, and we nearly collided with Griffin's ship." He propped his elbows on his knees and scraped his dripping hair away from his forehead with a moan. "I was not meant to be a seaman."

She turned up the flame of the lamp and saw the waxy, pale green tingeing his skin again. The guy really should stay on dry land.

"Here." She unearthed her fanny pack from the depths of the bunk, then fished out the box of Dramamine. If they didn't have smooth sailing soon or a quick end to this trip, her little yellow "pellets" would be history.

She popped two from their blisters, then pulled the water pitcher from the cabinet where Alec had stowed it hours earlier. She managed to slosh water all over the place before she got a glass filled and the pitcher safely put away.

"Thank you," Alec sighed, then tossed the pills back as if he'd been doing it all his life.

"You need to get out of those wet clothes." She held out a hand to help him to his feet, but he looked at her as if she'd grown a second head. He ignored her hand and staggered to his feet on his own.

"I need to get back up on deck. The storm is passing, but they still need—"

"Don't be ridiculous. You're weak as a kitten. I bet you spent more time dry-heaving than you did helping." She waited for his reaction. "Didn't you?"

The clenching of his jaw told her all she needed to know. "Only after the medicine wore off."

"Look. Get into some dry clothes and give the pills a little time to kick in. Then when you feel better you can go back up."

She could tell he was going to be stubborn over this, so she did something she very rarely did. She got helpless.

"Okay. I'll admit it." She bowed her head and leaned into his arm. A chilly wetness seeped into her shirt. "I was terrified. I just want you to stay with me a little while. Just a little while. I'm so scared." She looked up at him with her best helpless look.

He sighed and dropped his head to his chest. With an air of resignation he peeled off his sodden jacket and unbuttoned the white shirt plastered to his skin. Shaelyn could see that just that effort cost him. The man wouldn't ask for help if he was dying.

Without thinking, she grasped the dripping shirt and helped peel it away from the muscular ridges of his stomach, across the expanse of chest and shoulders, then down the corded muscles of his arms. His wet skin glistened in the lamplight, a sculpture of light and shadow that begged for her touch.

He sucked in his breath when she ran her hands across his chest.

"You're freezing," she said, avoiding his gaze, feeling as if the heat of her hands would melt right into his icy skin. She fought the shiver that had nothing to do with a chill and reminded herself that he was cold and seasick and needed to be in bed.

She nearly groaned.

He insisted on staggering behind the small screen to remove the rest of his clothing. She rummaged through expensive chests of brass and leather until she found a towel and dry clothes, trying not to think about what he was doing back there. Not until he was completely dressed did he step from behind the screen. He hesitated at the sight of her.

She'd found a dry shirt for herself, and now sat in the middle of the bunk, buttoning the last buttons. Her fingers faltered as he stood there and stared at her.

"Well," she said after a long pause interrupted only by the howl of the wind, "you look better already. Not that it would have taken much."

She climbed from the bed and plopped into the leather chair before he had a chance to stagger there. She knew he wouldn't even sit on the bunk if she was still in it.

"Why don't you lie down and rest. You've been up all night."

He towered over her.

"I thought you needed company."

"Oh, I do. Just having someone here helps. It's so scary being alone."

"I can send Jimmy to—"

"No. I just feel better when you're here. Now why don't you lie down. I promise not to ravish you."

He rubbed his eyes and stifled a yawn, somewhat insulting her suggestion about ravishing him. He dropped to the bunk and scrubbed his face again.

"I suppose I can rest a few moments." He punched a pillow before falling into it. "Wake me if you need . . . comforting."

The tone of his voice told her exactly how much he'd believed her act, which was not at all. She just smiled to herself and watched him relax into sleep.

The lamp swung on its hinges, casting his face into light and then shadow. She stared at that face that had become so precious to her, and a bittersweet warmth curled in her chest.

She'd had to travel a hundred and seventy years to find the man who could complete her life. The person who filled that empty space in her, that Alec-shaped void. Even when she wanted to choke him, she wanted to kiss him. Even when he patronized her, she wanted to cuddle into his arms and have him hold her.

She should never have told him the truth about where she was from. He thought she was insane, or hiding something even worse. He might have fallen in love with her if she had kept her mouth shut, feigned amnesia, told him anything but the truth.

But then again, there was Faith.

*   *   *

Streams of early-morning sunlight bounced around the cabin until they fell across Shaelyn's eyes, nudging her awake. She pried one eye open to glare at the light, then snuggled deeper into the warm, solid nest of Alec's arms.

Alec's arms!

Both eyes flew open and she tried her best not to move. His deep, even breathing told her he still slept. If she tried really hard, maybe she could just slip right out—

His arms tightened and pulled her closer.

Damn. He'd have a fit if he woke up with her in bed with him. She'd never known that nineteenth-century men could be such prudes. But she'd been so tired, and she couldn't get comfortable in that darned chair. He should just be glad she didn't peel down to the buff, as she usually did.

Holding her breath and moving a fraction of an inch at a time, she lifted his arm, which rested across her rib cage, and slowly laid it along his side. He shifted and threw it right back over her ribs, then draped his leg over hers as well.

She wanted to scream.

Instead, she slowly moved his arm again, sat up, then slid her leg from beneath his. The second her leg was free she crept to the end of the bunk and dropped her feet to the floor. She yawned and stood, stretching until her knuckles scraped the low ceiling, mentally patting herself on the back for pulling one over on him.

When she turned to admire him while he slept, golden-brown eyes stared back at her.

Just exactly how long had he been awake?

The thunder of running footsteps on deck halted her question, then a pounding on the door had Alec leaping from the bed and pulling on his boots.

''Sir, the ship's been sighted,'' Jimmy's muffled voice yelled through the thick panel.

Alec threw open the door and nearly ran over the cabin

boy. He turned, shoving Jimmy out of the way, and stuck his head back in the cabin.

"Stay belowdecks, Shaelyn," he ordered with a look that brooked no argument. Then he disappeared at a run, with Jimmy at his heels.

"Oh, I don't think so," she said to the empty room. "Not this time." She scrambled for her boots, pulling one on, then searching for the other. She finally found it wedged under the desk, along with a few other victims of last night's storm. She pulled the second boot on and didn't even consider taking time to button the darn things.

She finger-combed her hair as she ran out the door. The pounding of feet and the shouts of the men grew louder as she reached the top of the steps. She opened the door a crack, then decided to stay put at the sight of Alec giving orders. She wouldn't put it past him to lock her in the cabin if he saw her.

But what in the world was this fuss all about, if he was meeting a ship the way he did when he picked up Robert and Naomi? The men acted as if they were preparing for a fight.

Alec shouted one last order, then marched toward the door she hid behind. Had he seen her? Could she make it back to the cabin before he got to the door?

She decided to stay and demand she be allowed on deck, but to her pleasant surprise he took the steps leading to the helm.

The minute he reached that deck she slipped through the door and dove for a stack of crates beneath the steps. No sense inviting an argument when she could avoid one. She crept to the other side of the steps and leaned over the rail.

The sight that unfolded before her was like something from an Errol Flynn movie.

Alec's and Griffin's ships bore down on a third, easily overtaking it within minutes and sandwiching the smaller vessel between them. Shaelyn jumped at a reverberating boom as a cannonball sailed over the bow of the hostage ship. Good grief! Was the captain of Griffin's ship firing on it?

The sails on the middle ship dropped and a man at the helm yelled across the brief expanse of water.

"State your business."

"We'll have your cargo," Alec boomed back.

Shaelyn gasped. Alec was going to steal this ship's cargo? She thought he was picking up some seasick slaves.

They were close enough that Shaelyn could see the fat, bearded spokesman's fists clench. The moment his hand went for his sword, another crashing boom sent a cannonball soaring over the stern.

"The next one hits the hull," Alec bellowed. "Gather your men and lay down your arms."

The captain on the third ship visibly quaked with fury, but after a moment's hesitation he signaled the men to gather.

Grappling hooks flew across the water and bit into the deck and rail on both sides of the hostage vessel. Within moments the ships bumped together and planks dropped across the rails to form a bridge. At the sound of someone stomping down the steps, Shae ducked back into the shadows of the crates.

Alec marched across the deck and crossed to the middle ship first. Shaelyn jerked at the sight of him.

He wore a black silk mask over his eyes, much like the one he'd worn to the masquerade ball, but this one fell to cover the lower half of his face as well. With a startled glance she realized all the men had covered their faces.

Those men now swarmed onto the ship from both sides, some prodding the hostage crew together, some disappearing into the bowels of the ship.

Shaelyn could make out nothing more than random shouts. Alec, Captain Finley, and the captain of Griffin's ship—both masked as well—oversaw the proceedings while holding the third captain at the point of a sword.

Hatches flew open all over the ship, and an incredible

stench suddenly permeated the air. Shaelyn gagged and covered her face, thinking this must be what an outhouse smells like. No, it couldn't smell that bad, because no one would ever go in one to use it.

Just as she thought she might lose last night's dinner over the rail, she drew in a choking gasp at the sight of slaves—men, women, and children—crawling weakly from below. Some needed help just to stand. All of them squinted and hid their eyes from the sun. Most of them wore scraps of rags that hung from their bodies, covering little. Filth clung to them all, the likes of which Shaelyn didn't even want to contemplate.

Alec barked orders, pointing to Griffin's ship and then to his own. Suddenly he went rigid. Shaelyn realized he was staring straight at her.

_Uh-oh._

She'd completely forgotten to stay hidden. No sense cowering now. She straightened her shoulders and stood tall.

He went back to barking orders, louder and angrier, gesturing toward Griffin's ship. The crewmen who had been leading some of the slaves toward Alec's ship stopped and turned, then herded the poor, weak group toward Griffin's.

What was he doing? Changing his plans because of her? She crawled out from behind the crates and headed toward one of the planks connecting the ships.

Alec shoved the fat captain facedown onto the deck and bellowed an order for the prisoners to follow suit. Not until they'd all disappeared behind the rail did he leave the helm and make his way toward her.

"If you so much as take another step, I will tie you to the bunk and lock you in your cabin," he gritted through clenched teeth as he leapt to the plank and marched across.

Ordinarily an order like that would have guaranteed that Shaelyn do as she pleased or die trying, but something stopped her this time. She had no doubt he would do just as he threatened.

He dropped to the deck in front of her, grabbed her arm, and hauled her out of sight of the other ship.

"You infuriating little fool! What the hell do you think you're doing?"

She yanked at her arm, but his grip remained ironclad.

"Let go of me, you big jerk! I was just watching. I wasn't doing any harm."

"You could be recognized! Why do you think we're all masked? Because we like to play pirate?" He held fast as she continued to try to break his hold. "Stop fighting me! Even now, one of that crew may have seen you. Not to mention the trap Franklin Tilburn has set for us. We'll be evading him during this entire trip."

She stopped fighting when the implications hit her. Alec could be recognized through her.

"Okay." Her mind raced for a solution. "Give me one of those masks, then bind my hands like I'm a prisoner and tie me to something out there so they can see me. If I'm ever recognized later, I can say I escaped."

He looked as if he might argue, but Shae could tell he was thinking over her plan. With a muttered, "Stay," he disappeared onto the bridge and returned with a black silk scarf.

He tied it below her eyes, then grabbed her hair, wadded it up, then shoved the curly mass down the back of her shirt. He pulled a piece of coiled rope from his pocket, bound her hands so loosely she had to hold the rope on, then made a display of yanking her roughly back into view.

"At least act afraid, blast it," he growled under his breath. "Curl into a ball and sit still. The less they see of you, the better." He looped the rope around a mast and acted as if he were knotting it. "If anything untoward happens, and I mean *anything*, Shaelyn, run like hell to the cabin, bar the door, and get the firearm from my desk."

"Yes, master." She looked up at him and gave a mock quiver of fear. A muscle in his jaw twitched and he clenched his fists as if he wished they were around her throat.

He turned on his heel.

"Ten lashes to the imbecile guarding the prisoner," he roared as he stormed back to the other ship. As one, the men turned and looked at Jimmy, who stumbled at the looks and made a great show of cowering when Alec drew near.

They boarded the pitiful human cargo onto Griffin's ship, then several of the men transferred casks of fresh water from Alec's to Griffin's.

"Give them water to bathe," he ordered, "and all they want for drinking. Best make their meals bland at first."

The bedding for the captain and crew of the hostage ship was taken for the slaves, as well as what clothes could be found.

Shaelyn watched all these proceedings, wishing like heck she had her mini-recorder. The moment the slaves had emerged from that putrid hold, she'd known what Alec had done. He hadn't been out to rescue a couple of seasick slaves on the underground railroad. He'd taken a shipload of them coming straight from their native land, before they ever hit the shores of this country. The thought of him battling severe seasickness of his own to rescue these poor wretches made Shaelyn's heart swell with pride.

She watched, trying to memorize every minute detail. If only she could get over in the middle of the action. But if she even looked like she was going to slip from the ropes, let alone cross to that ship, she had no doubt Alec would have her locked in the cabin before she could manage to stand upright.

She couldn't see much of what was going on aboard Griffin's ship. From what she could tell, the slaves had huddled together, obviously not realizing they'd been rescued.

Jimmy, Harker, and the first mate, Welford, as well as some of Griffin's crew, passed buckets of drinking water through the fearful crowd, gesturing patiently that they could accept without fear of recriminations.

Once all the slaves had been boarded and control seemed to reign, Griffin's crew stowed the planks, removed the grappling hooks, then pushed away from the slaver.

Alec's men cut the sheets to the slaver's sails, then the men swarmed back onto their own ship as quickly as they'd left it. Alec was the last to leave. He jumped atop a bridging plank, then turned and pointed his sword at the fat, furious captain.

"Follow and you die."

As the man sputtered with rage, Alec jumped to the deck and marched toward Shaelyn.

She tried to stifle her smile, then realized no one could see it behind the black scarf anyway.

While the men shoved away and followed Griffin's ship, Alec whipped Shae's ropes loose, pulled her to her feet by her forearm, then dragged her toward the cabin.

Chapter 16

Alec PUSHED THE infuriating woman into the cabin and slammed the door behind him. She stumbled and caught herself on the desk, then spun around and yanked the silk kerchief from her face.

"Criminy, Alec! You can cut the caveman act now. Nobody can see us."

"This is not an act, Shaelyn. When I give you an order, I expect it to be followed."

"Oh, that." She waved her hand as if his orders were nothing more than pesky insects to be batted away. "You have to remember, I'm a journalist. That was history in the making. I couldn't possibly have sat down here and not witnessed a shipload of slaves gaining their freedom."

An aching throb hammered at his temples as he fought to keep from throttling her.

"I mean, think about it. Things like this go down in the history books. We made history today."

"*We* may be recognized, thanks to you and your very noticeable face!" Though he wanted to choke her, he couldn't stop the coil of pleasure in his chest at her use of *we*. And he had not failed to notice that she'd included herself on that first day at sea when she'd said Smith didn't suspect them.

Instead of seeming upset for possibly compromising their identities, she blinked with a smile and self-consciously pulled her hair from the back of her shirt. She gave the curly mane a gentle shake with her fingers.

"You think I have a noticeable face?"

Oh, if she only knew.

"Saint's blood! The reason I saw you was because half of Griffin's crew were gawking."

"Well, geez, the guys on the slaver probably didn't see me without the mask, and if they did they'll just think I was a prisoner. Besides, aren't ships recognizable? What will keep them from identifying your ships?"

"There are hundreds of vessels on the water identical to the two we used. We never use the same ship twice, and we cover any name or identifying marks."

She raised her eyebrows and pursed her lips. "Makes sense." She paced a few steps and turned. "Why did you load all the slaves on Griffin's ship? Some were moving toward this one until you saw me."

He sighed. "Quite frankly, until I saw you, I'd forgotten you were on board."

"How flattering," she muttered. He ignored her.

"I realized you might not be safe, so I ordered—"

"I can take care of myself," she stated with exaggerated patience.

"I am painfully aware of that." Just the thought made his groin ache. He glared at her, part of him itching to choke her, part of him noticing how her hair sparkled with glints of red and gold when the sun came through the port-hole. "This is not the first time I've rescued these poor devils, and until they realize they are safe, some of them bear watching. They speak no English, so there is no way to tell them except through kindness. And the vast majority of them have never seen a white woman."

"Oh. I hadn't thought of that. You're right." She paced

away and he started to chastise her again about not following his orders, but she turned back and looked at him, her
gaze downright worshipful.

"You were awesome out there today," she said. "I was
so proud of you."

Any harsh words evaporated like wisps of fog in the
sun.

"Well . . . I . . . I was just—"

"You were just wonderful. Standing up there, the wind
in your hair, that irate captain at the end of your sword."

He unconsciously straightened his shoulders and stood
a bit taller.

"The Dramamine must have really helped," she added.

His shoulders slumped.

She smiled at him with an impish twinkle of mischief
in her eyes. A twinkle the color of moss kissed by the
morning dew.

He reached up and smoothed a silky errant curl off of
her cheek. She closed her eyes at his touch and leaned into
his hand, sending a sweet ripple of heat through him, like
ever-widening circles on a pond. She opened her eyes and
looked at him, invited him. He cupped the back of her
head and drew her nearer.

"Sir," Jimmy's happy voice called from behind the
door. "I'm here for my ten lashes."

The past two days had been absolutely idyllic.

The past two nights had been hell.

Since Griffin's ship had all the passengers, Alec found
himself with little to do. He'd sought out Shaelyn, finding
her with Mr. Harker, helping to mend sails, or with Mr.
Ort in the galley getting a lesson on high-seas cooking.
Yesterday when he'd caught her climbing the rigging with
the lookout, Mr. Gilyard, he bellowed for Gilyard to bring
her down posthaste and risk a lashing if he ever took her
up there again.

While Shaelyn verbally abused him for his high-handedness, calling him some sort of male pig in her non sequitur language, he fought to swallow his heart back down into his chest. One small misstep and she could have been dead on the deck in front of him.

"How long will we travel with Griffin's ship?" Shaelyn asked. She sat cross-legged on the deck, barefoot, a clean pair of Jimmy's britches rolled up to her knees and another of Alec's shirts billowing on her small frame. The wind lifted her hair in swirls behind her. Alec's fingers tingled to bury themselves in the silky strands, to hold her head in his palms while he kissed her senseless. To lift her from the deck and carry her to the—

"Hello?"

"Hmm?" He dragged his mind back to her question. "Oh. We'll break away just south of Cape Helm. Captain Reynolds will take Grif's ship to an island cove and wait while Finley deposits us and takes on fresh water and food. They'll meet back up and sail together to Canada. The slaves will be given the choice to stay there or return to their homeland."

"Oh." She nodded. "Makes sense." She stretched her legs out in front of her and wiggled her toes.

"Really, Shaelyn. I still insist that it is most unseemly for you to show your calves and feet. The trousers are bad enough, but—"

"Don't start with me, Alec." She stretched like a cat, swung her feet around, then plopped her head in his lap and smiled up at him. "Why do I never hear you men complaining about too much cleavage from a woman's gown?"

"Well, that's different."

"How?"

"Well, it's . . . that is to say . . ." How could she expect him to think straight with her head in his lap, smiling up at him so endearingly?

"Uh-huh. I didn't think so."

And so had gone their relationship for the last two days,

since Jimmy had interrupted Alec's contemplations of kissing her and she had cursed under her breath.

She was like no other woman in the world. And, God help him, he realized she was the only woman he wanted.

How in the world would he deal with Faith?

"There's an elephant."

He looked down at her.

"I beg your pardon?"

"An elephant. Up there." She pointed skyward and his gaze followed her finger. "See it? That big cloud to the left of the sun. See? There's its trunk. And its ears. It must be African with ears that size. And there's its tail. Oops. No more tail."

Alec watched the elephant distort into a turtle and then into a mound of whipping cream. Shaelyn argued that it was an aardvark, but since he'd never seen one, he could hardly be a judge.

They picked out animals in the clouds until the last wisp of white gave way to flawless royal blue from horizon to horizon. The ship glided across glass-smooth waters, and for the first time in his life Alec found himself enjoying the gentle rock of the deck, the snap of sails in the breeze, the taste of the salt air on his tongue.

He leaned against a crate and relaxed. Shaelyn's eyes had drifted closed and she breathed as if she were sleeping. Her hair fanned across his lap and spilled onto the deck.

He ran his finger up one of the spiral curls, careful that she couldn't feel such nonsense. He closed his eyes and fought the ache in his chest that had plagued him for the past two nights as he'd tossed in his bunk until Welford had thrown a pillow at his head.

With a sigh he opened his eyes and looked down at Shaelyn. His gaze met the dark, mossy green of hers. Her eyes no longer twinkled with mischief, but studied him with a seriousness he'd seldom seen on her face.

She reached up and took his hand from her hair, then brought his fingers to her cheek. She leaned into them with

a look of sweet agony, then turned her head and pressed
a kiss into the center of his palm. The agony shot up his
arm and rocked throughout his body.

She looked up at him, her eyes bright with moisture.

"I'll miss you," she whispered.

The full lovers' moon mocked him as Alec paced the deck.
He hadn't even bothered to try to go to bed. Shaelyn's
words rang in his head like the ship's bell, and try as he
might, he could not wipe them from his mind.

She had resigned herself to leaving. She believed he
wanted to marry Faith. And just when he'd opened his
mouth to tell her he didn't want her to go, Jimmy had
come galloping up to show her the seals sunning themselves on a nearby island. She had jumped at the chance
to break the tension, and she and Jimmy had watched the
seals until the dinner bell rang.

He toyed with the notion of throttling his meddlesome
cabin boy.

And now, as she slept peacefully in Alec's cabin, he
paced the deck like a caged bear.

Where did she think she would go? She had contacted
no one and no one had come looking for her. What if,
even beyond the realm of possibility, she truly was from
the future? If she managed to get the ring off, would she
indeed disappear back to the time she claimed was hers?

He shook himself at the thought. He must truly be over-
wrought to even consider giving credence to her ridiculous
claim. But regardless of the fact that he didn't believe her
story, he admitted to himself that he loved her. Had fallen
in love quite possibly that first day when he'd watched her
stumble onto the deck, and he was still falling. Every time
she looked at him, every time she touched him, aside from
the torment she caused his tortured body, there was a right-
ness. As if two soul mates had come together at long last.

He scraped his hair back along his skull with both hands
and continued to pace.

But she was wrong for him, he argued with himself. She was infuriating, entirely too outspoken, unconventional, unpredictable. Mad. She would keep his life in constant turmoil.

He could marry Faith. Sweet, serene, sane Faith. His life would be ordered. Calm, organized, uneventful.

Boring.

As boring as poor Grif's was with Florence.

And he knew now that he didn't love Faith, at least not as he should. He had loved her twelve years earlier, as a youth loves a girl. But the love he felt for Shaelyn was the love of a man for a woman. A fiery, tempestuous, volatile love for the same kind of woman.

And she loved him, as well. She'd said as much the night she moved into the cottage. She'd left because it hurt too much to watch him with Faith.

Oh, how he regretted the pain he caused her.

But he would make it all up to her now. He would tell her in the morning how he felt.

No, by damn. He would tell her now.

He strode across the deck, threw open the door in the bulkhead, then clattered down the steps. He paused at her door.

It was the middle of the night. How long had she been sleeping?

Long enough.

He raised his fist to knock, but the door flew open before his knuckles ever met wood. Shaelyn bounced off his chest with an "Ooph!"

"What the . . . ? Alec! I was just coming to find you."

Shaelyn's mane of dark curls sprouted from her head at all angles. Her red-rimmed eyes looked as if she hadn't slept in days.

Saint's blood, she was beautiful.

She dragged him into the cabin and shut the door. Her ever-burning lamp glowed happily, but Alec noticed that the bunk looked as if a wrestling match had taken place there. He took a deep breath and turned to her.

"We need to talk," they both blurted.

"You first," they said in unison.

"No, go ahead."

"Be my guest." They managed yet again to speak at the same time.

Shaelyn gave him a pained smile, dropped into the chair, and wordlessly gestured for him to speak.

Now that he had the floor, he wasn't quite certain how to proceed. How did one go about telling his wife he loved her? He'd never expected to have that problem. Should he give her a gentle speech beforehand? Take her in his arms and hold her? Drop to one knee and try to think of something poetic?

"Shaelyn . . ."

She looked up at him with dread in her eyes. He took a deep breath.

"I love you," he exhaled.

Well, that was certainly one way to go about it.

The dread turned to a look of puzzlement, then realization, and then, much to his relief, elation. Before he even saw her move, she had her arms around his neck, nearly knocking him to the floor when their bodies met.

She pelted him with kisses on his face, his neck, his nose. When she settled on his mouth, the passion rocked him, weakening his knees, turning his brain to mush, coiling to burn in a part of him that wanted her as much as his mind did.

"Oh, Alec. I was so afraid. So afraid," she murmured against his mouth. Suddenly she jerked back. "Wait a minute. What do you mean by, 'I love you'?"

He stared at her. How could one misinterpret those words?

"I mean I love you and I want you to be my wife. *Remain* my wife. Blast it, you know what I mean."

She cocked her head. "Regardless of where I'm from?"

"Y-y-yes." He nodded slowly. This was not the topic

he wanted to discuss right now. "Regardless." *Of where you say you're from*, he added silently.

She studied his eyes, then ever so gently took his face in her hands and covered his mouth with hers, her kiss so achingly sweet it rivaled the one before it in the havoc wreaked upon his body.

He pulled her even closer and dragged her down with him, pulling her across his lap as he sat in the chair before his knees gave out. She snuggled closer, wrapping her arms tighter, her lips never leaving his, and he wondered if he'd put himself in an even worse position.

She brought her kiss to a slow, reluctant end, then leaned back into his arms and looked at him, a new worry obviously nagging at her.

"What is it?" He tried to draw her back, but she held him off.

She searched his face, then glanced at her lap before looking back at him. Torment darkened her glorious green eyes and sent a shiver of fear to his gut. What if she told him she no longer loved him?

"Alec," she began with a certain amount of dread. "Have you forgotten about Faith? I thought she was your first love."

He sighed in relief. *Thank you, God.*

With more gentleness than he had used in a decade, he took her hand in his.

How could he tell her that he was not so fickle as to fall in and out of love so easily? He never wanted her to worry that his love could be swayed by a prettier face or a better offer, as if either could exist in this world. But he was not prone to flowery words and emotional speeches. He had cultivated neither, once he'd resigned himself to a marriage of his father's choosing. However, he knew that what he said to Shaelyn right now would either set her at ease or forever leave her worrying.

"Shaelyn . . ." He brought her fingers to his lips and kissed them. "I did love Faith. I do love her."

Shae closed her eyes and miserably shook her head. He kissed her on the tip of her nose, then tilted her chin until she looked at him again.

"But I love her as a friend. As a man with fond memories of his first love. My love for Faith . . ." He bowed his head and prayed for adequate words. "My love for Faith was a gentle breeze in my life. My love for you is a storm. A wild, seething nor'easter that gets into my soul and lets me know I'm alive."

The smile slowly came back to Shaelyn's eyes, then she wrapped her arms around his neck and thoroughly kissed him, pulling him away from the back of the chair until they tumbled to the floor in a tangle of limbs.

"You're insane," he laughed while she giggled against his lips. Her response was to cling to him and roll across the floor until they reached the softness of the carpet. Of course, it was purely coincidental that he ended up atop her, pinning her to the floor.

He put his weight on his elbows and laughed down at her mischief, until their gazes turned serious. With infinite care, he lowered his head, brushing her lips once, and then again, and then settling against her willing mouth with a thrill he thought never to feel. This woman—his wife— loved him. That knowledge stole into his heart and started a sweet ache there that he hoped would never end.

Her kisses started an ache in other places.

He pulled her even closer as his tongue sought hers. She sighed in her throat, and that simple noise sent his heated blood crashing through him. Her hands wandered his back, stoking the fires that already raged.

"Shaelyn," he whispered into her mouth, "I love you." Did she hear the wonder in his voice?

Her fingers dug into his back. "Alec," she sighed.

That one word said it all.

He rose onto his knees, his fingers working at the buttons on her shirt. She tore at his, sending his blood thundering in his ears. He leaned down on occasion to taste the sweetness of her kiss while their hands worked in a frenzy at the fastenings. The more stubborn the buttons, the more frantic the kiss. He trailed his lips down the column of her neck.

"Sweet mercy," he groaned into the hollow of her throat, "to think I nearly lost you."

He continued his lovemaking for several long seconds before he realized Shaelyn had stilled.

He raised up and stared down at her.

"What is it?" he asked, his voice hoarse with want. He tried to kiss her again but she gently, reluctantly pushed him away.

"We can't do this, Alec. It isn't right."

He shook his head, trying to grasp the meaning of her words.

"Shae, we are married." He went back to nibbling her throat. "Nothing could be more right. The *time* couldn't be more right."

With aching tenderness she pushed him away from her neck and held his face in her hands.

"And what about Faith?"

Faith. He had all but forgotten Faith. He shook his head to clear his mind so muddled by desire, but the smoldering want still clouded his thoughts. Until Shaelyn's words threw cold water on them.

"Would you do this to Faith? Make me your wife before you settle things with her?"

Shaelyn nudged him away, then got to her feet, buttoning the shirt he had tried so hard to free. He couldn't help the sound of protest that escaped his throat.

"Alec, she deserves that much." Shaelyn's gaze scanned the open expanse of his shirt, looking just as disappointed as he felt. "A few weeks ago I wouldn't have given her a second thought—in fact, I'd be feeling darn smug right now. But Faith is everything you said she was. She's a good person, and if our roles were reversed, I would want that much consideration." She smiled down at him with just a hint of teasing. "You are not a man most women would choose to give up."

Her words salved his sting of disappointment somewhat. And he had to admit, however grudgingly, that he did owe Faith the truth before he made Shaelyn his wife in every way.

He stifled a groan.

Shaelyn knelt beside him and pressed her lips to his. "I want this as badly as you do," she whispered, running her palm beneath his shirt and across his chest. "But when we do this, I want nothing between us and our love. No regrets, no guilt. No nothing."

Her warm hand skimming his chest and the literal image of "no nothing" between them had him swallowing back another groan. He sighed and dropped his chin to his chest.

"Very well," he muttered.

When he stood, Shaelyn slid her arms around his waist and rested her head against his chest. She turned her face and kissed the bare skin there before looking up at him.

The woman had a talent for torture.

"Will you hold me the rest of the night?" she asked, pulling him toward the bunk. "After all, we *are* married."

Oh yes, he groaned. *Torture*.

Chapter 17

THE SUN HAD just burst over the horizon when Molly barreled through the front door of Windward Cottage, her skirts flying. Alec and Shaelyn had not even reined their horses to a stop.

"Welcome home!" she called, her eyes avid with curiosity. "Thank heavens you're home. I've had the devil's own time keeping Father at bay ever since Martin returned from the docks in an absolute . . . Shaelyn! What the devil are you wearing?"

Shaelyn looked down, then smiled at Molly's half-scandalized, half-impressed tone.

"Jimmy's trousers and Alec's shirt. You should try it sometime."

"She'll do nothing of the sort!" Alec ordered. "Her language already bears tending. I'll not send her home in britches."

Shaelyn turned a teasing grin to the man she loved more than life itself.

"Well, she didn't pick up that sort of language from me. Mine is much worse. And you're just cranky, so stop your pouting."

Alec narrowed his eyes at her, but she could see the amused glint in his golden-brown gaze.

"I am not pouting."

She winked at him. "Not for long, anyway."

Molly watched their exchange with little-sisterly glee.

"Why are you cranky, Alec? Did something happen on the voyage?"

Alec swung from the livery horse, then slid Shaelyn from hers.

"I am not cranky, pest." He hooked her neck with his arm and gave her an affectionate squeeze. "And *nothing* happened on the voyage. Absolutely nothing." His glance lighted on Shaelyn only long enough to have her biting her tongue to keep from laughing.

"How's Samuel?" she changed the subject, holding her breath to ask without giggling.

"Oh, he's greatly improved. I daresay you'll not recognize him, he looks so well."

That was a relief. She hadn't thought he would have a relapse without his daily therapy, but the possibility had nagged at her, nonetheless.

"Faith has been here every day. She has been a great help with Samuel, but I have had the devil's own—" She glanced at Alec. "I have been quite creative in explaining your absences. Shaelyn, you have had a nasty summer ague and remained at Harbor Mist so as not to expose us. Alec, you, of course, have been away on urgent business. Something vague about helping Griffin." She gave them a smug smile. "Father has been given the same information, somewhat more loudly, however, as to be heard over his bellows."

The news that Faith had been there every day robbed Shaelyn of some of her playfulness. They had a confrontation ahead of them that she didn't want to think about. Though Faith stood between her and Alec, Shaelyn truly liked the woman and hated to see her hurt. She never wanted to do to someone else what Aaron and Rachel had done to her.

Alec looked at Shaelyn at the mention of Faith. He winked and lifted his chin in an attempt to cheer her.

"Welcome back, sir." Ned arrived from the direction of the stables. His curious gaze scanned the length of Shaelyn's britches-clad body until his face turned the color of a brick.

"Thank you, Ned." Alec handed the reins over to the coachman and herded Shaelyn and Molly into the house. Shaelyn smiled. It seemed Alec was beginning to take her wearing pants in stride.

"Sir!" Martin came rushing from the back of the house when they entered the foyer. Shaelyn had never seen the staid family retainer so flustered. "I trust . . ." He glanced at Molly. ". . . the problem with the delivery was resolved to your satisfaction?"

Alec slapped Martin on the shoulder. The butler stumbled forward several steps.

"Resolved to everyone's satisfaction," he declared. "And I won't even hold it against you for allowing my wife to stow away on the ship."

Martin drew in a deep breath, then affixed his usual long-suffering expression and simply muttered, "Yes, sir. But I do have broad shoulders, sir."

Humor? From Mr. One Emotion?

"Thank you for escorting me to the docks, Martin," Shaelyn offered in an attempt to appease any pride she may have wounded by beating him to the ship.

"It was my pleasure, ma—" Martin's gaze turned to her, then flickered over her attire without the slightest change of expression. "Ma'am," he finished.

Well, well. She might liberate these men yet.

"If you'll excuse me, sir, I shall order two more places set for breakfast."

While Martin disappeared toward the kitchen, Alec took Shaelyn's arm and steered her toward the stairs.

"And if you will excuse us, pest, I would like to freshen up. And I'm sure Shaelyn wants to change into something more appropriate."

Shaelyn gave him an innocent smile and let him guide her up the steps.

"Don't make any bets on that, bubba."

Shaelyn fluffed the skirts of the sky-blue grosgrain morning gown. After days of loose pants and shirts and going barefoot on the ship, the yards of fabric felt as if they weighed twenty pounds, which, come to think of it, they very well might.

She'd decided not to try to liberate her husband all at once. No sense pushing her luck. Nor did she want to shock Samuel into a relapse by showing up in the sickroom in trousers.

She stood outside his room and knocked, then pushed open the door at his "Come in."

Nothing could have prepared her for the sight that met her.

Samuel sat outside on the balcony next to an open French door. He wore gray pinstriped slacks, a starched shirt and collar, and the very proper gray coat. His wheat-colored hair sparkled in the sunlight, a heart-lurching contrast to the healthy bronze tan of his handsome face.

"Wow!" Shaelyn strolled through the diamond-paned doors. "You do know how to recover, don't you?" The last time she'd seen him, he'd looked like something out of an Anne Rice book; pale as a vampire who hadn't fed in a couple of nights, and just as weak.

He smiled and colored just a bit.

"I have had good nursing. I fear I would have died if not for the care I received here."

Shaelyn waved away his gratitude. "I just got lucky, that's all."

"I'm glad you're feeling better yourself. Miss Hawthorne said you've been ill. I worried that I'd infected you with my illness.''

Shaelyn thought of her week-long ''illness'' and had to force herself not to smile.

''Oh, no. Just a bad cold. We Loo-siana girls ah just so delicate.'' She fanned herself and tried to look the part. Samuel's laugh turned into a cough.

After fetching him a tumbler of water and patting him gently, they settled into a nice little chat until Margaret brought him his breakfast tray.

''Faith . . . Mrs. Baldwin . . . insists I rest in the morning. What she doesn't know is that I take a little walk before breakfast.''

Shaelyn couldn't help a mischievous grin. ''Well, I won't tell on you. But if I don't get to the breakfast table, Alec will come looking for me.''

She made sure Samuel wanted for nothing before rushing to the dining room. She arrived in time to bounce off Alec's chest as he opened the doors in search of her. His arms caught her and pulled her back against him, holding her there like a pair of steel bands.

''Are you quite all right, my dear?'' he asked with teasing formality.

She rested her head against his shoulder and snuggled closer.

''I am now.''

Images of how he'd held her during the night flashed through her mind and sent an exquisite, aching heat curling through her blood.

He brushed a kiss across the top of her head and whispered, ''I imagine the pest is enjoying the show.''

Shaelyn stretched upward and peered over Alec's shoulder. Sure enough, Molly watched with a smile that rivaled the Cheshire cat's. She lifted her hand and wiggled her fingers at Shae.

Martin's arrival in the dining room broke up any more mushy stuff. Alec escorted Shaelyn to the table and seated her while Martin served the breakfast. Molly draped her napkin across her lap and watched them as if waiting for them to answer a question.

"What?" Shaelyn finally asked when she could no longer stand the staring.

"Well, are you not going to tell me what happened?" Molly said. "For it is very clear that something happened. Where did you go? Why were you on the ship? Did you share a cabin?"

"Molly!" Alec bellowed. The girl didn't even flinch.

Shaelyn looked at Alec, and his one cursory glance told her that Molly knew nothing of his "activities."

"Well, you *are* married," Molly reminded him with a roll of her eyes.

"This is not proper conversation for a girl of your age, young lady. The very idea of—OW!"

Shaelyn hadn't meant to kick his shin quite so hard.

"Stop being such a big brother, Alec. We went to Baltimore, Molly," Shaelyn lied. "And I was on the ship because they weighed anchor and we were too far out to sea to turn back by the time we realized it. And as for sharing a cabin, I can answer that in one word." She ignored Alec's strangled choke and leaned conspiratorially toward her sister-in-law. "Seasick."

"Oh." The avid gleam in Molly's eyes died, and she tossed her brother a look of disgust.

"Now see here, brat. I refuse to be an object of—"

A knock at the front door interrupted Alec's brotherly tirade.

"Good morning, Martin. How are our patients faring today?"

The voice sent Shaelyn's heart to her throat. Alec looked as if he suddenly faced a firing squad. Good heavens, they hadn't expected to have to deal with Faith so soon. They hadn't even discussed how they would go about breaking the news.

Martin assured Faith of Samuel's health, then an-

nounced that Alec had returned and Shaelyn had recovered
from her ague. Before Alec could do more than shoot a
reassuring glance at Shae, their visitor rushed into the
room.

If possible the woman had grown even more beautiful
in the past week. Shae, who had seldom felt dowdy in her
life, did so when around Faith. Her serene eyes glowed
with life and her flawless skin held a new, becoming hint
of pink. She would be an easy woman to hate if she'd
seemed at all aware of her devastating beauty. Shae liked
her all the more because she wasn't.

"Alec, welcome home! And Shaelyn, I am so pleased
to see you recovered. I vow you look as if you've never
been ill." Faith kissed Alec on the forehead, then rounded
the table to give Shae a sisterly hug.

That simple gesture of affection sent little knives of guilt
piercing Shaelyn's conscience. She turned and faced Alec.

He tossed his napkin to the table and scooted his chair
back, then nodded to Shaelyn at her unasked question.

"Pest," he gave Molly a look that did not invite curiosity, "you will excuse us. Shaelyn and I have something
to discuss with Faith in the parlor."

Faith's gaze shot to Alec and then to Shaelyn. She paled,
and dread replaced the happy light in her eyes as she
clasped her hands together at her waist. She followed Alec
to the parlor as if she were following the hangman to the
gallows; as if she knew that the man she loved was about
to deliver a death blow to their future.

Bringing up the rear, Shaelyn nearly writhed with guilt.
If there was anything she could have done to spare Faith
this pain, other than give up Alec, she would have. But
Alec had told her, in the wee hours of the morning as they
lay cuddled on the bunk, that even if Shaelyn had refused
him, he would not have married Faith.

Alec strode to the center of the parlor and gestured for
the ladies to sit. Faith slid miserably into the nearest seat.
Shaelyn tried to figure out how to crawl into a hole and

disappear. Alec eyed the decanter of whiskey with longing. He pinched the bridge of his nose and dropped his chin to his chest.

"Faith," he began. She continued to stare at her hands clasped in her lap. "I . . . I don't quite know how to put this . . ."

She looked up at him, the picture of abject misery when she spoke.

"It just happened, Alec. Before Thomas died. We never meant for it to happen."

Shaelyn looked at Alec, and Alec looked at Faith. The silence seemed to stretch on for hours. Shaelyn thought she would scream if somebody didn't say something. Alec closed his eyes and shook his head.

"What . . . 'happened'?" he asked, sounding totally confused. Shaelyn wanted to choke him, to hug him, to dance the dance of joy. Good grief! Men could be so dense! Faith looked as if she would agree.

"Samuel and I," she said. "We didn't mean to fall in love. But when he stayed with us to interview Thomas, it was as if . . . but of course we never . . . but I *was* fond of Thomas. Samuel and I vowed never to see each other again. But then I walked into the sickroom and there he was. And then Shaelyn took ill and I wanted to help. I had to spend so many hours in there with him. It is not Samuel's fault, Alec. It is all my fault. But it would not be fair to you if we married when my heart belongs to another."

"You'll not take the blame." Samuel stood in the doorway, obviously weak but with his shoulders squared. "If I had known Thomas had died, I would have gone to her immediately."

Faith flew to Samuel's side and Alec stared at them, as if not quite able to grasp the implications.

Faith's brow knitted in confusion. "Is that not what you wanted to speak to me about?" She turned to Samuel. "Did you not tell him of our plans?"

Samuel blinked and shook his head. "I was unaware of his return until moments ago."

Shaelyn stood and nudged Alec out of his stupor. "Why don't you tell them what we wanted to discuss? Or would you rather I do the—"

"Absolutely not," he said, realization finally dawning across that painfully handsome face. A smile graced his lips that had Shaelyn aching to kiss him. He waved the couple onto the couch before he spoke.

"This all seems rather superfluous now. You see, Shaelyn and I," he took Shaelyn's hand and winked at her, "well, we have fallen in love as well. We had planned to break—"

Faith let out an uncharacteristic squeal and jumped up to give Shaelyn a heartfelt hug. Samuel rose more slowly but made his way to Alec to clap him on the back.

The relief on all their faces was enough to start Shaelyn giggling. Faith looked at her, then allowed her own laughter to gild the air.

The two women hugged, as if the oldest of friends. The men clapped each other on the back and shook hands.

When Martin walked by the open doorway, Shaelyn was the only one to notice the tiniest hint of a smile on that long-suffering face.

Chapter 18

ALEC HAD THOUGHT the day would never end. After they celebrated his and Faith's nonbetrothal, he had wanted nothing more than to scoop his wife into his arms, lock themselves away in his bedchamber, and do what his tortured body had wanted to do for weeks.

But his blasted household was filled to the brim with extraneous people. He could hardly take his wife to bed in the middle of the morning with Samuel and Faith roaming the house, not to mention his little sister, whose whereabouts could never be predicted.

And now, blast it, Shaelyn had disappeared after dinner.

The ladies had retired to the parlor to leave the men to their port—a suspicious gesture on Shaelyn's part to begin with. But when he and Samuel had emerged from the dining room, the parlor was empty and the ladies were nowhere to be found.

"Well, what do you make of it, Smythe?" Alec asked after they'd conversed an indecent amount of time, trying to ignore the absence of the women.

Samuel shrugged. "If there is one thing I have learned

about the opposite sex, it is that it is best to leave the mysteries of the female gender a mystery.''

Alec had a feeling he would have no choice in the matter when it came to Shaelyn.

Just as he was about to suggest they go in search of the wayward women, the sound of feminine footsteps echoed in the hall.

Faith entered the parlor, followed by Molly. Alec watched for Shaelyn, but she failed to appear.

''I am extremely exhausted, dear brother.'' Molly made a great show of stretching in a most unladylike manner. ''I believe I shall retire early. Good night, everyone.'' Before he or Samuel could utter a response, she'd disappeared up the stairway. He turned to Faith, expecting an explanation of Shaelyn's whereabouts.

She avoided his gaze.

''Samuel, darling, I am tired as well. And you look fatigued. I believe it's best I go home and allow you your rest.'' She kissed him on the cheek. ''Will you walk me to the door?''

Alec watched, incredulous, as Faith bid him goodnight before strolling with Samuel toward the foyer.

''Just one moment!'' he bellowed.

Faith stopped and turned back to him, obviously fighting to keep her face emotionless.

''Oh, yes,'' she said, still avoiding his gaze. She pulled an envelope from a pocket in her skirts. ''Shaelyn asked me to give you this.''

A fist of fear closed around Alec's heart and squeezed. Why would Faith not look at him? Had Shaelyn changed her mind? What other reason was there to send him a note?

He tore open the vellum with a savage rip, then gaped like an idiot as a shower of flower petals sprinkled the floor and the toes of his boots.

''What the devil . . .'' He stared at the fragrant, multi-colored petals, then noticed a veritable trail of them leading back through the rear of the house. He looked at Faith, who sighed and rolled her eyes, then turned him toward the trail and gave him a shove.

Forgetting all but the rainbow of petals at his feet, he followed the fragrant path through the house to the back terrace. The knot of fear in his chest dissolved into a fiery, liquid ache that surged through his blood.

The trail continued through the garden and along the path leading into the trees. He no longer needed to see the petals to know where they led.

His anxious stride quickly covered the distance between the sparse woods and the guest house. The carpet of petals continued up the steps and through the open doorway.

He smiled to himself. He would be surprised if there was a flower left blooming in the gardens.

The floral trail led up the stairs outlined by glowing candles. The petals crushed beneath his boots as he climbed the steps, the air perfumed with a mingling of wonderful scents, but his fevered mind hardly noticed.

When he rounded the top step, all the blood rushed from his head and traveled south. He swallowed hard and fought to draw breath into lungs that had forgotten how to breathe.

Shaelyn stood at the open door to the balcony, illuminated by a dozen candles and haloed by the silver reflection of the moon off the water. Her white, filmy nightclothes fluttered softly in the breeze.

Her smile hit him full in the chest. What little breath he'd managed to find escaped his lungs when she shrugged out of her robe and let it fall to the floor in a puddle of silk.

Had that groan come from him?

He took one hesitant step toward her, and then they were in each other's arms. Her tongue sought his, sending exquisite waves of torture undulating through his being to coil into a mind-numbing ache. While her kisses wiped away all coherent thought, her hands divested him of his jacket, then loosened the knot of his tie.

He yanked off the tie, then the collar, then helped her free the buttons of his shirt while their lips stayed joined, frantic and hungry, until finally her hands skimmed the bare skin of his chest. He thought he would die of the sheer pleasure.

A small sigh escaped her throat and she pulled at his shirt while he fought with the accursed ribbons that formed the straps of her nightgown. With a seductive, knee-weakening smile, she stayed his hands and backed away.

The flickering candles bathed her in gold while the sea-kissed breeze from the balcony molded the silk of her gown against her many curves. He all but gulped when she dragged the ribbons over one creamy shoulder. Her heated gaze invited him to remove the other strap at his leisure.

A shiver of need racked his body. He found his hand toying with the remaining ribbon, caressing her throat, her collarbone, her cheek, and finally he hooked the ribbon with his finger and slowly slid the silk down her arm.

His heart stopped in his chest when the gown fluttered to rest upon the carpet of petals. Only when his lungs started to burn did he remember to breathe.

She took his hands in hers and drew him toward the bed. The gesture pulled him out of his trance until he scooped her into his arms and laid her atop the frilly covers so invitingly turned back. She looked up at him, the love in her eyes forming a knot in his throat. Had he ever dreamed his wife would look at him with such love?

In a matter of seconds he had rid himself of his boots and clothing and pulled her into his arms, savoring the feel of heated flesh upon heated flesh. She sighed when he covered her mouth with his, and his mind swirled with blinding need. She welcomed his touch, giving as much as he, kissing him with dizzying, eye-watering fervor. They explored each other with newlywed wonder. It was as if they were both untried; both making love for the first time.

He forced himself to be gentle. He prolonged the sweet agony as long as he could, and then finally, when he could bear it no longer, he took her.

Within the hazy, blinding lust that clouded his mind, he realized no barrier stopped his entry. He opened his eyes and looked down at her. She gazed up at him, apologizing with her eyes, the tormented apology sinking into his heart and dissolving his shock until it made no difference that he was not her first. He would forgive this woman anything; for this woman he would die a thousand deaths.

He buried his face in her neck, murmuring words of love, until her nails dug into his back and he joined her on that heavenly precipice, hovering there for an excruciating moment, and then soaring with her into ecstasy.

Shaelyn watched him sleep, her love for him welling in her chest with each breath she took.

She'd seen the look on his face when he'd realized she wasn't a virgin. And she'd seen his acceptance even in this time when men valued that trait in women above all else.

She would have given anything if he could have been the first. Heaven knew, she had bitterly regretted giving in to Aaron's pressuring. She had wanted to wait. She had waited longer than most. But she'd finally given in, and then two months later she'd read in the paper that he and Rachel had applied for a marriage license. By the time he had returned from his "business trip," he had a pregnant bride on his arm.

For the first time since their betrayal, Shaelyn smiled at the memory. She really should thank them someday, for if not for their betrayal, she most likely would have never ended up on that ship, or had the opportunity to slip the ring on her finger, or had this maddening, wonderful man trick her into marrying him.

She sighed and rolled over, backing up against his solid warm chest, curling to fit the curve of his body. Even in sleep, his arms drew her closer.

The only thing that marred her blissful happiness was the thought of her parents and Brianne. Contemplating never seeing them again was as painful as losing them to death. And she couldn't bear the thought of the agony they would suffer, knowing that her disappearance would forever go unsolved, that her parents would never know what happened to her.

But even if she were able, even if she had the option, how could she ever leave Alec behind to return to the future?

She shook her head and snuggled closer to her husband. She would not let these thoughts ruin the euphoric hours she had just spent with Alec, nor ruin the ones ahead.

She twined her fingers in his and kissed the masculine knuckles of his big, gentle hand. She relived what those hands had done to her throughout the night, still tasted his kisses so tender she had nearly wept.

He had loved her in ways she'd never dreamed, taken her places she'd never been. Not until Alec had shown her, did she realize how selfish Aaron had been. If she could thank Aaron for anything, it would be for teaching her the worlds of difference between a selfish lover and a giving one.

She closed her eyes and sighed, a smile curving her lips.

"You let me go to sleep." Alec nuzzled the top of her head while he pulled her tight against his chest. "We could have spent the time doing things much more interesting."

She rolled over into his arms and nestled her head in the hollow of his shoulder.

"I figured it was either let you sleep or have you passing out from sheer exhaustion."

He growled into her hair. "You underestimate me, Mrs. Hawthorne. I need no rest with you in my arms."

She looked up at him and brushed a kiss across his lips.

"Prove it," she whispered.

He growled once more and took up her challenge, proving his words with heart-stopping finesse, until they both lay exhausted and she teasingly conceded defeat.

Not until the blinding sun on the water nudged her awake did Shaelyn even realize she'd slept. She slipped from the bed and freshened up, then crept back into Alec's arms and tried to kiss him awake. She nuzzled his neck and kissed his chest. She smoothed his dark, mussed hair away from his forehead. She leaned over him and kissed his lips while her hands roamed free across the muscled expanse of his body. Not until she saw the tiniest twitch to the corners of his mouth did she realize the man had not fallen into a coma.

"You faker!" She shoved at him, but the steel bands of his arms wrapped around her. His laughter rumbled in his chest.

"Guilty as charged, madame. But you made the crime so worth my while." He dragged her across him and kissed her soundly. When he finally ended the kiss, he sighed. "There aren't enough hours in the night to love you properly."

Shaelyn squinted at the silvery sunlight reflecting off the water. She trailed her hands along his muscles and tortured him a little.

"So, is there a law against using the hours in the day?"

He looked at her, and then at the sun. A seductive smile spread across his face, and then he pulled the covers over their heads and spent the next few hours answering her question.

The days flowed like sweet wine, one into the other, heady and dizzying, while Shaelyn and Alec ignored the world and honeymooned in the guest cottage by the sea.

Shaelyn saw a side of Alec he'd never revealed. She met the man who woke her with kisses, only to drag her onto the balcony to see the misty bars of sunlight piercing the shadows of the woods. She met the man who could lie for hours in the grass, her head on his shoulder, and watch the clouds scud across the sky. The same man who would chase her down the beach, throw her over his shoulder, then march up to the bedroom and toss her on the bed, to love her so gently it caused an ache in her heart. She met the man with a sense of humor so bawdy he managed to make her blush.

She met the man who was everything she'd ever dreamed of.

But after a week, reality returned when they made the mistake of visiting the house.

Molly squealed at the sight of them, obviously delighted and openly curious. Shaelyn could tell the girl teemed with questions that would have Alec roaring. Somehow she managed to stifle asking them, but Shae had no doubt that once Molly got her alone, Shae would be fielding the questions herself.

"Faith and Samuel married yesterday," Molly announced. "He said he would return to thank you properly for your care and hospitality."

That insecure little part of Shaelyn couldn't help but study Alec's face for any sign of regret. He slid her hand into his and gave her a smile loaded with love ... and a devilish little smirk.

"Thoughtful of them not to interrupt us."

Molly chattered on, guiding them onto the back terrace as if they were visitors, insisting they stay for the noon meal. As they finished their dessert, Alec told Molly they would be moving back into the house that night.

"Hmm," Molly said. "Do you suppose we can keep the news of your marriage ... or, rather your ... well ... your *marriage* ... from Father? I fear he'll see no point in my chaperoning you then. Indeed, he'll most likely find a way to blame me for your ... well ... your ..."

"You have made your point, pest. And as much as I would like a reprieve from Father as well, I see no way to—"

The slam of the front door and the roar of "Alec!" bouncing through the house killed any hope they had of even one more day of peaceful bliss. The cliché "Speak of the devil" crossed Shaelyn's mind.

Margaret, who had been collecting dessert plates, snatched the last of the china and literally ran toward the kitchen. Martin appeared at the French doors.

"Sir, I believe your father has—"

William Hawthorne shoved the butler out of his way and stormed onto the terrace. Jane Hawthorne appeared behind her husband, doing her bothersome-gnat impersonation.

"What the devil have you done, boy?" he demanded with all the quiet of a sonic boom. If there had been any china left on the table, Shaelyn was sure it would have rattled.

Alec tossed his napkin on the table and leaned back into his chair.

"I have done quite a few things of late, Father. Would you care to be more specific?"

The man sputtered, his face turned from brick red to an alarming purple, then, if possible, he bellowed even louder.

"You have let Faith Almany's fortune slip between your fingers! No doubt for this little nobody who tricked you into marriage!"

Alec shot out of his seat so fast the chair tumbled across the terrace. He towered over his father, clenching his fists.

"My wife is not a nobody," he said, his voice low and barely controlled, "and she never has been. There are no 'nobodies' in this world, Father, except for small-minded, bad-tempered, greedy men like you."

Jane squeaked.

"I have spent thirty years," he went on, "honoring my father, bowing to your unreasonable demands in a misguided sense of duty. But I will bow no more. I told you, it was I who tricked Shaelyn into marriage, not the other way around. And now I thank God I did. I would not have married Faith. *Especially* not for her fortune. Saint's blood, Father, how much money does one man need?"

William quivered with rage as Jane fell into a chair, fanning herself.

Shaelyn vacillated between wanting to crawl into a hole and wanting to throw herself into Alec's arms.

"You will treat my wife with the respect she deserves," Alec continued, "or you will not be welcome in our home."

William stood there, his face changing a rainbow of hues. Shaelyn wouldn't have been surprised if the man had keeled over from a heart attack or stroke. She wondered if she could stomach giving him mouth-to-mouth if he did.

He quivered, speechless with rage. He turned his gaze on Shaelyn, a gaze so full of loathing she unconsciously shrank back in her chair. Before she had a chance to stiffen her spine and return his look, he wheeled around and stormed back through the French doors.

Jane rose slowly from her seat, all resemblances to a flapping goose gone. She looked at Alec, then Molly, then Shaelyn, tears glistening in eyes that must have once been alive with life.

"I am so sorry," she whispered, then ducked her head and hurried after her husband.

The only sound that broke the silence was Alec's muttered curse.

"Damn him."

Chapter 19

WEEKS WENT BY —heavenly weeks marred only by that one encounter with Alec's father. His look of pure hatred haunted Shaelyn for days, but unpleasant thoughts couldn't last long under the onslaught of Alec's love.

Alec seemed actually relieved after the confrontation, as if he'd known the meeting was coming for years, and he was glad to get it over with.

Molly, of course, was summoned home, but she managed to circumvent her father's wrath and come for regular visits. No doubt the carefree girl had no compunctions about lying through her teeth in order to visit her beloved brother. Even Jane braved any consequences from her husband and showed up a few times, showing a hint of backbone and apologizing for William's behavior.

Faith and Samuel visited several times before going back to New York. Samuel was man enough to admit he'd been wrong about Shaelyn's journalistic endeavors and asked her to write several articles for his paper. Not until she'd settled down at the desk in the bedroom to write the first in a series on the political issue of slavery did she realize how sorely she missed her laptop, her word-processing program, her online research. And what she wouldn't give for her spellchecker.

Times like these were when thoughts of her parents haunted her. She missed the twentieth century and all the wonderful conveniences, but she would gladly live without the luxuries in exchange for Alec. But even her blinding love for her husband couldn't keep her from missing her parents. From worrying about them. From wishing they could see their grandchild.

As if the thought stirred the nausea, Shaelyn threw down the quill pen and made a dash for the closest receptacle. She made it to the porcelain bowl on the washstand just in time.

No doubt about it. There was going to be a grandchild. She didn't need a pregnancy test to confirm what she'd suspected for the past couple of weeks.

Considering she'd never thrown up in her life, and now she had a record going of twelve days in a row of tossing her cookies, she felt pretty confident that her diagnosis was correct.

A baby. A little piece of Alec. The thought thrilled her, yet saddened her, knowing her parents would never see this child.

For the first time since before the voyage with Alec, she unconsciously twisted the ring on her finger.

She froze when it slipped onto her knuckle.

Her head spun, whether from shock or from the effect of the ring on her knuckle, she didn't know. She shoved it back into place, willing away the dizziness, fighting to slow her staccato heartbeat.

The ring would come off!

She shook her head, trying to clear her mind. What did this mean? She hadn't lost weight. The thing would have slipped off her finger as easily as it had slid on. She almost felt as if it had kept her there in the past until she and Alec had fallen in love, and now it gave her the freedom to go home.

What kind of game was Fate playing?

She slowed her breathing and forced herself to calm down. It may have been a fluke. Maybe she'd imagined it.

She tugged again on the ring, and again her head spun as the ring eased onto her knuckle.

This couldn't be happening. She almost wished it had kept her trapped there, with no decision to make; no being torn between two worlds.

There had to be a reason it had kept her in the past, and there had to be a reason it now freed her to go home. Perhaps, as she'd thought before, she could remove the ring and go home to see her parents, and then put it back on and return to Alec.

Her head throbbed at her temples. She couldn't deal with this right now. For all she knew, she could wake tomorrow morning and find the ring back to being tight as a drum. No, she wouldn't think of this right now. She would wait to see what the future brought and decide how best to deal with it then.

In the meantime, she had something she needed to tell her husband.

Alec rubbed his aching temples, massaged his eyes, pinched the bridge of his nose. Every time he worked at the shipping offices, he remembered why he preferred to work at home. But some things could only be done in town, so he'd been forced to spend the day at Hawthorne Shipping.

Bumping into his father.

He made one last entry in the books, stoppered the ink, and shoved away from the desk. What he needed to remove this throbbing headache was a healthy dose of Shaelyn.

His secretary, Ezra Cartwright, leapt to his feet when Alec left his office.

"Take those books for you, sir?"

Alec handed over the ledgers. "Check my figures, Ezra.

I would not swear they are accurate. I've been fending off a headache all day.''

"So I've noticed, sir. He just went into his office.''

Alec's bark of laughter relieved some of the pain in his temples, but Ezra flushed to a brilliant red when he realized what he'd said.

"Oh, sir! I didn't mean to imply—''

"Oh, no, Cartwright. You were correct the first time.'' He slapped his blushing secretary on the back and strode from the room, his mood improved already.

The simple act of putting distance between him and his father loosened the knotted muscles in his shoulders and neck. The closer he got to Windward and Shaelyn, the more his spirits lifted.

Before he'd reined Irish to a stop, the front door burst open and Shaelyn flew into his arms the moment he dismounted. The feel of her arms around him, the scent of her hair as he nuzzled the top of her head, wiped away the last vestiges of his daylong headache. She gave him a kiss that threatened to melt his knees, then smiled up at him with mischief.

"Welcome home,'' she purred.

He bent his head and dotted kisses on her face.

"With a welcome home like this, I might be inspired to work in town more often.''

"Oh, no you don't.'' She took his hand and dragged him into the house. "I like our arrangement just the way it is.''

She had ordered dinner to be served in their rooms, and after a hot bath, in which she tormented him by helping him bathe, they settled down to feed each other their meal.

He smiled at this woman and thanked God yet again that He had delivered her to him. Where she came from didn't matter. Where she stayed meant the world.

After she fed him the last bite from her plate, she took him by both hands and pulled him toward the bed.

"Care for dessert?''

Her words erupted a dizzying tidal wave of want. He didn't need to answer her. She already worked at the buttons on his shirt, and he returned the favor by freeing the laces of her gown.

She shoved him onto the bed and pushed him to his back. He lay there, playing along with her little game, letting her have her way with him until he thought she would drive him mad. When he could stand no more, he rolled atop her and paid her back for her mischief until they both lay exhausted, satiated, euphoric, wrapped in each other's arms.

He tucked his chin and looked down at her.

"What is that misty look for?" he asked, his lips against her temple.

She sighed and cuddled closer. Alec thought she could curl right into his heart.

"I was just wondering what we'll name him."

"Name who?" He rubbed his cheek against the top of her head and wondered if she was too tired to . . .

He jerked his head back and stared down at her. She gave him an angelic little smile.

The unspoken words slammed into his brain, then rattled around in there like echoes off a seacliff wall. A baby? A baby!

A thousand emotions raced through him. Shock. Joy. Stark terror. Fear for Shaelyn.

Was he equal to the task of being a father? Would he crush the spirit from his children as his father had tried to do? Would Shaelyn have the problems Griffin's wife had had?

A baby!

His head swam with visions of Shaelyn, swollen with his child, of her straining to push it into the world, of him holding the tiny evidence of their love. Riding him on his shoulders. Buying him a pony. Taking him fishing. Teaching him how to be a man.

His heart swelled and rose in his throat. He thought he

would burst from the love for this woman. He wrapped her in his arms, tried to pull her right into his very being.

"I love you," he whispered against her hair, too choked with emotion to utter more.

"And I love you," she whispered back, and then added, "Daddy."

His heart did a joyful somersault as he lowered his lips to hers.

Shaelyn hugged the chamber pot, laid her head against the cool porcelain, and wondered why in the world anyone would get pregnant a second time, knowing what they went through with the first.

Another wave of nausea hit her, but there was nothing left on her stomach. When she thought the worst was finally over, she stood on shaky legs and rinsed her mouth, brushed her teeth with their nasty tooth powder, rinsed again, then staggered to the bed for her third nap of the morning.

When Alec walked in, she almost groaned. Her morning sickness scared him to death. She couldn't convince him that it was completely normal. But he'd been so cute. A regular little mother hen. He wouldn't let her lift anything heavier than a sheet of paper and her ink pen. He nearly hand-fed her when he didn't think she'd eaten enough, even though she'd remind him that the bulk of the food would end up in the chamber pot. When he started making noises about moving their bedchamber into one of the downstairs parlors so she wouldn't have to climb the stairs, she'd put her foot down, reassuring him that the morning sickness should be over in a couple of months, and pointing out that if she didn't get enough exercise, she'd soon look like a beached whale.

"You've been sick again," he stated with his astute diagnosis of the obvious. Shaelyn just groaned at him and rolled over.

"You did this to me," she moaned, trying to keep her

face straight and the smile off her lips. Just having him this close put ideas into her head, now that she felt better.

He looked miserable when he sat on the edge of the bed and smoothed back her hair.

She smiled up at him. "Would you do it to me again?"

His look of misery turned into a playful glare.

"You are incorrigible."

She let her hands wander freely along the firm peaks and valleys of his body as she looked up at him through her lashes. "Did you say incorrigible, or *encourageable?*"

The words were no sooner out of her mouth than she found herself flat on her back.

"Never let it be said," he growled in her ear, "that I passed up a chance to *encourage* you."

A solid knock on the bedroom door had them cursing in unison.

Shaelyn repaired what little damage he'd had time to do to her gown, while Alec stomped to the door, muttering under his breath.

"What?" he barked as he yanked open the door.

Martin stood on the other side, his impassive face flaming.

"I am sorry to disturb you, sir, but a messenger came with this." He handed Alec an envelope. "He said he's not to leave until you've read it."

Alec ripped the paper open and scanned the contents.

"Tell him I'll leave before dawn. Send word to the *Zephyr* to prepare to set sail."

While Martin left to deliver the message, Shaelyn scrambled off the bed.

"Who's it from?"

Alec handed her the note. "It's from Griffin, Shae."

Her stomach did a little flip at this shortened use of her name. He didn't use it often, and she loved to hear him say it. She ignored the urge to drag him back to the bed.

The note simply said that Griffin needed Alec's help, and to come in his fastest ship.

"Well, that's rather cryptic. When do we leave?"

Alec took her face in his hands and kissed her once. "Not we. Just me."

This time her stomach flipped from alarm.

"What do you mean, just you? You can't take off on a trip to Louisiana without me! In this day and age it would probably take a month!"

She watched his jaw clench at her vague inference that she knew another time besides this one. He still wouldn't accept her story. She jerked away from his hands and glared at him.

"Shaelyn, whatever the reason, Griffin's need is urgent, and probably dangerous. We shall be traveling with all haste, and I have no idea what to expect along the way. And you're with child! I'll not let you take a chance with your health."

She narrowed her eyes and dug in her heels. There was no way he was getting out of here without her.

"Pregnancy is not a disease, Alec."

He sighed and pulled her onto his lap when he sat down.

"Shaelyn, I have to go. Griffin would not send a message like that if it were not urgent. But please do not ask me to be distracted by worry for you from what needs to be done. If it weren't for the baby, I would carry you on board myself. But you've been so ill every day. I cannot imagine that a sea voyage in hurricane season would be conducive to your health."

He looked so miserable, so torn, that Shaelyn knew she couldn't ask him to take her. He was already beside himself with worry, having only Griffin's stories of his wife's miscarriages as a basis of knowledge. Every time she so much as sneezed, Alec wanted to fluff pillows around her and build her a little nest.

"Oh, all right," she sighed. He gave her a little-boy smile that melted her heart. Would this baby wrap her around its little finger as its father had done?

He gave her a long, slow kiss, then scooped her up and

carried her to the bed. He untied her lacing, unfastened a couple of his buttons, then hovered over her, his lips against her neck.

"Now. Where were we?"

Shaelyn stood on the dock blinking back tears, her stomach twisting in knots, her heart in her throat as the men loaded Alec's trunks onto the ship.

Ghostly gray fingers of dawn crept across the inky horizon, but she knew that before the sun could begin to rise above the waters, Alec and the ship would be long gone.

"Don't do that," he whispered, then kissed away one lone little tear that had found its way onto her cheek. Her combination laugh-sob only sent another one spilling over her lashes. "I don't want to carry with me the memory of you crying." He wiped away the second tear with his thumb, then tilted her face to his. "I want to dwell on that mischievous smile of yours. That outrageous twinkle in your eyes."

She ducked her head and took a deep breath. She would *not* cry when he left.

Blinking her eyes dry, she raised her gaze to his, the best fake smile she'd ever managed pasted across her face.

"How's this? Mischievous enough for you?"

He laughed, but she could tell his heart wasn't in it, any more than hers was in that plastic grin.

"Mr. Hawthorne." The captain nodded that they were ready to sail.

She *would not* cry.

"Here," she managed to choke out, then handed Alec the last four Dramamine. "That's all I have. Make them last."

He took the blister pack from her fingers, then brought her hand to his lips and kissed the center of her palm.

"I love you," he whispered, his voice almost hoarse.

She swallowed, blinked, choked on unborn tears.

"I love you more."

He crushed her to him, brought his mouth down on hers. She clung to him, trying to absorb the taste, the feel, the smell of him; something to pull out and remember while she waited for him to return.

Finally, reluctantly, he raised his head.

"I'll be home as soon as I can," he whispered.

She smiled and nodded once, not trusting her voice to behave.

He placed his hand low on her flat stomach, above where the baby nestled.

"You take care of little Bubba."

His unexpected humor brought a laugh to her lips and a sting to her eyes. She swallowed hard and nodded.

He kissed her on the forehead, the nose, the mouth, then wheeled around and marched up the gangplank, taking her heart with him.

The moment he reached the deck, the captain gave the order to cast off.

Shaelyn stood where he'd left her and watched the ship set sail. Alec stood at the rail, staring back.

Not until he was too far away to see did she let herself cry. And when the tears came, the sobs racked her body until she knelt on her knees and curled into herself.

A silent Martin put his arms around her and held her like a father, and then he and Ned helped her into the carriage and took her home.

Chapter 20

"WHEN DO YOU expect him home?" Molly sipped her tea and took another bite of her biscuit. Shaelyn's stomach lurched at the sight. A month had passed since Alec left, an endless, lonely month, and still the morning sickness plagued her.

"His message said he'd be heading home within a few days, so, God willing, it shouldn't take him much longer to get here than it took the message."

"So, my dear brother might be home before the end of October. I must admit, I have missed him and his badgering." She smiled at Shaelyn and gave her a playful smirk. "But I'll deny it if you tell him."

Molly slathered a thick layer of butter onto her biscuit, then added a generous dollop of jam. The moment the girl's even, white teeth sank into it, Shaelyn's stomach rebelled. She muttered, "Excuse me," then made a dash for the stairs.

"Shaelyn!" Molly yelped.

Shae wondered if it were possible to wear out a chamber pot. She'd thought several times that the pink painted roses looked a bit faded where she usually held on with a death grip.

"Shaelyn!" Molly called from the doorway as Shae retched again. She ignored her sister-in-law and concentrated on not throwing up a vital organ.

"Oooh," she moaned. A heavenly cool wet cloth fell across her neck, then Molly handed her another and told her to put it on her throat.

"Why on earth did you not tell me?" Molly asked when Shaelyn sat back on her heels. The girl's eyes literally glittered with excitement.

Shaelyn dabbed at her face and took a deep breath.

"At first I wasn't sure, and then when I was, I guess I was afraid I'd jinx myself."

"Oh, Shaelyn, this is wonderful. You and Alec. Parents! Oh, my goodness! I'll be an aunt." She flopped into the bedside chair, then jumped to the edge. "Does Alec know?"

Shaelyn smiled and nodded as she got to her feet to pour a tumbler of water.

"I told him about a week before he left." She smiled at the memory and her hand automatically went to her stomach. "I think I scared him to death."

Molly giggled. "I can well believe that. And I can just see him trying not to let it show."

"Oh, you know your brother well."

"Speaking of brothers," Molly chattered while Shaelyn brushed her teeth, "Father received a message from Charles. He and Mary will be returning from their wedding trip in a few days. I believe they visited every country in Europe, they've been gone so long."

"Wonderful. I'm anxious to get to know them, if your father will let them near me."

"Oh, I think Father's days of ruling his sons are over."

About time, Shaelyn wanted to say. Instead she took Molly's arm and walked with her downstairs. Martin was just coming out of the parlor.

"Mr. Sheffield is here, ma'am. I told him Mr. Alec is away, but he said he would speak with you."

What did Alec's lawyer want with her?

At Shaelyn's invitation, Molly followed her into the parlor. Lawrence Sheffield rose from his chair when they entered.

"Mr. Sheffield, it's nice to see you again." He took her hand and brushed his lips against her knuckles.

"The pleasure is all mine, I assure you. And Miss Hawthorne, how are you this fine afternoon?"

"I am exceedingly well, sir," Molly answered. "And yourself?"

"Fit as a fiddle." He slapped his hands against his waistcoat. "My Lori keeps me hopping."

"Would you like some tea?" Shaelyn asked as she sank into a chair. Her knees had not quite recovered from that last bout with the chamber pot.

"No, no, my dear. I came by to deliver some good news." He fished a packet of papers from his pocket and handed them to Shaelyn. "There was no need to file for the divorce. Your annulment has been granted."

Shaelyn's heart stopped beating in her chest and the papers fluttered to the floor from numb fingers.

"But Alec stopped the proceedings. He sent you a message the day after we returned from the voyage."

Lawrence frowned and shook his head in denial. "I never received a message from Alec, my dear."

Her breath caught in her throat. The room suddenly grew hot, stifling. A white haze clouded her vision and muddled her thoughts, right before she slid to the carpet in a dead faint.

Molly had all but moved back in with her. She stayed there all day nearly every day, and returned home only to sleep. Shaelyn didn't know how Molly was getting around *Der Fuehrer*, but she was eternally grateful to have her around.

The news that she and Alec were no longer married—

indeed, in the eyes of the law had never *been* married—
had thrown her into a tailspin until Molly simply suggested
that they could marry again when Alec returned. Amazing,
how being upset can muddy the simplest solutions.

"Are we going to the docks today?" Molly put down
the book she'd been reading and looked to Shaelyn for her
answer. They'd been going to the docks nearly every day,
awaiting word on Alec's ship, or, please God, the ship
itself.

Shaelyn nodded. "I thought we might go to the inn for
lunch, if my stomach's on it's best behavior."

It had been nearly two weeks since she'd gotten Alec's
message that he would leave within days. She figured he
had to be arriving any day now, and she wanted to be
standing on the dock when his ship came into sight.

The sound of a horse galloping up the drive drew Shaelyn to the window.

Alec!

"Oh, Molly! He's home!"

She tossed her pen atop the journal she'd been writing
in and flew to the door and onto the drive. And then her
heart sank in her chest.

Charles, not Alec, dismounted in front of the house. She
fought back tears of disappointment. She'd grown fond of
Alec's brother and his wife since their return. Perhaps
Charles brought news of the ship.

"Good morning, Charles." She tried to sound happy to
see him. "Have you heard from Alec?"

Charles took her arm and led her toward the house.

"Let's go in and sit down," he said, all but pulling her
up the porch steps.

Shaelyn followed, then dug in her heels in the parlor
when she realized Charles had not once looked at her.

"What is it? What's happened?"

Charles scrubbed his eyes with the palm of his hand,
just like his older brother.

"Please sit down, Shaelyn."

Alarm bells rang in her head. "I'll sit down when you tell me what's wrong."

Charles finally raised his head and looked at her with eyes red-rimmed and full of pain.

"No!" She sank into the nearest chair, her heart in her throat, a buzzing in her ears.

"His ship went down," Charles choked through tears. "There were no survivors."

"No," Shaelyn whispered, her heart ripping from her chest, her head shaking in denial. No survivors. No survivors. "You're wrong," she insisted. The humming grew louder in her ears.

Molly had buried her face in Charles's chest, sobbing uncontrollably. Shaelyn wanted to tell her to stop it. That Charles was mistaken.

He took a slip of paper from his coat and handed it to Shaelyn. One paragraph leapt out at her.

It is confirmed that the ship the Zephyr, *of Hawthorne Shipping, went down with all hands off the east coast of the Territory of Florida during a hurricane. Five unidentified bodies recovered. Will ship to Cape Helm, Maine, on next ship north.*

"Noooo!" The wail seemed to come from somewhere outside her, but her mind screamed the word of denial. She crumpled the paper in her fist, then wrapped her arms around her stomach, rocking back and forth, letting the sobs well up from the deepest part of her soul.

He couldn't be dead. Not Alec. Not someone so full of life. Not now that they'd found each other.

Images of him being battered by the storm flashed in her mind. Of the deck slipping below the water, of him struggling in a thrashing sea. Of him nuzzling her neck. Kissing her stomach. Talking to the baby.

Oh, God, no! No!

The tears came, faster than they could spill onto her

cheeks, burning her eyes and dragging the agony in her soul up with them.

Masculine arms pulled her against a hard chest. She turned into Charles and wept into his shoulder. Wept for the love she had lost, for the love she would never know, for the man whose arms she ached to be in.

She cried so hard she feared she would lose the baby. She calmed herself, held the pain inside until she could deal with it better. She couldn't lose this tiny piece of Alec. The fruit of the tender love they'd shared.

"I'll be fine." Her voice caught on the words as she sat up and dried her eyes with the back of her hands. Numbness settled over her brain like a thick blanket of fog. The welcome numbness allowed her to let Charles help her rise and guide her up the stairs to the bedroom. She heard a sobbing Molly call for Martin, and then murmuring voices followed by Martin's agonized gasp.

She couldn't listen anymore. She couldn't listen to others mourn her husband when she felt as if she could never mourn him enough herself.

She curled up on the bed and denied Charles's suggestion to have Margaret sit with her. She just wanted to be left alone with her misery.

When the door shut quietly, closing her off from the world, she dragged a pillow to her and wrapped her arms around it. The pillow smelled like Alec, even though the bedding had been changed. The scent brought fresh tears to her eyes and she buried her face in its softness, breathed in the perfume that was the essence of the man she loved.

How could he do this to her? How could he die when she loved him so much? When they had their whole lives ahead of them? How could she bear this life without him?

Shaelyn sat in the church, dressed in black from head to toe, flanked by Molly on one side and Charles and Mary on the other. William and Jane sat across the aisle, William, for a change, subdued, with the appearance of actually mourning his son. He even held his grieving wife's hand and patted it on occasion.

Shaelyn blocked out the words of the minister. She couldn't sit there and listen to him talk about Alec being dead. There was no body to bury, no grave to visit, nothing tangible to help her through the grieving process. Just this memorial service.

Charles had viewed the five recovered bodies and sworn that none of them was Alec. There had been over twenty men on the ship. At least fifteen other families were going through this as well—bidding farewell to a loved one whose grave was miles and miles of saltwater.

Charles stirred beside her and held her elbow. The service must be over. She rose and let him guide her down the aisle. A sob broke from her throat. She'd never walked down the aisle with Alec. And now, as she viewed that space through the black haze of her mourning veil, she realized she wasn't even a widow in the eyes of the law.

The knife that had pierced her heart for days now twisted with a vengeance. She leaned on Charles and would have given in to the wracking pain if not for some of Alec's last words to her, ringing in her mind.

Don't do that, he'd whispered. *I don't want to carry with me the memory of you crying. I want to dwell on that mischievous smile of yours. That outrageous twinkle in your eyes.*

She blinked back the ever-present burning and straightened her shoulders. She would never tell him good-bye. But when she left this church and the service in his memory, somehow she would walk out with a smile beneath her veil.

She thought the people would never leave. They filtered through the house for hours, extending their condolences, reminiscing about Alec. They thought they were helping ease her pain, and maybe if she and Alec had shared a long life together the stories might have helped. But she'd only had him to herself for little more than two months, barely time to build her own memories. She didn't even know these people.

She shook her head and told herself to be strong.

Molly, Charles, and Mary had stayed by her every minute. William and Jane had even come for a while, but Shaelyn could tell that William was there strictly for appearances. They had left when Jane broke down in tears.

Lawrence Sheffield entered the room with a tiny, porcelain-doll woman on his arm. He towered over her like a lumbering bear.

"Shaelyn, my dear, this is my wife, Lori."

The woman gave her a sympathetic smile and patted her hand. "I am so sorry, dear."

"Thank you," Shaelyn repeated for the millionth time that day.

Sheffield knelt beside her on the floor, and still she had to look up into his eyes.

"I know this is a terrible time, my dear, but I feel I must speak to you in private."

Shaelyn had a feeling she didn't want to hear this conversation, but at least it would give her a break from the never-ending condolences. She rose and led the way to the library. The scent of Alec still clung to the air in the room, tugging at her heart. She swallowed hard.

Lawrence waited until she'd seated herself before he began.

"William questioned me about the annulment today. Considering the legalities involved with the dispensation of Alec's property and the fact that he had no will, I had to admit to him that the annulment had been granted."

Shaelyn took a deep breath and released it. "Don't worry about it, Lawrence. You had no choice."

"You realize what he's planning, do you not?"

She closed her eyes and nodded. "He's going to take Alec's property under the grounds that we weren't married."

Lawrence nodded. "He is within his rights," he said, "but not within the bounds of honor, as far as I'm concerned."

She looked at the kindhearted attorney and decided to unload some of her burden.

"I'm pregnant, Lawrence."

The man's eyes widened and he bowed his head.

"It happened after we spoke to you. We realized we loved each other and only then did we consummate the marriage. We were so happy, and we thought you'd stopped the annulment proceedings."

"This doesn't surprise me, my dear. And you'd have been damned fools not to recognize that love. But promise me one thing."

Shaelyn nodded her promise.

"Don't tell William you are with child."

The implications of his warning shocked Shaelyn to the core.

"Molly's the only one who knows. William will find out only when I can no longer hide it."

He patted her hands and walked to the door. "You're exhausted, child. Stay in here and rest, and I will dispel this crowd in my own charming way."

She gave him a weary smile. "I love you."

Shaelyn stared at the grandfather of her baby and wondered how such a bastard could have a son as wonderful as Alec.

Just a matter of days had passed since the memorial service, but William had wasted no time in evicting her from the house. He had just given her notice that he wanted her out by the end of the week.

She stood, officially ending their meeting. "I will be gone by morning," she said as she walked to the door. She turned, unable to resist her parting shot. "And you will never lay eyes on your grandchild." She gave him a level look and lowered her hand to her stomach.

He leapt to his feet, veins bulging, but she merely turned her back and closed the door. By the time he stormed out of his office, Shaelyn's carriage was two blocks away.

She had said her good-byes to everyone, though they would not know it until they found her letters.

She walked through the house, touching things that Alec had touched. When she was done she wrapped a shawl around her shoulders, picked up a small oil lamp, and took her time walking to where they'd spent those first endless, blissful days of making love.

The early November air had turned cold and the leaves on the trees blazed during the day, but now they were waving black shadows against a nearly full moon. Alec would have pointed them out to her, and they would have leaned against each other and watched them for a while. He would have rested his chin on her head and hugged her to him . . .

She bit the inside of her cheek and blinked away the burning in her eyes.

She let herself into the guest cottage in a swirl of dried leaves. The quiet parlor welcomed her like an old friend after a long absence. She moved around the room, looking out at the view one last time, dragging her fingertips across the desk where she'd written her first article for Samuel and started her journal detailing her thoughts.

She moved to the stairway and climbed the steps to the bedroom where the tiny life within her had been conceived. The dim light of the lamp fell across the frilly bed, and she could almost see Alec lying there, waiting for her.

A sob rose in her chest. His spirit still lived in this room. Their love would forever haunt the confines of Harbor Mist. She willed it to be so.

With a calm that surprised her, she set the lamp on the table and curled up on the bed.

"I'm going home, sweetheart," she told the spirit of her husband. "Your father will try to take our baby if I stay."

She grasped the ring on her finger. "I won't let him do that. And without you here, I have no reason to stay."

She closed her eyes and took a deep breath.

"I love you, Alec. I will love you forever." She swallowed the tears clogging her throat and tried to ease the pain in her chest with a shaky breath. "Wait for me."

She pulled the ring from her finger. It slid free with such ease that it flew from her hand and clattered to the floor.

"No!"

She tried to scramble from the bed, but already the vertigo struck with such force it pinned her to the mattress. The world swirled around her in a nauseating kaleidoscope of shadows. Forces she couldn't see buffeted her, and then suddenly she felt a rough wooden floor beneath her hands.

She opened her eyes and looked around, recognizing the companionway of the ship where she'd found the ring. She was on her hands and knees, in the same position as when she'd slipped the band on her finger. The dim light from the oil lamps illuminated the black scorched floodlight on the wall.

A door opened above and the companionway filled with light as she rose to her feet.

"Hey there, missy. The groom's waitin'."

Chapter 21

SHAELYN STARED AT Pete in his fraying knitted cap. He scanned her from head to toe and gave a low whistle.

"They went all out for that costume, didn't they? I may just take the groom's place, the way you look in it."

All she could do was stand there and blink.

"Hey, don't tell me you've got stage fright. All you gotta do is stand there and say 'I do.' "

It couldn't be possible! Had she traveled back to the same moment she'd left? Had she traveled back to July twenty-ninth?

The baby!

She clamped her hands to her abdomen. Was she still pregnant?

She felt the same tiny bulge that had been there just that morning, which reassured her somewhat. But the first thing she planned to do was go in search of a pregnancy test.

"You all right there, missy?" Pete started down the steps, but Shaelyn shook her head.

"I . . . I'm all right, Pete. I'll be there in a minute. I just dropped something. Would you leave the door open?"

"Sure thing."

When he disappeared out the door, Shaelyn whirled around and searched the floor for any sign of the ring. She scanned every corner, got down on her hands and knees and searched every crack and crevice, hoping against hope she would find it wedged where she had found it before. All she found was her notebook and recorder.

With a heart that felt as if it were ripping in two, she slowly rose to her feet. Not only had she lost Alec, but she'd lost that which had taken her to him. And now she had to go through the ceremony that had started it all. Could she bear to stand there in a mockery of what she and Alec had done?

She closed her eyes and took a deep, fortifying breath. She was back in 1999. She had a job to do. She needed to make money for herself and the baby. She would do this, and then she would write about it.

And then she would cry it out of her system.

She lifted her skirts and climbed the steep steps with the ease of someone with experience. When she stepped onto the deck, a crowd of tourists turned to watch her, and she saw her first glimpse of the twentieth century in more than two months.

Pete came up to meet her and escorted her toward the crowd. One by one the tourists moved out of her way until they parted to reveal the captain and the back of a tall man with shiny black hair.

Her heart nearly exploded in her chest. She stumbled and Pete tightened his grip on her arm.

"Alec!" she cried.

The man turned to her, a question on his face, recognition absent from his eyes.

He wasn't Alec. He didn't even come close.

She took a deep, quivering breath and stared at the furled sails, willing the tears away. Somehow she found herself standing next to the man. The captain launched into the mock ceremony in a booming voice using names she'd

never heard of. She repeated her vows like a robot, giving
him her hand when instructed to do so. Eventually he
leaned over and gave her an embarrassed peck on the
cheek, then led her to the gangplank and off the ship amid
a round of applause.

He said something to her, his voice indistinguishable
above the roaring in her ears. She looked at him and forced
a smile, mumbling something in response. When he left
her and returned to the ship, she turned and headed for her
condo, ignoring the strange looks people gave her gown.

She needed to get home. She needed to see her parents.
To see Bri. She needed to go somewhere and try to heal
this pain that time would never erase.

"I've made you an appointment with a doctor, sugar. I
think it's time you saw one."

Louisa Sumner handed her a slip of paper with the name
Dr. Stetler, and the date of August thirtieth at 1:30. Shaelyn finished writing out her check to the children's home
to cover all her curses within the past several months.
She'd lost count of her "balance," so she figured five
thousand dollars ought to do it. She sealed the check in an
envelope, slapped a stamp on it, then picked up the slip of
paper. The name wasn't familiar.

"This isn't Dr. Noble, Mom. I have an appointment
with him next week."

Her mother shifted in her chair at the kitchen table in
Shaelyn's Baton Rouge home.

"This one's not an obstetrician, Shae. He's a psychiatrist."

"Damn it, Mother." Shae tossed the paper back onto
the table. "I'm not crazy. I'm not imagining this. If you
don't believe me, that's fine, but I'm not going to a shrink
so he can pump me full of anti-delusion drugs."

"Just talk to him, Shaelyn. Even if it's just about those
nightmares that have come back."

"No!"

She scraped her chair back and stood.

"I come home to find comfort with my family, and all I get from you and Dad and Bri are raised eyebrows and offers to have me committed. Everything I told you is true! I lived in 1830, I married the man of my dreams, and he is the father of this baby!"

"Shaelyn, we spoke to you just five days ago!"

"I already told you . . . Oh, never mind. I don't blame you for not believing me. I wouldn't if I were in your place. But I will never, I repeat, *never*, see a psychiatrist about it."

She shoved her chair to the table and turned to leave.

"Shaelyn, where are you going?"

She waved her hand as she walked out of the room.

"I'm going back to Maine, to find proof that what I've said is true."

Why she didn't think of this before, she didn't know. Her only excuse was that her mind had been numb with grief.

She rubbed the tiny bulge beneath her jeans. "Come on, little Bubba. We're off to the courthouse."

She found her way to the office that held the records of Cape Helm's births, deaths, and marriages. It didn't take her any time at all to find the record of marriage between one Alec Hawthorne and one Shaelyn Sumner, joined in holy matrimony on the twenty-ninth day of July, in the year of our Lord, 1830.

Tears flooded her eyes at the sight and the unexpected ease with which she'd found the record. An ache grew in her chest and she let the tears flow free, sitting there at the microfiche viewer.

"Are you all right, ma'am?" a young clerk in a bow tie asked.

She chewed her lower lip and swiped at her eyes.

"Yes. I'm fine. I just found what I'm looking for."

He peered at the screen, took one more long look at her, then walked away.

While she had the records open, she decided to scan the next few years and see if there were records on Molly and Charles.

She found nothing on Molly, but she discovered that Charles and Mary had had four boys and three girls in the space of eight years.

"Criminy, Charles," she muttered with a watery smile. "You should have given the girl a breather."

With a little reticence, she scanned the death records to see how long *Der Fuehrer* had lived to torment his other children. She found the record much sooner than she'd expected.

> *William Charles Hawthorne*
> *b. Feb. 15, 1775*
> *d. Feb. 17, 1832 of natural causes*

So, nobody ever got around to killing him. She read on.

> *Survived by wife, Jane Elkin Hawthorne, sons Alec Christopher Hawthorne and Charles Elkin Hawthorne, and daughter Molly Ann Hawthorne.*

The words jumped off the screen and slammed into her brain.

Survived by Alec Christopher Hawthorne!

Oh, my God! *Oh, dear God!* Had he survived? Was this a mistake in the records?

Heat tingled across her neck and up the back of her spine. The room spun for a moment and she thought her heart would explode in her chest.

She put the microfiche back in their holders, shoved them into the bow-tied clerk's hands, then ran from the building and didn't stop until she got to the library.

"Newspaper articles from 1830," she panted to the librarian. "Do you have them on microfiche?"

The plump little lady with her short helmet of hair

slowly shook her head no. Shaelyn wanted to scream.

"We've put them all on CD-ROM."

Shaelyn could have kissed her.

The woman took a maddeningly long time to find the disk she was looking for.

"Now you put this in the little drawer on the left and—"

Shaelyn grabbed the CD from the woman's hands and ran for the computer bank.

"I know how, thanks," she called over her shoulder.

She dashed to the nearest computer, which had a teen-ager browsing the web. The next had an eleven-year-old playing a video game. At the third, a mother with two children hanging on her arm tried desperately to look up something between whines.

Shaelyn was going to physically remove one of the people if she didn't find a computer.

That, or commit homicide.

A free computer fell into her line of vision and she ran to it with all the determination of a quarterback going for the goal line. Woe to anyone who got in her way.

She slid into the seat just as a gum-popping teenage girl put her hand on the back of the chair.

"Sorry," Shaelyn said while she dropped the CD into the drawer. "I'm in a hurry."

"What*ever*," the girl huffed in irritated teenage-ese.

Shaelyn bypassed all the months leading up to November 1830. She found the article reporting the sinking of the *Zephyr* and the deaths of all onboard, including the ship's owner and pillar of the community, Alec Hawthorne. She'd read that a hundred and sixty-nine years ago.

The next article froze the blood in her veins. It was written two days after she'd left.

LOCAL SHIPOWNER ALIVE

Alec Hawthorne, reported lost at sea after his ship went down during a hurricane, arrived in Cape Helm yesterday, shocking his family as well as the community.

He reported having become ill early in his voyage home and disembarked on the tip of the peninsula that makes up the Territory of Florida, to recover from his illness and continue his journey overland.

Shaelyn laughed out loud. He'd been seasick! A chorus of "*Shhh*s" sent her back to reading.

Hawthorne's homecoming proved to be bittersweet, however. He was shocked to learn of the loss of the ship and its men, but most upsetting is the mysterious disappearance of his bride of three months, Shaelyn Sumner Hawthorne. She had been missing for little more than a day when Hawthorne returned from the grave. It is said that Mrs. Hawthorne was despondent over the loss of her husband, and the family fears . . .

The words blurred in front of Shaelyn's eyes, and blood roared in her ears.

He was alive! And she was here. Molly knew the truth, but Alec would never believe her. She had to get to him. She had to put the ring back on and go—

The ring! Oh, dear God. The ring.

Why, *why* had she taken off the ring? If she had waited just twenty-four hours, she would be in his arms right now, the happiest woman on earth.

She had to find the ring.

Yanking the CD from the computer, she raced to the desk and shoved it into the nearest clerk's hands, then ran out the door and back to her condo.

Bills, shopping lists, and newspapers went airborne as she searched for the phone book.

She tore the list of antique dealers and jewelers out of the Yellow Pages. You couldn't walk ten feet in that part of Maine without stumbling into an antique store, and she would comb every one of them, as well as any jeweler who dealt in antique jewelry, looking for her ring.

Five days later she had visited every place of business on that list, plus some others, and no one had ever seen a ring of that kind.

She was dangerously close to being clinically depressed.

She needed a break. She would go back to the courthouse and the library, get copies of the marriage record and the newspaper article, and then go home to Baton Rouge and try to clear her head and come up with another plan.

There had to be another way to find that ring.

Griffin stood in the doorway to Alec's library, glaring. He had sailed in just a day after Alec's arrival, in mourning and prepared for a funeral.

"Drinking won't bring her back, Hawthorne."

Alec waved him off. "I appreciate it, Grif, but I need to be alone right now."

Griffin started to speak, but instead just shook his head and closed the door behind him.

Alec poured another drink and tossed the contents down his throat in one swig. He waited for the blessed numbness to creep into his brain, cloud his thoughts and give a few longed-for moments of forgetfulness.

So far it hadn't worked.

A week had gone by since his return to Cape Helm. He had thought of nothing on the trip overland save holding Shaelyn in his arms and never letting her go. He'd also vowed never to set foot on a ship again.

His seasickness had increased in direct proportion to the storms around them. Finally, when he'd grown so weak he could barely rise, he'd swallowed his pride and instructed Captain Hancock to put him ashore before they had to bury him at sea. Though the waters had been rough, never had he dreamed that the ship would go down just days after they left him on dry land.

And then to return, not only to find Shaelyn gone, but to discover that they were no longer married, and that his father had ordered her out of Alec's house.

That very day Alec had spoken to Lawrence Sheffield and ordered what he had built of the business to be separated from Hawthorne Shipping. He would not work another day, let alone earn another cent, for the man who had treated his wife so heartlessly.

And she *was* his wife, no matter what the law declared.

He scrubbed his eyes with the palm of his hand, then dragged it down to rasp against his days-old beard. He had barely eaten or slept since his return, let alone bothered to shave.

Where the hell could she be?

He, Griffin, and the men he'd hired had ridden much farther than she'd had an opportunity to travel, checking every direction, every place of lodging, every means of conveyance: ships, coach lines, railroads. He'd even checked livery stables for a woman meeting her description hiring a horse.

And what had she taken? Margaret had inspected Shaelyn's wardrobe and declared that the only clothing missing was what she'd worn the day she'd disappeared. Indeed, the little maid had found some very odd-looking apparel stuffed into a boot that could only be a very abbreviated version of undergarments. One more mystery to add to the enigma that was his wife.

And then they'd found the ring, lying in the middle of the floor in the bedroom of the guest cottage. That alone caused his heart to shift in his chest.

He'd demanded in those early days that she remove the ring, and he had witnessed her trying desperately to do so, even when she didn't know he watched her. How did she get it off? And why did she leave it behind?

He raked his hands through his hair, then slammed his fist against the desk.

She loved him, damn it.

A growing fear, the seed of which had been planted days ago, took root against all his efforts to stop it.

Molly and Charles—indeed, everyone who had paid their respects—had told him how the news of his death had devastated her.

Had she taken her own life?

Even now he had men watching the shoreline for her body, and had a litany in his head praying they would find nothing.

He wouldn't believe it. He *couldn't* believe it and live with himself.

Of course, Molly chose to believe another story. He'd read the letters Shaelyn had written to everyone. All of them saying good-bye. Only Molly's had more details. Shaelyn had told her she was returning to her own time. The ring had suddenly decided to slip from her finger, and she would return to her time and her family rather than allow William to try to win custody of their child and make its life as miserable as he had made everyone else's.

Molly was convinced this was fact. Alec was convinced it was a desperate, far-fetched attempt to confuse any search his father might have made for her.

The library door burst open and bounced off the wall. He expected to see his father in the doorway, and he prepared to physically remove him, but Molly marched into the room, as ladylike as a raging bull. She slammed a leather-bound journal down in front of him.

"Read it."

He looked at the small book, then back to his sister.

"What is it?"

"It's Shaelyn's journal. I started reading it to see if she'd left a clue as to where she might have gone. This proves what I have insisted all along."

"Molly—"

"Read it!"

Rather than argue with her, he opened to the first page and read.

The journal gave Shaelyn's innermost thoughts. He watched her fall in love with him, and he agonized over how he'd hurt her at times. His heart ached when he realized how early she'd known she loved him, and he mourned the time he'd lost with her while refusing to acknowledge his own feelings. She devoted pages and pages to how she wished he would believe she was from the future. How she wanted to tell him about cars and airplanes, men walking on the moon, microwaves, genetic engineering, cloning, computers, telephones, e-mail. The list grew as he turned the pages. When he finally read the last entry, he closed the book.

"Well?" she demanded, all signs of his playful little sister gone.

He looked up at Molly and stared at her, his stomach twisted in a sick knot.

"This proves nothing."

She yanked up the journal and waved it under his nose.

"How can you say that? Why would she write these things when she thought no one would ever read them?"

"What did she write, Molly? That she loved me? That she was blissfully happy? I already knew that. But what are those other things she wrote about? Those things from the future she wanted to share with me? The only 'thing' she mentioned that I could understand was men walking on the moon. For God's sake, Molly, think about it. The only way to interpret that is that she is claiming that people have traveled to the moon and walked upon its surface! Why in the world would she make such a preposterous claim?"

"Why indeed?" Molly yelled at him. "Unless it were true. Any person in their right mind would never make a claim such as that unless they could somehow prove it!"

His jaw popped when he clenched his teeth.

"And where is her proof?"

He thought for a moment she might slap him. She literally quivered with rage.

"All right, answer me this." She slapped both hands onto the desk and leaned so close to him he could see his reflection in her eyes. "How is it that Shaelyn told me, in August, that the steam engine *Tom Thumb* would race a horse to Baltimore, but the engine wouldn't finish the race because of a mechanical problem? I am sure you read about it in the newspapers, but Shaelyn told me what would happen weeks before the race. And how did she know the town is going to bury a time capsule, as she calls it? They just announced their decision to do that last week."

Alec shook his head, amazed at his sister's gullibility.

"That would not be hard to guess. Those engines have never been reliable. Or perhaps Shaelyn is gifted with the Sight. I can believe she could foretell the future before I can believe she traveled from there."

Molly glared at him through eyes shining with tears, a resentment in her gaze he'd never seen before. She shoved away from the desk and marched to the door, then turned and pierced him with a look of disgusted pity.

"Shaelyn would never take your baby's life. And did it ever occur to you that you've never heard of those things in her journal because they haven't been invented? Think with your heart, Alec, not your mind."

She closed the door before Alec could tell her that Shaelyn had taken his heart with her when she left.

Chapter 22

SHAELYN FOUND LITTLE comfort in the fact that Brianne and her parents believed her now. They'd done so with a lingering amount of skepticism, until her father had left on an unheard-of "business trip" and returned with a new attitude toward her story. She had no doubt he'd followed her footsteps to the Cape Helm courthouse and library. She couldn't blame them, though.

They worried about her depression. Her mother still wanted her to see a counselor, to help her through her grief.

Shaelyn refused. She didn't want to accept her loss. She wanted it to spur her on to continue looking for her ring, though in the back of her mind she knew her quest was nearly hopeless. But if she gave up that hope, she would be giving up her hope for any happiness in life as well.

She'd made no secret of the fact that if she ever found the ring, no matter how long it took her, she would put it on and return to Alec. Her parents had nodded with tears in their eyes. They'd looked at each other with love and that unspoken language they'd always used, then told her that if she ever found the ring, she should waste no time in good-byes. "Don't take a chance on having it stolen or lost, princess," her dad had said. "You put it on and go to Alec."

With a lump in her throat she could barely swallow past, she'd agreed. But she'd also promised to try to find a way to come back and see them from time to time.

She came home in early September with the proof of her and Alec's marriage, then spent the next four months grieving and angry at the world. Thanksgiving had been hard, but Christmas had been unbearable. She would have given ten years of her life to be spending the holidays curled in front of a fire with Alec, his head in her lap as he spoke nonsense to their baby.

She swallowed hard and smoothed her hand over the growing mound so precious to her. She would soon have to abandon her oversized clothes and move into bona fide maternity wear.

She wheeled the rental car into the parking lot of Cape Helm's quaint little inn. She'd very nearly chosen to stay in Baton Rouge for New Year's Eve, but the heart of the story that had taken her to Alec to begin with was the turning of the millennium in small-town America. She could hardly write the final installment of the article without being there for the event.

After checking in, she slogged back through the snow to her car and headed north on Route 1. She had decided on the plane ride to Portland that she would try to find Windward Cottage and, in one last-ditch effort, see if she could trace the ring from there.

It took her longer than she'd anticipated, but she found the house at the end of a road that wound toward the ocean through acres of dense trees.

The home loomed above the water, majestic as ever, its diamond-paned windows still glittering in the sun, the view as magnificent as the last time she'd seen it, one hundred and sixty-nine years ago. A sign swung from hooks in the front yard.

Windward Cottage Bed & Breakfast
Daniel and Bethany Hawthorne, proprietors

A wave of dizziness rocked Shaelyn to the core. Daniel Hawthorne. Was he a descendant of Charles? Or had Alec remarried? She could not even let herself think about that.

She pulled the car to a stop in front of the house and sat there, staring at the home so dear to her heart.

She had to see it. She had to walk once more through the rooms that had been filled with her and Alec's love.

A pretty, bright-eyed girl with flaming red hair answered her knock and invited her in.

"Would you like a room?" she asked, wiping her hands on a dish towel. "You'd pretty much have your pick. We don't get a lot of traffic this time of year."

Shaelyn forced a smile and looked around, swallowing back tears at all that looked familiar, and all that had been changed.

"I have a room at the inn in Cape Helm, but when I stumbled across this place, I thought I might stay here instead." She looked back at the girl with eyes the color of violets, subconsciously thinking those had to be contacts. "It's funny. I've spent summers here for years and never knew this place existed."

"Oh, we've only been in business a year, since my husband's father died. I'm Bethany Hawthorne, by the way."

Shaelyn took the girl's hand and wondered if she was looking at a very distant niece.

"Shaelyn Sumner. Do you mind if I look around?"

Bethany waved her toward the parlor. "Feel free. You have the run of the house. I have some bread baking that's about ready to come out of the oven, but I'll find you when I'm through and answer any questions."

Shaelyn walked from room to room, fighting back tears and watching vignettes of her and Alec playing in her mind. By the time Bethany found her, it was all Shaelyn could do to keep the tears at bay.

"How do you like our humble home?" Bethany bustled into the bedroom Molly had used.

Shae smiled but bit hard on the inside of her cheek.

"I can tell it's had lots of happy memories."

"Oh, yes. Daniel grew up here. He loves the place, and so do I."

Shaelyn narrowed her eyes and gave her a curious look.

"Hawthorne. I researched the Hawthorne family in the area once. Did your husband descend from Alec or Charles Hawthorne?"

Bethany visibly searched her mind, then shook her head.

"I couldn't really say. Probably. He could tell you, but he's in town, helping prepare for the festivities tonight. They really plan to do this New Year's Eve up right."

Shaelyn nodded, not wanting to even think of any more holidays without Alec.

"Do you have any other rentals on the property?"

Bethany looked at her with surprise.

"As a matter of fact, there's a little cottage about an eighth of a mile up the shore. It used to be the guest house. It's really popular with couples. Has a personality all its own. It just seems to breathe with a sense of . . . I don't know . . . love. You probably think I'm crazy. But Daniel and I loved it so much we spent our wedding night there."

Shaelyn turned the sob that escaped her throat into a delicate cough.

"Could I possibly see it?"

Bethany studied her, then her eyes softened.

"Sure. I'll get the key and you can give yourself the tour. I can't leave the ovens for long."

Shaelyn felt the ghosts the moment she walked through the front door of Harbor Mist. Little had changed except the weathered aging of the house. The furniture, though of course different, was the same style. The colors were nearly the same. The paint scheme the same. The house had been updated with plumbing and a furnace, but the essence of the cottage remained wonderfully old.

She took the stairs to the bedroom, thinking of how recently she'd climbed them last, yet it had been seventeen decades ago.

The ghosts hit her full force at the top of the stairs. Alec's smiling face appeared in her mind as clearly as if he stood before her. She could almost feel his arms around her, his lips on hers. The modern bed that stood where their wedding bed had stood beckoned her, and she could not resist going to it, smoothing her hands across the bedspread.

The pain raged, a living, scorching ball that burned in the depths of her soul.

She'd thought coming back would comfort her, but it had only poured salt on the raw, angry wounds that threatened never to heal.

She rushed from the cottage, shoving away the ghosts that only caused more pain. By the time she reached the terrace at Windward, the tears had nearly frozen on her cheeks. She paced until she calmed her thudding heart and her eyes watered only from the biting cold.

The warmth of the kitchen enveloped her like Alec's strong, warm arms. She sucked in a fortifying breath of air scented with freshly baked bread, then handed the key to Bethany.

"Your home is wonderful," Shaelyn told her, meaning every word. But then she hedged, not wanting to hurt the woman's feelings, but knowing she could never bear spending a night in either house. "I'll check with the inn and see if they'll let me out of the rest of my reservation tomorrow. Can I call you then and let you know?"

"Sure. That's no problem. As I said, we don't usually have to hang out our No Vacancy sign this time of year."

Shaelyn nodded and started out the back door, but then she stopped.

"By the way, I'm doing a story on interesting pieces of jewelry . . . I'm a journalist, if you haven't guessed." Bethany smiled. "Anyway, the article is about pieces of jewelry with a legend behind them: a curse, a spell, a good-luck charm. I heard about a ring just the other day connected with the Hawthorne name. Would you know anything about it?''

Bethany flopped onto a stool next to the counter.

"I didn't know anybody even remembered that old thing. An emerald-and-diamond ring, right?''

Shaelyn's heart leapt to her throat and pumped so hard she thought she would faint. Surely Bethany could hear it thundering in her chest.

"I believe so. Can you tell me more about it? Do you know what became of it?''

"There are several pieces in that set of jewelry. A bracelet, a necklace, earrings, a brooch. My mother-in-law has several of the pieces, but I'm not sure if she has the ring. Delores is a little . . . possessive about the jewelry. Refuses to talk about it. But if anyone has it, I'd guess it's with her other pieces in her safety deposit box at the Bank of Cape Helm. If not, she might know where it is.''

Delores Hawthorne. Where had Shaelyn heard that name? She racked her brain, and suddenly she could hear Pete telling her he'd talked to Delores Hawthorne, the town's historian.

Shaelyn nearly wept with relief. Had she found it?

"Do you suppose your mother-in-law would allow me to interview her about the ring? Perhaps take some pictures of her with it?''

If she could only get her hands on the ring, she would slip it on and then arrange for it to be handed down through the same family. It should reappear the moment Shaelyn went back to Alec.

Bethany tilted her head with skepticism.

"I wouldn't bet on it. She's a little freaky about the silly thing. She refuses to talk about it. Daniel's dad always told these wild stories of strange things happening to the people who wore the jewelry, and when he died and we had to get into the deposit box, she came with us, snatched the jewelry case from inside the minute we opened it, and held the thing until we locked the box back in the vault. When I asked her about it there at the bank, she opened the case only long enough for me to get a glimpse at a pile of jewelry, then snapped it shut and refused to say anything about it.'' Bethany shook her head with wonder. ''Delores isn't usually that . . . weird.''

Shaelyn refused to be defeated. Refused to let her heart drop even a fraction of an inch.

''Would you ask her, or could I? I'm pretty persuasive, and I would love to include the piece in my article.''

Bethany shrugged. ''She's in town with Dan. She's the master of ceremonies, but I'll ask her when I see her tonight. Will you be there?''

Shaelyn nodded and smiled her first genuine smile since October, 1830.

''I'm doing a story on it.''

''Great. Maybe I'll have an answer for you, or else you can try sweet-talking Mother Hawthorne herself.''

When Shaelyn left the house, she felt as if she could float back to Cape Helm.

Revelers gathered in the square, bundled in layers of scarves, sweaters, boots, and L. L. Bean attire from the nearby outlet.

Shaelyn searched the faces for Bethany, but she'd never dreamed such a mob would attend the festivities. The streets swarmed with people, and finding one muffled face would be like finding a needle in a haystack.

Speeches were made. Different ceremonies performed. Children ran around with sparklers burning, giddy with excitement.

Shaelyn was just as giddy as the children.

Where the heck was Bethany? Maybe she could have her paged.

An orchestra played patriotic music while the mayor announced the unearthing of the time capsule.

"Bethany!" Shaelyn caught a glimpse of fiery curls springing from beneath a ski cap. The girl turned, searched the crowd, then waved and elbowed her way toward Shaelyn.

"I've looked for you everywhere! I talked to my mother-in-law."

A drumroll grew near the stage.

"What did she say?" Shae's heart hovered at the top of her throat.

"She . . . money . . . take it out . . ." The drumroll drowned out Bethany's words.

"What?" Shaelyn yelled, pointing to the orchestra.

"She said there's not enough money in the world to persuade her to take the jewelry out of the vault!" Bethany yelled back. "I swear, Delores really believes those old family tales."

Her last words echoed when the drumroll suddenly stopped, and her words echoed in Shaelyn's mind as well. Did the woman have some sort of firsthand knowledge of the ring? Shaelyn had to convince her to let her see it, even if she offered to go to the vault with her.

"Where is she? I'll ask her myself."

"Ladies and gentlemen, what you've all been waiting for. Mayor Dempsey will now open the time capsule!"

Shaelyn cursed the damned announcer and the PA system for drowning out her question. She touched Bethany's arm and drew her attention away from the stage.

"Where is your mother-in-law? Can you point her out?"

Bethany looked back toward the stage.

"She's the woman on the left, next to the mayor."

The gray-haired lady who'd been emceeing the proceedings stood, bundled like an Eskimo, on the left side of the platform next to the mayor.

"Thanks," Shae called, then plowed her way toward the stage. The crowd had grown quiet in anticipation of whatever was going on. Shaelyn wanted to get to the woman before the ceremony was over and she lost her in the crowd.

The air seemed to hum with silent excitement. She would get to this woman. She would convince her to show her the ring.

The mayor's voice boomed across the PA system, breaking the tension of the crowd. Shaelyn ignored him and fought her way through the sea of people.

"Shaelyn Sumner Hawthorne?"

She froze. Had that been the mayor's voice, hesitant and confused, blasting her name out of the speakers? Had Delores had a change of heart and had her paged?

"Is there a Shaelyn Sumner Hawthorne in the crowd?"

She looked at the stage, then pushed her way forward. The crowd parted until she ran the last few steps. She bolted onto the platform and stood, panting, in front of the gray-haired woman.

The mayor turned to her at the microphone.

"Are you Shaelyn Hawthorne?"

She slowly looked at him and nodded.

"Do you have some identification?"

She blinked and fished her driver's license from her purse. She handed it to him and pointed at the name.

"I . . . I'm a newlywed. I haven't had time to get my license changed. Why?"

The mayor looked at the license, then handed her a package.

"This is for you," he said, his voice filled with disbelief and confusion.

She looked down at the parcel wrapped in brown paper. Her gaze fell on familiar handwriting. Handwriting that belonged to the one man in the world she would love with all her heart.

To be delivered to Shaelyn Sumner Hawthorne at the opening of this capsule, December 31, 1999.

With a choked sob she tore the twine from the package and opened the envelope within. Through a blur of tears she read the letter.

My beloved Shaelyn,

What began as a beautiful dream has turned into a hellish nightmare. I am alive, Shae, but only in body. Come back to me and resurrect my soul, the soul that died the day I returned and found you gone. Don't make me live the rest of my life without you. Don't make me live with only memories of that mischievous smile. Come back to me.

With all the love I can send across time,

Alec

The sobs welled up to ache in her chest. She kissed the letter penned by Alec, held it to her heart. He was alive! He believed her. He was waiting for her.

She scrambled for the wad of brown paper she'd dropped when she'd seen Alec's letter. Within the crumpled ball she found a tiny flat box.

Her fingers fumbled as she blinked away tears and whimpered like a child. The top sprang open. Nestled on a bed of black velvet lay the ring.

A gasp came from the gray-haired woman as a laughing sob burst from Shaelyn's lungs. She shoved the letter into her leather jacket, keeping a death grip on the box.

With shaking hands she pulled the ring from the velvet, slipped the box into her pocket, then slid the ring over the tip of her finger.

Tears cut icy rivers down her cheeks as she closed her eyes and took a deep breath.

" 'Bye, Mom and Dad. Good-bye, Bri. I love you." That one sliver of pain in the joy of her overflowing heart dulled and then melted like ice floating on a warm sea. It would be all right. Everything would be all right. She could almost hear her parents' voices. *Don't take any chances, Shae. Go to him.*

She opened her eyes and took one more look at the twentieth century. The chimes on the clock at City Hall bonged. She scanned the crowd, who all stared at her, silent, and then a roar started as the clock continued to bong.

With her heart soaring in her chest, she slid the ring over her knuckle.

The dizziness hit as the roar of the crowd grew to frenzied cheers. Fireworks erupted as a voice boomed over the speakers. "Ladies and gentlemen, welcome to the third millennium!"

The world spun around her, staggering her, buffeting her in a blur of noise and shapes and lights. She heard gasps and screams. She planted her feet to keep from falling. She closed her eyes and fought the nausea of vertigo.

And then the world grew quiet.

Deafeningly quiet.

"Shaelyn."

The music of his voice, hoarse, choked with emotion, curled around her heart and forever took possession.

She opened her eyes to the most beautiful sight she'd ever witnessed. The sight of her husband standing before her, cheeks ruddy with cold, eyes brimming with love, shock, wonder. Tears.

A small crowd of merrymakers ignored them, their attentions focused on a speaker standing on a low platform. Alec stood over freshly turned soil, exactly where the time capsule had been unearthed . . . or in Alec's case, buried . . . only moments before.

With one final sob she flew into his arms. He clasped her to him and held her fast as his mouth crushed hers in a kiss that exploded hot, twinkling stars in her blood, unleashed the love she'd stored for months, released the desperation she'd held at bay.

She whimpered in her throat, laughing, crying, as the

kiss went on for an eternity, as he held her, clung to her as a dying man clings to life.

"I love you. I love you," she chanted against his lips.

He brought his mouth down on hers again, trailed kisses across her face, kissed her eyelids, then raised his head and spoke to her soul.

"I love you more."

Epilogue

BATON ROUGE, LOUISIANA
JANUARY 6, 2000

"LOUISA! LOOK WHAT came in a FedEx package!
From a woman named Delores Hawthorne. It's a newspaper article from the *Cape Helm Herald*. Listen to this."
Jack Sumner read the article aloud, tears of sorrow, joy,
and relief glistening in his eyes, with a certainty in his
heart that their daughter would find a way to visit again.

*Last night, in a bizarre turn of events assumed to
have been a publicity stunt, a package was removed
from the time capsule opened in the town square, ad-
dressed to one Shaelyn Sumner Hawthorne. A young
woman claiming to be that person took the package,
opened it, then according to witnesses, put on a ring
from that package and disappeared into thin air.*

*It is not known how the package was placed into
the sealed capsule ahead of time, and as of this print-*

ing no one has come forward to claim all this free advertisement, but this reporter is willing to pay for a ticket just to see that stunt again.

CAPE HELM, MAINE
JANUARY 1, 1831

Alec took the ring from Griffin—the diamond-and-emerald ring he'd had made to match the first—then smiled at Shaelyn's gasp of surprise. He slipped the band over her knuckle and nestled it against the one that had brought her to him. Twice.

He looked into her eyes, thanked God that He had returned this precious gift to him. When his gaze swept to where her gown draped over her rounded stomach, he swallowed past a knot of emotion that threatened to unman him. He would spend the rest of his life in this woman's arms, giving thanks for the fates that had brought her to him.

She smiled up at him with that mischievous grin, her features blurred through the white, filmy veil of her wedding gown. Oh, yes. For the rest of his life.

"With this ring," he repeated after the minister, "I thee wed. Forever."

About the Author

Jenny Lykins, bestselling author of Jove's *Waiting for Yesterday*, *Echoes of Tomorrow*, *Lost Yesterday*, and *The Ghost of Christmas Present* in the *Christmas Spirits* anthology, makes her home in Tennessee, with her husband and two teenage children.

Her favorite pastimes are curling up with a good book, riding her motorcycle, and traveling.

You can write to Jenny at P.O. Box 382132, Germantown, TN 38183-2132.

TIME PASSAGES

_CRYSTAL MEMORIES   Ginny Aiken   0-515-12159-2

_A DANCE THROUGH TIME   Lynn Kurland
                                        0-515-11927-X

_ECHOES OF TOMORROW   Jenny Lykins   0-515-12079-0

_LOST YESTERDAY   Jenny Lykins   0-515-12013-8

_MY LADY IN TIME   Angie Ray   0-515-12227-0

_NICK OF TIME   Casey Claybourne   0-515-12189-4

_REMEMBER LOVE   Susan Plunkett   0-515-11980-6

_SILVER TOMORROWS   Susan Plunkett   0-515-12047-2

_THIS TIME TOGETHER   Susan Leslie Liepitz
                                        0-515-11981-4

_WAITING FOR YESTERDAY   Jenny Lykins
                                        0-515-12129-0

_HEAVEN'S TIME   Susan Plunkett   0-515-12287-4

_THE LAST HIGHLANDER   Claire Cross 0-515-12337-4

_A TIME FOR US   Christine Holden   0-515-12375-7

Prices slightly higher in Canada   **All books $5.99**

Payable in U.S. funds only. No cash/COD accepted. Postage & handling: U.S./CAN. $2.75 for
one book, $1.00 for each additional, not to exceed $6.75; Int'l $5.00 for one book, $1.00 each
additional. We accept Visa, Amex, MC ($10.00 min.), checks ($15.00 fee for returned checks)
and money orders. Call 800-788-6262 or 201-933-9292, fax 201-896-8569; refer to ad # 680

Penguin Putnam Inc.	Bill my: ☐Visa ☐MasterCard ☐Amex_____(expires)
P.O. Box 12289, Dept. B	Card#_____
Newark, NJ 07101-5289	
Please allow 4-6 weeks for delivery.	Signature_____

Foreign and Canadian delivery 6-8 weeks.

Bill to:

Name_____

Address_____City_____

State/ZIP_____

Daytime Phone #_____

Ship to:

Name_____	Book Total	$_____
Address_____	Applicable Sales Tax	$_____
City_____	Postage & Handling	$_____
State/ZIP_____	Total Amount Due	$_____

This offer subject to change without notice.